Praise for Katriena Knights' *Starchild*

"With *Starchild*, Katriena Knights blends social awareness with a first-rate, danger-filled, science fiction story."
  ~ *Vi Janaway, Romance Reviews Today*

"This story fulfills everything you could want in romantic sci-fi. Ms. Knights' characters are expertly developed. Her wonderful storytelling puts the reader right there with them."
  ~ *Lototy, Coffee Time Romance*

"*Starchild* is more sensual than spicy, but at about 82k words, it's a satisfying read with plenty of excitement to keep you turning pages."
  ~ *Seanachie, Erotic Romance Reviews*

Look for these titles by
Katriena Knights

Now Available:

Earthchild
Where There's a Will

Starchild

Katriena Knights

A SAMHAIN PUBLISHING, LTD. publication.

Samhain Publishing, Ltd.
577 Mulberry Street, Suite 1520
Macon, GA 31201
www.samhainpublishing.com

Editing by Linda Ingmanson
Cover by Scott Carpenter

First Samhain Publishing, Ltd. electronic publication: January 2008
First Samhain Publishing, Ltd. print publication: November 2008

Chapter One

"Yes, Admiral, I received the updated estimates as soon as I arrived at the space station."

The fact he spoke via a vidphone link didn't stop Harrison Fairfax from pressing thumb and forefinger to the bridge of his nose, trying to quell the dull headache that only worsened his nausea.

"Is there a problem?" Admiral Derocher's brusque tone counteracted the pleasant cadence of his Jamaican accent.

Fairfax looked up, hoping he wouldn't lose his meager lunch in front of the admiral. "No, not at all. Four billion is still well within my range. I've already got my accountants working on it. If you'd like to check back around five o'clock, I can give you an update."

"That would be fine." Derocher cleared his throat. "I hope you have a pleasant trip."

Fairfax swallowed, smiled wryly. "So far it's been a living hell. But thanks anyway."

Derocher nodded once. Fairfax, assuming the admiral was finished, broke the vidphone connection and carefully stretched out on the narrow couch. One hand fumbled in the overnight bag on the floor, eventually emerging with a large dark blue bottle. The space station's doctor had given him a prescription, but Fairfax had left the little foil packet of pills in the bathroom. He'd tried those pills before—they were useless.

He tipped the bottle to his mouth and took a swig. A product of Fairfax Pharmaceuticals, the travel sickness medication lacked a patent and a few levels of government approval, but it worked.

Ever since his parents and older brother had died in a plane crash fifteen years ago, Fairfax hadn't been able to fly in any vehicle without medication. Fortunately, the nausea had begun to fade when he'd reached the space station. Apparently his subconscious didn't differentiate between airplanes and space shuttles, but the big, stable space station was acceptable. Hopefully the big behemoth of an interplanetary vessel wouldn't upset him, either.

He sat up gingerly, and the room didn't spin. Good. Flipping on his computer pad, he dialed into MediaNet.

Not for the first time, he wondered exactly what kind of situation he was getting into. Two days ago he'd been sitting at home in New SanFran hacking into State Department files when Admiral Derocher had called. Nothing to do with the hacking, thank God. Rather, he'd been interested in discussing an investment opportunity. One extended by EarthFed President Schumann himself. Could Fairfax be on a shuttle in twenty-four hours?

Of course, Fairfax could. Even billionaire financier Harrison Fairfax didn't say no to EarthFed President Schumann. So here he was, over twenty thousand miles above the Earth, waiting for his accountants to work up a plan for investing in the Earth colony of Denahault.

He still wasn't completely sure why.

He took another swig from the bottle, probably putting himself well over the recommended daily dosage. His search of MediaNet had provided a nice selection of public domain files. He scanned the information, nodding to himself from time to time.

Information on the Denahault colony was spotty, but there was no mention of financial problems. Access to the detailed records, unsurprisingly, had been denied. So why was Derocher in charge of courting Fairfax's investment? It wasn't the kind of thing admirals usually dealt with, and the colony didn't even appear to need the money.

Fairfax had his suspicions. There was nothing for it but to see how things played out.

The next set of files held more immediate interest.

The departure of the EarthFed starship *Starchild* had been

delayed until late tomorrow to accommodate Fairfax's arrival. The ship's captain was one Trieka Cavendish. She'd graduated with honors from the EarthFed Academy, maintaining a spotless record since. Not necessarily a good sign. Unquestionable loyalty, as far as Fairfax was concerned, spoke rather poorly for her.

Then again, he probably knew things she didn't.

He read the rest of her rather impressive professional bio and turned off the computer. He was scheduled to meet her at six p.m.—he'd size her up then, see if he could get some sense of what she might know.

Not that he expected to be able to trust her. In his position, Fairfax could afford to trust no one.

Captain Trieka Cavendish was fifteen minutes early for her evening one-on-one briefing because she hated to be late and had little patience with those who were. Hopefully, her guest wouldn't be so punctual, so she could vent some of her annoyance on him.

"Mr. Fairfax," she pictured herself saying. "You may be a civilian, and you may own half the United States and selected chunks of Europe, but while you're on my ship, you'll obey my rules. And one of those is punctuality."

Trieka smiled a little, crossing the small private dining room to look out the viewport. She wasn't normally so vindictive, but it had been a long and frustrating day.

The port at the moment afforded a view of Earth, partially obstructed by a protuberance of the space station. Watching Earth drift behind the space station with the rotation of EarthStar II, Trieka thought not of the distances and what she would leave behind, but of her desire to begin her mission.

She turned away, her smile turning wry but not quite bitter. Thanks to Admiral Derocher and the too-rich-for-his-own-good Mr. Harrison Fairfax, she'd have to wait another twelve hours.

The door slid open and Trieka glanced toward it, expecting

Fairfax. Instead a waiter breezed in, carrying a large tray of fruit and cheese. Mabel's Station Café had supplied private wait staff to go with the private room. If Trieka had been briefing any other passenger, she would have had to do it shipboard, in one of the claustrophobic closets reserved for the purpose.

"Is this acceptable?" the waiter asked, setting the big silver tray on the big silver table. "Commander Anderson suggested it."

Trieka nodded, eyeing the cheese squares hungrily. "This is fine. Apparently our guest won't be up to rumaki." She wasn't exactly up to rumaki, either—liver wasn't a favorite, wrapped in bacon or not.

The fresh-faced waiter smiled engagingly. "The commander suggested a change to the entrée as well. The cook settled on a bland pasta dish."

Trieka nodded. Now Fairfax was ruining her dinner. She'd been looking forward to that filet mignon. "Sounds appropriate. Thank you."

"Can I bring you anything else?"

"Just water, please." Fairfax wouldn't be up to wine, and Trieka was on duty.

"Good enough. There's a call button under the edge of the table if you need anything else."

"Thank you."

As soon as the waiter was gone, Trieka pounced on the cheese. Busy with preboard all day, she hadn't had much for lunch. And then she'd gotten the call from Admiral Derocher.

Her departure had been delayed to accommodate Fairfax, who would be joining the two hundred and forty-eight colonists traveling to Denahault, by direct request of EarthFed President Schumann. EarthFed had apparently decided to court private investors to support the colonization effort, and Fairfax was the first target. It was an important development that would draw media and put Trieka in the kind of political position she generally tried to avoid.

The strong white cheddar practically melted in her mouth. No dehydrated, reconstituted shipboard rations here. She glanced at her watch: 1610. He was late.

Trieka wasn't surprised. She'd spent part of the afternoon

watching media vidclips of Fairfax and thought she knew
something about him. Poised, handsome, self-assured, richer
than God, he wasn't the kind of man who would care
particularly if he left someone like Trieka hanging. She picked
up another cheese square and let herself seethe.

The door slid open again and Trieka turned. The waiter
returned, behind him her late guest.

"We've arranged for a private dining room, Mr. Fairfax," the
waiter said, setting two carafes of water down on the table.
"Dinner will be served in about half an hour."

"Thank you, Carl." Fairfax stepped back to allow the waiter
to walk past him out of the room. Trieka quirked an eyebrow.
The waiter hadn't worn a nametag. This guy was good.

Fairfax turned his attention to Trieka. "Captain Cavendish,
I presume?"

"Correct," Trieka replied as Fairfax extended his hand.
Trieka took it. She had to look up to meet his eyes, but she did
it squarely.

He shook her hand once in a comfortably firm grip. "Good
to meet you. I'm sorry I'm late. I was tied up on the phone with
Admiral Derocher."

So, not only was he polite, but he had a good excuse. "I
suppose I can't fault you for that. Have a seat."

He moved past her to sit at the table. He was taller than
she'd expected, an inch or two over six feet. Not quite as
handsome as she'd thought, either, since the vidclips de-
emphasized the too-long nose and slightly weak chin. Though
well tailored, his gray-blue suit still hung a bit. Trieka didn't
know much about men's fashions, but she knew enough to
realize the suit plus the shoes would have cost her a couple
months' salary.

She waited until he'd settled before choosing her own chair.
He smiled a little as she sat. A nice smile. His mouth was
beautifully shaped, his eyes the color of an autumn storm-sky.
Perhaps he wasn't the perfectly handsome and incredibly
eligible bachelor the media made him out to be, but Trieka had
to admit he certainly wasn't ugly.

"How are you feeling?" Trieka asked. "Medical told us you
had a rough trip."

"Better," he said, "but not quite up to Mabel's famous chili."

Trieka smiled. "That's all right. We're having a nice, bland pasta dish."

Fairfax nodded and made a questioning gesture toward the cheese.

"Help yourself."

He picked out a few cubes of white cheese, avoiding the yellow ones, and placed them in a neat row on the table in front of him. Then he picked up a grape and looked at it.

"Air travel's never really agreed with me," he said. "Apparently shuttle trips are no better." He rolled the grape between long fingers, then set it down. A plain gold band circled his left ring finger. Why? She was fairly certain he was a widower, and the vidclips she'd studied to prepare for his arrival had been careful to mention his bachelor status as often as possible.

"Then may I ask why you decided to invest in off-planet property?" she asked.

"They told me space travel wasn't as likely to cause me any problems." He picked up the grape again and put it back on the tray. "They lied."

"You didn't have to leave Earth to invest," Trieka persisted.

Fairfax looked at her, his eyes a bit too shrewd for her liking. "I never invest in property I haven't seen."

"I see."

Trieka poured herself a glass of water, then filled Fairfax's glass without asking him if he wanted any. He nodded thanks and drank.

"The trip on the *Starchild* will be considerably different from the shuttle trip," she said. "Have you heard of hyperspace sickness?"

She found his grimace perversely rewarding. "Please tell me I'm not going to spend the entire trip in the head."

"Probably not. It's just something you should be aware of. Acute sickness can cause hallucinations and severe disorientation. It has to be caught early." He seemed to be listening as he switched a slightly too-small piece of cheese for a larger one. She went on. "A list of symptoms is posted on the wall of each passenger's quarters. Sickbay personnel are available at a moment's notice if there are any problems."

He shifted a few more cheese cubes into a pyramid. He still hadn't eaten any of them. "That's acceptable."

Trieka pressed her lips together. "I run a tight ship, Mr. Fairfax. You'll be expected to follow orders without question. There's to be no interference with my crew. I'll go over the basic rules of conduct while we eat. Any breach of these rules could get you confined to quarters at my discretion."

She paused for breath, and Fairfax leaned forward, looking directly at her. A lock of hair fell down to curl against his forehead. Trieka stopped halfway through the breath, captured in his gaze.

"Captain Cavendish," Fairfax said mildly, "if you've brought me here to tell me not to try to run your ship, you're wasting your time, because I have no intention of doing so. If, however, you'd like to tell me how to avoid this hyperspace sickness, or explain to me exactly how much more vomiting I can expect to endure before we reach Denahault, then talk away, because I consider that useful information."

Trieka opened her mouth, then closed it with a snap. He was walking all over her, and quite politely, too.

Fairfax leaned back in his chair, pointing at the pile of dark yellow cheese squares. "Is that sharp cheddar?"

"No, it's fairly mild," Trieka answered, still a little off-balance.

Fairfax picked up a few yellow squares and added them to his pyramid. Trieka took advantage of the moment to collect herself.

"I apologize. It's been my experience that people of your stature are supremely bad at taking orders. Especially from women. I wanted to be certain there were no misunderstandings. I hope I haven't offended you."

"I'm not easily offended, Captain." He had one too many cheese squares for his structure. He ate the extra piece, making a face as he swallowed.

Trieka studied him. She'd transported a few world leaders to various space station summits and they'd carried a similar aura, one Trieka found compelling. It was an unconscious, easy self-confidence that pulled ordinary mortals into unwilling orbit.

He looked at her again and his power struck her full force. She refused to look away, unwilling to cede even the slightest fraction of authority.

"I get the feeling," he said, "that you don't want me on your ship."

"Earth-lubbers don't belong on colony ships. The people I'm taking to Denahault worked for two years to prepare for this trip. I don't think it's appropriate they should be delayed in this way, and if the order hadn't come from the president I probably would have protested." She paused. "And now you can relay that back to Derocher, and I'll lose my job."

To Trieka's surprise, Fairfax laughed. "I don't think so. Derocher told me basically the same thing. That I should expect a somewhat less than warm welcome. That your concern is first and foremost for the safety and welfare of your crew, and that I wasn't likely to contribute a great deal to that." He added a few more squares of cheese to his growing pyramid, still laughing softly.

Trieka bit down hard on her pride to keep it from escaping. After a moment of recovery, she said, "I don't like politics and I never have. I suppose I'm a disappointment to him in that respect."

Fairfax looked at her, still smiling, and with unwarranted warmth in his eyes. "On the contrary, I got the impression he would have been disappointed if you'd responded any other way."

"I think he knows me a little too well." She folded her hands neatly on the table. "I apologize, Mr. Fairfax. I suppose I have no business telling you how to run your affairs."

"No more than I have any business telling you how to run your ship. I assure you, I'll be as little trouble as possible."

"Maybe not to me, but I think you'll keep medical busy."

Fairfax grimaced. "That's the least welcome prediction I've heard today."

He ate a few pieces of cheese, slowly demolishing the carefully stacked pyramid. Each succeeding piece seemed to go down more easily. Trieka wondered if the pyramid had been an avoidance tactic. She picked a few strawberries from the tray, feeling her stomach rumble. She hoped Carl would bring the pasta soon.

"Anyway, in the spirit of not causing trouble, I *am* going to have to ask you for a favor." Fairfax gave a slight shrug, as if in apology. "This whole situation has caught me rather unprepared. I need to download some information from the EarthFed public archives to complete my overviews, so I've brought my own computer equipment."

Trieka nodded. "I can help you with that. It's a bit tricky downloading from space, but it can be done."

"I appreciate any help I can get."

Trieka smiled a little. "Dairy products are helpful."

He looked up questioningly, obviously unsure how dairy products could help him download from the EarthFed public archives. "For what?"

"Hyperspace sickness. Dairy products usually help."

"Now *that*," he said, his mild voice becoming suddenly emphatic, "is something I need to know."

❊ ❊ ❊

Later, Fairfax walked the corridors of EarthStar II, unable to sleep. He and Cavendish had eaten, then she'd finished the briefing, explaining the standard operating procedures of her ship and a little bit about the colony on Denahault. Not that Denahault would matter much to him in the long run. It was just a means to an end, both for himself and EarthFed.

Finally she'd dismissed him, subtly making sure he understood the situation was exactly that. He didn't mind, and hadn't bothered to battle her for dominance. He'd gotten the feeling it had annoyed her.

Now he walked and admired the sleek lines of the space station's interior architecture, the smooth, reflective silver of the walls. He recognized the space-forged alloys—one of his companies owned several of the patents—but he'd never seen them in action. The smooth merges from walls to floor to ceiling and the dull reflections combined for an effect that was disconcerting but strangely comforting. The not-quite-familiar material stood as a reminder that he walked a corridor several thousand miles above the surface of the earth. But, at the same time, it threw back at him the most familiar element in his world—his own face. The architect in him, which had come out when he'd funded the post-quake reconstruction of New SanFran, wondered if there was any way to recreate that effect with Earth-based materials.

Finally he stopped in the observation lounge. There was an empty table near the window wall. He took a seat, looking out at the blue-and-white curve of the Earth. The simple beauty of the spectacle arrested his thoughts. If he angled himself in his chair just right and leaned forward, he felt like he might topple right through the window and fall until he embraced the smooth surface of the planet beneath.

"May I get you a drink, sir?"

Jerked out of the spell, Fairfax looked up to see a tuxedo-clad waiter standing next to his table. "Scotch and soda," he answered. The waiter nodded smartly and departed.

The waiter's near-military posture brought Cavendish to Fairfax's mind. Smallish and slim, polished to a military sheen that was oddly offset by her short red curls and the freckles on her narrow nose, Captain Cavendish carried with her an aura of complete control and self-confidence. Fairfax found her intimidating. He hadn't been intimidated by anyone since the day he'd met Katharine.

An investigative journalist with a reputation worthy of a pit bull, Katharine Maier had been the last person Fairfax had wanted to see on his doorstep that day. But the story she'd come to investigate had proven to be smoke, and she'd dissipated it with aplomb. She'd bought him flowers, and later they'd dated, and married, and then she was gone. She and her father and a private plane, gone as if they'd never existed.

The waiter returned with his drink and Fairfax took a long swig, feeling the alcohol sear his throat. He still found it difficult to think of Katharine, even after seven years.

Which was, of course, why he was here.

Cavendish had agreed to help him with the computer—she'd had no reason not to. He could acquire the last few files en route to Denahault. The picture should become clear then, and the only hurdle left would be how to pass the information on.

Absently rotating his wedding band with his thumb, he looked again at the tranquil planet turning in the wide window, thinking about what lay hidden beneath the peaceful drifts of white clouds. Katharine would be proud of what he'd accomplished so far. Soon, he'd have all the facts. He'd lost his entire family and the cosmos had offered him no explanation. In the loss of his wife, he would have answers no matter what it took.

Strangely, his mind turned again to Cavendish. That wasn't right. She sat in his brain as a distraction, and he didn't need that.

But what if she was involved? She could be—she was obviously intensely dedicated to EarthFed and her longtime association with the colonization program made it all too likely. But she'd also seemed basically decent.

He'd have to find out for certain before he could make a judgment. And, if she was in any way involved, he would take her down without a second thought.

Chapter Two

The day of departure dawned as did all days on EarthStar II—with the official opening of Mabel's and the slow return of life to the empty corridors. Trieka, preparing to indulge in one last bottomless cup of coffee and stack of pancakes at the café, spied Commander Jeff Anderson and Lieutenant Robin Wu, her navigator, doing the same.

She gave them a wave and a mock salute. Under other conditions, she might have joined them, but since they were soon to be locked up together in a relatively small ship for a week and a half, she thought it best to give them a break from her presence. She removed her wrist comm and laid it down on the table, then turned it on and tuned to MediaNet.

WorldNews was covering their departure. Though people had been traveling to the colonies on a regular basis for over a decade, it was still novel enough to be newsworthy. One of the feeds came live from the docking bay. Trieka was glad she'd decided to stop here for breakfast instead of going straight to the ship. The media was informally—but effectively—banned from Mabel's.

Trieka listened with half her attention as the newscaster interviewed Trieka's cargo master. Ensign Solomon explained the use of cryogenics in supplying the colonies with livestock. Trieka absently nodded approval of his explanations as she pulled up the latest manifest in another window.

"May I join you?"

Surprised, Trieka looked up. Fairfax grinned down at her, holding a tray of waffles. He wasn't wearing a suit today, but the handmade Aran sweater and crisp wool trousers had probably cost him nearly as much.

Trieka started to say no, then reconsidered. Passenger fraternization usually wasn't encouraged, but in this case she thought Admiral Derocher might have a different view.

"Of course," she said.

He sat down across from her in the small booth and arranged his plate. "Any good news?" He gestured to the wrist comm with his fork.

"They're interviewing my cargo master." She looked at the screen again. "Oh, wait. Now they're talking about you."

"Must be a slow day."

"Do you want to hear it?" Trieka turned up the volume— *she* wanted to hear it.

"Not particularly."

Trieka shrugged and scanned the manifest while she listened to the broadcast. According to the report, the Denahault colony was in dire need of funds. This was the first Trieka had heard of it.

"'Wealthy Financier Harrison Fairfax'," Trieka repeated. "Is that your official title?"

"It is this year. I supposed it's an improvement on 'Wealthy Eccentric Recluse'."

"But not as good as 'Wealthy Eligible Bachelor', which is what was on the disk jacket of *People to Watch* this week." She paused to chew. "Funny how they always work the 'wealthy' in there."

"I'm in that rag again? Who was I seen with?"

Trieka shrugged. "Could have been me for all I know. I didn't read it." She keyed off the news and pulled the manifest into the main window. There had been a few more cargo changes, but the list was now keyed as stable, and the passenger list read "Final".

"That might have made an interesting story," Fairfax said.

Trieka glanced up. "What?" Focused on other things, she'd completely forgotten what they'd been talking about.

"My being seen with you," Fairfax reminded her patiently. "After all, I haven't been photographed with a woman since...for a very long time."

19

A stab of not-so-old pain filled his eyes. That would explain the wedding band, Trieka thought.

She turned her mind back to her work and scrolled through the manifest. "Maybe you should get out more."

"Maybe I should."

Something in his voice made her look up. He seemed to stare right through her, his eyes distant. Slowly, they came back. The lines next to his mouth had deepened and, as his gaze met hers, it seemed to bore into her, looking into things she kept hidden. She looked back at the wrist comm, wondering what exactly he'd been thinking, and why she reacted to him so strongly.

When she ventured to look up again, he had returned his attention to his breakfast.

Trieka swallowed, gathering her bureaucratic air back around her.

"I'd like you to board early with your computer equipment. Commander Anderson can help you set things up. We need to be sure you're compatible and that nothing will interfere with the ship's systems."

Fairfax stared blandly at his breakfast. "What time?"

"Thirteen-hundred would be good. Then you can get off if you like and stretch your legs. Formal passenger boarding starts at sixteen-hundred."

"That seems reasonable." He pushed the last piece of waffle across his plate, looking like he'd lost all appetite. "I'll leave you to your work, then. I'm going to stop by the duty free shop today—is there anything I can pick up for you?"

Trieka tried not to gape at the strange shift in conversation. Fairfax looked up, and something dark passed across his face— thought or memory, Trieka wasn't sure.

"Sure," she said. "Champagne and caviar."

To her surprise, Fairfax smiled. "I'll see what I can do." He picked up his tray and stood. "I'll see you at one." The smile shifted to a grin. "No, sorry—thirteen hundred."

Trieka put Jeff in charge of Fairfax's preboard. Hopefully Fairfax wouldn't be offended. Jeff was better qualified to set up Fairfax's computer, and Trieka felt she needed to put some distance between herself and her Wealthy Financier. He was treating their acquaintanceship just a bit too unofficially.

She had other things to do, in any case, from going over preliminary jump site readings with her navigator to running a final check of the ship. Finally, an hour before boarding was to begin, she went out into the waiting area to mingle with the passengers.

The waiting area overflowed. It had been built to hold about a hundred people. Currently, it looked as if all two hundred and forty-eight passengers were packed in, shoulder to shoulder, standing on the chairs and each others' luggage. An air of eager anticipation filled the room.

Some captains of colony ships liked to deliver rousing speeches before takeoff. Leaving Earth to live on a distant planet was a great and heroic undertaking, worthy of such histrionics, but Trieka wasn't very good at speeches. So she'd decided to mingle.

Her presence quieted the crowd a little as they parted to let her pass. Then they mumbled in surprise as she stopped to speak to anyone who showed interest. By the time she returned to the ship, the frantic edge to their eagerness had calmed.

Trieka, on the other hand, was charged with their enthusiasm. In the midst of the details and drudgery she'd forgotten she was fulfilling dreams with this voyage.

And one of those dreams was her own. On the way up the corridor to the cockpit, she glanced out a portal and wondered if her mother would be watching coverage of the liftoff from her house in Chicago. Watching and thinking of Trieka's father, who'd died thirty years ago on the first ship to Farhallen.

An hour and thirty minutes later, well ahead of schedule, boarding was complete. Jeff, who'd been in charge of the boarding crew, returned to the cockpit shortly thereafter.

"Are we ready?" Trieka asked.

Jeff sat down at his console and buckled himself in. "All set. All passengers present and accounted for, in their cabins and hopefully strapped in."

"Good. Lieutenant Wu, see if we can get clearance for an early departure."

Clearance granted, they prepared to depart. The last connection to EarthStar II was severed, and the *Starchild* was on her own. With a gentle acceleration, she moved out into space, out of Earth's orbit, into the first leg of their trip to Denahault. As the ship turned, a vast starscape moved into view, filling the front ports with infinity.

"We are away," Jeff announced.

Trieka allowed herself a smile of pride. She really wanted to whoop and holler a little, or at least jump up and down. Instead she keyed the ship's intercom.

"Attention passengers. This is Captain Cavendish. We've completed separation from EarthStar II and are approaching our initial heading. You may unfasten your seatbelts and move about your cabins, but please do not leave the cabins until further notice. Thank you." She switched off the intercom and looked at Lieutenant Wu. "How long until we reach heading one?"

The navigator bent her dark head over her console. "Thirty minutes, sir."

Trieka nodded. "Steady as she goes."

Fairfax had his harness unbuckled almost before Captain Cavendish finished her announcement. Commander Anderson had told him to key up the sequence for his first set of downloads as soon as they completed separation. This would fit his data transfer request into the first window through which he could reach the EarthFed archives by satellite. He wanted to be sure he didn't miss the opportunity. If he didn't get this data, everything was shot.

He'd loaded the request ahead of time, so it took only a moment to send it off after he'd logged in. But he wasn't done. He had more data to track down, and this request had nothing to do with survey information from the EarthFed public archives.

"*Do it during takeoff,*" Madison had told him, practically on Fairfax's way out the door. "*With all the navigational information going back and forth, they'll never notice the breach, and you'll have the orders downloaded in a matter of seconds.*"

He and Madison had worked their way into the EarthFed databases a few months ago and had collected compelling evidence, but never the orders, which should lie somewhere in Admiral Derocher's private files.

Then, last week, Fairfax had logged in through a public archive user ID and hacked his way through a backdoor in EarthFed's high security databases. He'd found Derocher's logs, but at the time hadn't been prepared to snag them. He'd intended to download the information the next day, after setting up a series of safeguards. Then the president had called and given him twenty-four hours to be on a shuttle.

Now, in the midst of the uplink confusion created by the *Starchild*'s navigational needs, he copied three files from Derocher's private log digest. Seconds later, he was out and logged off, with only the request for survey information from the public archives still running. If anyone cared to look closely enough, the unauthorized entry might be traceable, but hopefully by the time they found him out, this would be over, and EarthFed would have more important things to worry about.

"Mission accomplished," Fairfax said to no one. He pulled the disk out of his computer and put it in his shirt pocket.

Six hours after takeoff, the *Starchild* followed a steady course for the nearest hyperspace jump site, which had been established just past the moon's orbital path. Exhausted, blinking grit out of her eyes but too wired to feel the effects of the weariness, Trieka turned the cockpit over to the night crew and went to her quarters.

The room still smelled like disinfectant. Trieka changed from her uniform to a pair of silk pajamas. Just the feel of the cloth against her skin relaxed her. An aroma generator sat on the desk. She slid a disk into it and, within moments, the room smelled like a spring morning after a rain. With a little disinfectant thrown in on the side.

She sat down in front of the computer and flipped it on.

"Good evening, Captain Cavendish," said the computer. Trieka had programmed it with a dark velvet male voice that made her toes curl whenever she heard it.

"Good evening, Lance. Open file 'Cavendish Logs, Denahault', please."

"It is, as always, my pleasure."

Trieka smiled. Lance was always so polite. Just the kind of man she liked—one who did exactly what he was told when he was told to do it.

"File opened," the computer went on after a moment, and Trieka began to dictate her log. White words walked letter by letter across the blue screen as she spoke, turning into sentences, paragraphs, pages. It had been an eventful day; she had a lot to record and she might as well get it done in the few minutes she had left before her adrenaline crashed.

Sure enough, after a few pages she found herself struggling for words she knew shouldn't be that difficult to dredge up. She laid her head down on the desk to gather her vocabulary. The words returned gradually, then scattered again. She lifted her head.

Someone was behind her. Slowly, she swiveled her desk chair around.

Fairfax stood behind her in a shadow. He smiled a little as she turned, a small, sensual movement of that beautiful mouth. A lock of brown hair dangled across his forehead. He wore a blue wool sweater.

"Good evening, Captain," he said.

"What are you doing here?" She hadn't heard him come in. Her door was supposed to buzz when anyone requested entry. Well, actually, it was supposed to chime, but her request to have the buzzers replaced had been ignored.

He took a step toward her, looming over her where she sat in the low chair. He seemed to fill all her vision, the room itself disappearing in her complete awareness of him.

"I came to see you," he said.

"It's past midnight."

His gaze trailed from her face down her body. "I know. I was hoping you'd still be awake." He bent down, grasping the arms of the chair, his face only inches from Trieka's.

"I'm allergic to wool," she said.

Fairfax smiled again, showing even teeth. He straightened and peeled the sweater off, tossing it across the room. Then he leaned back over her.

"Is that better?"

Trieka cleared her throat. "Well, at least I won't sneeze."

The brown hair of his chest curled mere inches from her nose, but all she could smell was the aroma disk. Fairfax's hands lifted from the chair, closing firmly around her arms. He drew her up, lifted her and sat her down on the desk next to the computer.

"What are you doing?" It occurred to Trieka that she probably should have slapped him by now, but she had no particular desire to. Her hands didn't seem to be moving at her request, anyway.

"What would you like me to do, Captain?"

He spoke the words against her ear, then leaned back to look into her face. She stared at him, at his mouth, unable to see anything else.

Finally, in the tone of someone accustomed to having her orders followed without question, she said, "Take off your pants."

He did. She wasn't sure how he did—his hands didn't seem to move from her arms—but a moment later, he stood completely naked and completely aroused. So completely aroused, in fact, Trieka wondered how he'd managed to keep it in his pants.

"You're huge," she said, with no small amount of awe, and he grinned.

"What would you like me to do now, Captain?"

Trieka opened her mouth, not certain what she was going to say. And destined not to find out, because at that moment the door burst open again and Admiral Derocher stalked into the room, his expression a mixture of shock and stern disapproval.

"Captain Cavendish!" he exclaimed. "What's the meaning of this?"

Her mouth still open, Trieka turned to face Derocher. "Well, Admiral, you did tell me to keep him happy—"

"Logging off in forty-five seconds. Forty-four. Forty-three..."

At the sound of Lance's voice, Trieka jerked awake. The word processor screen still glowed blue, the cursor blinking after the end of the last word. According to the computer's internal clock, she'd been asleep nearly twenty minutes.

"Good grief," she said.

The images of the dream replayed in her mind and her face grew hot. At the end of the unfinished entry, she typed, "To be continued. I need sleep."

She saved the file, shut down the computer and went to bed.

Chapter Three

The annoying buzz that was supposed to be a chime jarred Trieka out of a more restful sleep eight hours later. Bleary, she looked at the clock on the shelf by her berth: 0459. As she stared, eyes barely focused, it clicked over to 0500 and began to beep.

Whoever was outside her door activated the buzzer again.

The situation should have made sense, but in her semi-unconscious state, Trieka couldn't fit the pieces together.

"Captain!" That was Jeff's voice. "Breakfast."

"I'm coming," Trieka replied reflexively.

She swung out of the bed as she gradually remembered she'd set her alarm a half hour later than usual. She didn't go on duty until 0600, and had figured the extra sleep would do her some good. Quickly, she shed her pajamas and stepped into her uniform. She folded the pajamas and laid them on the bed, shoved a hand through her hair to put the riotous curls into some semblance of order, then went to the door.

Jeff and Lieutenant Wu stood outside. Jeff, as always, was pressed and pleated within an inch of his life, his dark blond hair crisply combed, boots so shiny you could touch up your mascara in the reflection. Robin at least looked like she'd recently been asleep, her fine, dark hair entertaining a not-quite tamable cowlick.

"Rough night, Captain?" Robin asked.

"No rougher than usual on the first night out."

"Weird dreams?"

"Very." She had no desire to go into detail, especially with her crew, but Fairfax had continued to haunt her dreams, naked and otherwise. She didn't make a habit of using sleep enhancers, though it was fairly common for crews on long voyages, but she was beginning to wonder if it might not be a bad idea.

Although crew and passengers had been scheduled to eat in shifts, the small mess was filled to capacity. Ensign Rico had held their table while Jeff and Robin went to fetch Trieka. Trieka helped herself to the food at the counter, then joined her crew.

"How did it go last night?" Trieka asked Rico.

Rico shrugged. "Smooth. No catastrophes."

"That's always a good sign. How about you, Jeff? How was Fairfax's preboard? He give you any trouble?"

"No, not really. Asked a lot of questions."

"Good. I think Admiral Derocher would appreciate it if we were nice to him. The government wants his money."

"Is that why he's here?" Robin looked as if she had just solved a particularly annoying puzzle.

"That's right. So kiss his ass as much as possible."

Robin grinned slyly. "May I take that literally?"

"Only with his permission."

Jeff cocked an eyebrow at Robin. "Best be careful, Lieutenant. We don't want any lawsuits."

Robin shrugged it off. "Not likely. I just think he's cute, that's all. And being rich doesn't hurt anything, either. What do you think, Captain?"

Trieka had her mouth full of toast, which was fortuitous since the question caught her off guard. She chewed and swallowed, trying not to think about the dreams.

"I think he's skinny and he has a big nose."

Jeff looked at Trieka in amazement. "I think that if I were talking about a woman like that, you'd write me up."

"Oh, please—" Robin protested, but Trieka interrupted her.

"No, Jeff's right. It's highly inappropriate. Lieutenant, write yourself up for unbecoming conduct."

"Write myself up?" Robin gaped, only half-serious.

"Well, it would save me the trouble."

Jeff, on the other hand, had worked up a snit. "I'm offended you're not taking this seriously."

Trieka laid a conciliatory hand on Jeff's arm. He'd been a good friend since academy days, so she hated to chastise him. In fact, she'd requested him as her second-in-command because he was smart and dependable and maybe a little cute. But his too-proper attitude didn't fit in with her concept of a colony ship. She wanted things more relaxed. On the other hand, he'd probably make a great admiral someday.

"I wouldn't write you up for talking about a passenger, Jeff. After all, I didn't even reprimand you for what you said about me at the holiday party last winter."

Jeff slid from self-righteous to uncomfortable. "I was drunk."

"Even so, I think you were responsible for your own actions."

"I apologized once, and I'll apologize again."

Trieka grinned. She'd gotten quite a bit of mileage out of that little indiscretion. "It's all right. Though I have to say it's the first time I've ever heard my breasts compared to any kind of fruit, much less—"

Jeff waved surrender. "All right, all right. Fairfax is cute and he has a big nose. Can we please change the subject?"

"Sure. How are the passengers settling in?"

Apparently the passengers were settling in fine. Trieka listened as Jeff related the mild fiasco of the boarding procedure, half her attention focused on her own thoughts.

She had a great deal to accomplish today, with only the usual twenty-four hours to work with. She arranged her schedule in her head, Jeff's words sinking in just far enough for comprehension.

She wasn't sure what made her look toward the door, but when she did, Fairfax walked through it. Inexplicably, Trieka's heart sped up, then settled into a slow, very hard rhythm that left her breathless.

He was bleary-eyed and mussed, the dark red-brown hair

standing up at his crown. From the pattern of the wrinkles in his shirt, she could tell it was silk. It looked like he'd slept in it. He collected his breakfast, then sat down at a table with a group of passengers, greeting them with a weary smile.

No, Trieka wouldn't call him cute, though the long nose gave him a bit of a sad puppy look. Not cute, but definitely not ugly. Unable to stop the thought, she wondered how accurate her dreams had been once the clothes had started coming off.

"Captain?" Jeff said.

Trieka realized he'd asked her a question. Quickly, she cast back, trying to remember what it was. Funny how she could arrange her schedule and listen to Jeff at the same time, while Fairfax's presence seemed to crowd everything else out of her head.

"I'm sorry," she said to hide the hesitation while her mind filled in the gaps. "I was thinking." She considered a moment. "There are a couple of empty passenger cabins. We had some last-minute pullouts. If these people really can't stand each other, you could separate them."

Jeff nodded decisively. "Good. That gives me some flexibility."

Trieka returned an equally firm nod, hiding her amazement that she'd supplied a relevant answer. Jeff returned his attention to his meal, and a comfortable silence settled over the table.

Trieka's coffee had gone cold, and she wrinkled her nose at the tepid, bitter taste. She enjoyed strong black coffee when it was hot—cold, it needed sugar. She reached across the table for a sugar packet, looking up as she did so.

Fairfax's gaze riveted to hers from across the room. He smiled a little, and Trieka found herself staring at his mouth. His jaw was wider than his temple. His smile broadened, showing a flash of teeth. Automatically, Trieka smiled back, then, suddenly self-conscious, looked away.

A surreptitious glance a few moments later found him involved in his breakfast and the conversation of the woman sitting next to him. Resolutely, Trieka put him out of her mind and resumed planning her day.

* * *

Fairfax was exhausted. Even five cups of black coffee couldn't keep his eyes open. He should have tried to exchange his early breakfast shift with someone else. It had occurred to him, but it had also occurred to him that Captain Cavendish would probably eat at the early shift. For whatever reason, it had seemed worth the loss of sleep to exchange that smile with her across the room and see her look away as if it had affected her.

But he was paying for it now. Finally, after drifting into semi-unconsciousness one too many times, he excused himself from the breakfast table and returned to his room.

The berth in the small cabin barely allowed him to stretch out to his full six foot one inch frame. He lay very still on his back for a time, trying to let his mind drift. Unfortunately, the drifting kept finding a target. He opened one eye to look at the computer pad sitting on the small desk. If he reached out, he could pick it up without even stretching...

No. He'd been up all night struggling with the encrypted files he'd snagged from Derocher's logs. It wouldn't do him any good to struggle more with them today. The little pad just didn't have the processing power to break the encryption. He'd have to access the shipboard computers to take advantage of their power.

He needed to get into Cavendish's logs as well. He had to know if she carried orders from Derocher—something other than the simple delivery of a few colonists to their destination. He had to know, and not just because it would add to the pile of evidence if she did. In fact, he hoped she didn't.

Madison had taught him a lot about ship's computers, too. Fairfax began to run the most common configurations through his head, theorizing where the weakest points might be in the system's security. The theoretical networks became pictures—spinning, mesmerizing webs. He wasn't certain when they caught him, but they did, and he fell into sleep.

* * *

The first items on Trieka's agenda for the morning were meetings with the passengers. The group of two hundred and forty-eight was divided into five roughly equal groups, each headed for a different settlement on Denahault. Each group had appointed a leader who was in charge of making sure everyone got where they belonged with all necessary supplies and information.

Trieka would meet with each of the five leaders today, briefing them on the latest news from Denahault Prime. Everyone had to know exactly what was expected. Part of Trieka's job was to be sure the colonists' assimilation went as smoothly as possible.

Then there was Fairfax. She really didn't have time for him today, but in the interest of diplomacy, she'd decided to give him a meeting as well. As she'd stressed to her cockpit crew, it never hurt to kiss a little ass.

So it was that, at 1900 hours, matters settled with the team leaders and jump site readings verified in the cockpit, Trieka stood pushing the buzzer that should have been a chime on Fairfax's door.

"Who?" Judging only by the tone of his muffled voice, Trieka guessed he must have gotten some rest since this morning.

"Captain Cavendish," she replied briskly.

There was a moment of silence, then the door slid open. Fairfax stood in the doorway, smiling. "Come in, please."

Trieka stepped past the welcoming sweep of his arm. The lights in the small room were dim, presumably so he could more easily see the computer terminal, currently displaying a detailed map of Denahault Prime.

"To what do I owe the pleasure?" Fairfax said.

"Your final briefing. It's part of the routine." She bent to look at the computer. "Are these the maps you downloaded from the public archives?"

Fairfax stepped up behind her, looking over her shoulder. "Yes. Why?"

"These are six months out of date. We have current maps on our system. I'll have Commander Anderson show you how to access them."

"Thank you." Fairfax sounded surprised. He moved away from her, sitting on the narrow bunk.

Trieka turned toward him and sat in the desk chair. "There are games on our system, too. I'm sure you could use some diversion."

Fairfax smiled. "Yes, I could." He leaned sideways across the length of the bed, snagging the handle of the coldbox at the foot with two fingers. He wore a black sweat suit and white sports socks. The shirt rode up as he reached, exposing a few inches of his stomach.

Trieka found herself staring at the small piece of bare flesh. The shirttail rose just past his navel. The brown hair on his stomach was curly and not too thick, the stomach itself flat. Something about the way the sweat suit fit him made him look less thin and more athletic, lanky through the leg, like someone who might play basketball.

"I have something for you," he said. He pulled a long-necked bottle out of the coldbox and picked up a small jar from the shelf above.

Trieka blinked, jerking her eyes back to his face. "Something for me?"

He handed her the bottle. "Champagne," he said, "and a jar of caviar. EarthStar II's duty free shop is surprisingly well-stocked."

"You're kidding, right?" Trieka was flabbergasted—she'd never intended him to take her seriously. But the bottle was clearly labeled, and the little glass jar held ebony roe.

"You said you wanted it," said Fairfax with a shrug.

"I was kidding."

"I know. Crackers?" He held up a box of water crackers.

Trieka shook her head. "I suppose you have champagne glasses, too?"

"Well, they're plastic, but they'll do in a pinch."

"I can't accept these."

"Then share them with me."

Trieka studied him. She felt very strange. She might have called it giddy if she hadn't sworn off giddiness at the age of twelve. "There's got to be a regulation somewhere that says I shouldn't," she admitted, "but I can't think of it."

She looked down at the bottle and the jar, then up at Fairfax and his inquisitively raised eyebrows. She set down the champagne.

"Tell you what." With her free hand, she unfastened the insignia pin above her left breast pocket. It didn't change the fact that she was in uniform, but as a token gesture it seemed a good one. "Now it's unofficial."

"Is that a yes?"

"Yes."

It wasn't the best arrangement for indulging in expensive snacks, since there were no chairs, no table, and no plates or utensils. But they had the plastic champagne glasses, and Fairfax produced a pocketknife with an attachment that worked quite well for transferring caviar from the jar to the crackers. Trieka sat at the desk, sipping champagne, while Fairfax sat cross-legged on the bed.

"So," he said. "Since it's no longer official, I guess that means you can't brief me."

Trieka shrugged. "I could, but since you're not planning to become a permanent resident, the best thing you could do as far as briefing would be to read the ship's files on Denahault." She scooped caviar onto a cracker and bit into it delicately. The rich salty caviar blended perfectly with the bland cracker. "This is very good caviar."

Fairfax snorted vaguely. "I should hope so for what I paid."

Trieka peered up at him, suddenly uncomfortable. She laid the cracker down and stood. "Maybe this isn't such a good idea, after all. I'll be sure Commander Anderson sees you first thing in the morning—"

Fairfax slid from the bed to stand in front of her, partially blocking her path to the door. "I'm sorry. I was trying to make a joke."

"That's not how it sounded."

"I know. Please sit back down."

There was something strange and uncomfortable in his eyes. This discomfort, though, made her want to stay. Slowly, she sat. Fairfax slid back onto the narrow bed.

"The fact is," he continued, "you intimidate the hell out of me. And that makes me say stupid things."

Trieka's right eyebrow twitched up. "I intimidate you? Then why all this nonsense?" She gestured with cracker and champagne glass.

His gaze slid away from hers, and he looked almost embarrassed. "You've gone to a lot of trouble to accommodate me. This is just to say thank you."

He wasn't telling her the truth. Or at least not all of it. She said nothing, waiting. He stared at the wall, and a muscle bunched along his jawbone. Then he faced her, his expression almost desolate. "The last time I found a woman this intimidating, I ended up marrying her. I just...thought it might be worth pursuing."

Trieka stared at him. That was the last thing she'd expected to hear. She suddenly wondered what that gorgeous mouth would feel like pressed to hers, what it would taste like sweetened by champagne and salted with caviar. To her own surprise, she felt not a hint of a blush, but blood rushed to other places in her body.

"I'm flattered," she said, "but I don't make a habit of dating passengers."

"Maybe after we land?"

Trieka couldn't suppress a laugh. "Maybe."

He smiled and lifted his glass. Hesitant, Trieka tapped hers to it. If he said, "To us," she was leaving.

"To nothing in particular," he said.

"I'll drink to that."

Trieka sipped her champagne, then stood again, pinning the insignia back to her shirt. "I'll tell you what. How about that ship's tour I promised you?"

Fairfax nodded. "All right. Sounds like a lovely evening."

Trieka led him through the front portion of the ship,

providing a behind-the-scenes look at the mess hall, then giving a brief overview of the cockpit. On the way back to the engine room, they found themselves caught in a mild traffic jam as the night shift took over. Trieka glanced at her watch. As of now, she was officially off duty.

They ducked back into the mess hall to stay out of the ebb and flow of people. Trieka sat down at a table, Fairfax settling down next to her.

"How long will this take?" he asked.

Trieka shrugged. "They're probably done by now. But, frankly, these new boots are killing me."

He laughed a little. "So how did you get involved in this line of work?"

"Why?" Trieka couldn't resist taking the bait, whether he'd offered it intentionally or not. "Don't you think it's an appropriate career for a lady?"

His grin flickered again, but he restrained it, obviously not completely sure she was joking. "I didn't say that. I'm just curious, that's all."

Trieka considered. Very few knew what had driven her to this path. She didn't talk about it often, especially since the fiasco with Jake. But, thinking of Fairfax's own losses, she thought he might understand.

"It was my father."

He nodded. "A military man?"

"He died before I was born." She stretched her legs, thinking of the media disks, the photographs, all stacked in a cedar chest in her mother's closet. "He was one of the first chosen to colonize Farhallen. It was an experimental ship without the safeguards we have today. He looked out a portal during the hyperspace jump. His mind went and never came back. He died while they were shipping him home."

"I'm sorry."

She shrugged a little, pleased he felt the need to acknowledge a loss so distant. "He walked away from my mother and me to follow his dream. I could have hated him for it, but I didn't. When I got old enough to understand, I realized I had the same dream. So I followed it. I'll never have a family of my own, but I'll have my dream."

"And his." Fairfax's gaze bored through her, but caressed her as well.

Trieka swallowed and looked at her hands, folding them on the table in front of her. "Perhaps. But I can say for certain that it's also mine. Always has been."

"Yes, I believe you can."

He reached across the table and touched her hand, his finger grazing the curve of hers. Trieka stared at the long, graceful line of his hand, and at her own hand, which seemed suddenly to belong to someone else. Heat curled inside her.

This was, she decided, a very dangerous man. Too much like Jake in too many ways. Too much like herself.

She moved her hand a little and he withdrew. It had been nothing, just a touch, barely any contact at all. She could still feel it.

"What about you?" she said. "I hear you made your money the old-fashioned way."

The tension fell apart, which was what she'd hoped.

"That's right," said Fairfax with a grin. "I inherited it, and then I worked my ass off to keep it."

"It must have been difficult coming into so much money so suddenly."

"Losing my family was more difficult."

His candor surprised her. Looking at the glint of gold on his left hand, she decided to ask. "And your wife?"

"I don't know." The studied calm of his features hurt more than any show of emotion could have. "She and her father disappeared seven years ago. I still don't know."

"I'm sorry," she said. "I shouldn't have asked."

He made a slight wave with his left hand. "It's all right."

But it wasn't all right, because he pushed his chair a little away from the table. "If your feet have recovered, maybe we should get started again. It's getting late."

Fairfax was in deeper trouble than he'd thought. A few days ago, in the duty free shop on the station, the champagne and caviar had seemed like a great joke. An expensive joke, but still a joke. But a few hours ago, watching Cavendish sip the champagne and delicately nibble the crackers and roe, it hadn't seemed at all funny. In fact, it scared him.

After the interlude in the mess hall, Cavendish had withdrawn a little, finishing the ship's tour with consummate professionalism. She'd established appropriate eye contact, directed his attention here and there without touching him. He'd paid careful attention, nodding occasionally, asking pertinent and intelligent questions.

But as the evening wound on, he became more and more aware of her—the shape of her small breasts under the dark blue uniform, the slim, boyish body and long legs. Her short, curly red hair looked untamable, as if there was no point trying to comb it so she'd hacked it off instead. And her eyes were a shade of hazel that seemed to change from moment to moment.

He'd spent seven years avoiding women, nursing the empty pain still hanging behind his heart. He'd clung to everything about Katharine—the useless hope she might still be alive, even the wedding ring friends had told him he should abandon. Now, suddenly, he found himself entranced.

Fairfax rolled over in bed, burying his face in the bend of his elbow. The lines of the encrypted files ran over and over through his mind, burning meaningless characters on the backs on his eyelids.

What if he found the captain's name in there somewhere? What if he downloaded her personal logs and order journals and found out she was involved? He wouldn't spare her—he couldn't, knowing what he knew—but would he ever forgive himself?

Please, he thought, moving his lips silently around the words. *Please let her be clean.*

Trieka lay awake for a long time. She'd cleaned her teeth before turning in, but she could still conjure the taste of the evening: sweet champagne and salty caviar.

She could conjure other things, as well. The way Fairfax's eyes crinkled almost shut when he smiled. The inherent grace to his hands. The line of his back beneath the sweatshirt. The curve of his buttocks beneath the sweatpants. The strip of bare skin exposed whenever he moved the wrong way.

And most of all, the sound of his voice speaking those unexpected, inexplicable words: "I just thought it might be worth pursuing."

Trieka hadn't been pursued in a very long time. She could count on the fingers of one hand the number of dates she'd had since taking on the *Starchild*, and she'd even have some fingers left over. The one serious relationship she'd had in her life had broken up very messily. She hadn't been in any hurry to start another.

But that had been nearly a decade ago. Maybe it was time to face down Jake's emotional ghost.

She rolled over onto her stomach, burying her face in the pillow. Maybe she wouldn't send Jeff to help Fairfax with his computer in the morning. Maybe she'd just go herself.

Chapter Four

As it turned out, Trieka had to send Jeff after all. As they neared the jump site, an anomaly in its readings set off minor alarms. Trieka spent most of the morning with Robin, analyzing the readings, then making scheduling changes and clearing them with EarthFed. The site was still in an unstable cycle, which should have passed a few days ago. They'd have to sit stationary until the site stabilized—hopefully a delay of no more than a day. Sometimes predicting jump sites could be as exact a science as predicting the weather.

With some time on her hands, she went to check in with Fairfax right after lunch, carrying a box of cheese and milk. Her buzz at the door was greeted by an immediate, "Come in."

He was stretched out on his berth, reading a book. He wore loose black cotton pants with elastic at the ankles and a dark blue silk shirt. The shirt was only partially buttoned, crookedly, so one side gaped open. His feet were bare, heels butted against the end of the berth. He had long toes and narrow ankles. Trieka wondered why she noticed.

"Captain," he said with a smile, sitting up. "What can I do for you?"

Button another button on that damn shirt. She could see far too much of the soft brown hair on his chest. "I just wanted to see how things went with Commander Anderson this morning."

"Oh, they went fine. I was looking over the files earlier, but I needed a break."

"Good. If you need anything else, let me know." She set the box down on his desk. "I also brought this."

Fairfax looked quizzically at the box. "What is it?"

"Cheese and milk. It looks like we'll be making the hyperspace jump sometime tomorrow, so you might want to get started eating."

Fairfax nodded. "Thank you. That's very considerate."

"The other passengers have their own supply. I collected this from the crew. Most of us don't need it."

Fairfax looked concerned. "Are you sure? I don't want anybody giving the stuff up if they need it."

"I'm sure. Most of this is mine. I've never had hyperspace sickness, and I don't even take the crew shots." For whatever reason, the demon that had taken her father had shown no interest in her.

"Maybe it isn't a genetic predisposition?"

So he remembered the personal snippets she'd let slip during the ship's tour. That pleased her, strangely, but also made her uncomfortable. "I don't know. Unfortunately, nobody knows what causes hyperspace sickness, so there's no set cure. But men seem to be more susceptible than women, and taller men even more so."

"That's encouraging," Fairfax said dryly.

"Don't worry. We'll take care of you. Just hit the emergency button next to the berth if you need to contact medical. Speaking of the berth, it looks a little short. Are you comfortable?"

"It's fine. Thanks for asking."

"All right." She hesitated. Surely there was something else, something she had to ask or tell him, some reason to stay a few minutes longer. But nothing came to mind. She patted the box. "Enjoy."

He smiled. "I will."

※ ※ ※

A beep woke Fairfax from half-sleep. He had dozed off, sitting in his desk chair watching the computer run a decryption program. He couldn't do anything at this point, but he was afraid someone might notice he'd linked his little pad up to the ship's computers. So he'd sat and watched, ready to log off at any indication the intrusion had been noted.

Now the coded garbage had begun to unscramble into readable text. He glanced at his watch, surprised to see it was three a.m. The last time he'd checked, it had been just past eleven. His eyes burned and pain stabbed behind his left eye. Obviously the snatches of sleep hadn't been enough.

He went to the coldbox and poured a glass of the champagne. Lifting the glass toward the computer, he said quietly, "For you, Kathi." He sipped, then sat back down.

The computer finished the last file, presenting him with a screen full of text. Fairfax bent forward to read.

The champagne hadn't been a good idea. The few swallows had hit him hard, leaving him warm and weak and a little dizzy, not to mention even sleepier. He set the glass aside and opened a carton of milk.

The files were everything he'd expected. More and, at the same time, less. Straightforward, emotionless descriptions of orders given and carried out, of raped ecosystems, of entire planets bent to the will of EarthFed in the name of progress and colonial expansion.

They had plans for Denahault as well. To tame the extreme weather, to eliminate from the local fauna anything that might threaten the establishment of a human colony. Bile rose in his throat, thick and burning. Hadn't humanity learned anything in the last century, when whales and elephants and every kind of lemur had teetered on the edge of extinction?

But he'd forgotten. This wasn't humanity. This was politics.

In any case, the evidence was damning, descriptive and ultimately usable. It didn't matter how he'd gotten it—if he leaked it to the right sources, the ball would start rolling. And eventually roll right over EarthFed's head.

What about Cavendish, though? Did her involvement in the colonization program automatically indict her? Her name appeared several times in the logs, but only in the most obvious contexts.

Then he found it.

"The Denahault situation has actually proven fortuitous." This from Admiral Derocher himself, to a colleague in the State

Department. The man who'd replaced Kathi's father, in fact. The electronic memo had initially been sent under Class Eight security encryption, then collected and put into a digest with the whole file coded Class Nine. "It could prove the perfect tool to eliminate a number of problems." Including himself, Fairfax thought.

"I concur with the plan as stated," the State Department man had replied. "Recommend a ship and someone you can trust to keep this quiet."

And Derocher's answer: "I recommend Captain Trieka Cavendish. Her loyalty is, in my mind, unquestionable."

But did that really mean anything? Just because Derocher trusted Cavendish's loyalty didn't mean Cavendish was in the know. She could just be one tool of many, usable because of her dedication. She saw EarthFed in terms of her father, not in terms of worms like Derocher.

He had to know.

He'd broken into the ship's systems once, to add to his processing power. It wasn't much of a jump to get into Cavendish's personal logs.

Fairfax glanced at his watch. Four a.m. Shrugging, he resumed tapping the keyboard. Who needed sleep?

At noon the next day Lieutenant Wu pronounced the jump site stable. It had been so for three hours and was projected to be so for another nine. The second leg of the journey could begin.

Preparations for the hyperspace jump were minimal. The passengers should be prepared already; they'd been briefed in detail and run through various tests to judge their reactions to the interdimensional leap as a part of the screening process before they'd been accepted into the program. The crew was ready, and so was the ship. The only questionable element was, as usual, Fairfax.

To add to the uncertainties about his readiness, no one had seen Fairfax all day, and attempts to contact him via the shipboard comm had proved fruitless.

"Maybe he's sleeping in," Lieutenant Wu suggested.

Trieka glanced sidelong at Robin and frowned.

"I suppose the admiral will be displeased if we let him get squashed against a bulkhead. Jeff, run to his quarters and make sure he buckles up."

"Yes, sir."

A few minutes later, Trieka's intercom buzzed. She thumbed the button. "Go ahead."

"We're all set here," Jeff's voice said. "I'll be up front in five."

"Confirmed." Trieka turned to Robin. "Start the final warm-up on the engines. We'll hop as soon as Jeff gets settled."

"Aye, sir."

A soft hum rose in the cockpit as Robin activated the engines. Trieka leaned back in her chair to listen. The sound was almost musical, but dissonant, like bagpipes heard from a distance.

"I'm back."

Trieka barely moved her head toward Jeff to acknowledge his return. He settled into his seat and buckled up.

Hearing the sound of the engines rise a notch, Trieka drew her own chest and waist belts into place. "What was Fairfax up to, anyway?"

"Still in bed. He said he was up all night playing games on the computer."

Trieka grinned wryly. "That sounds familiar. Start the countdown, Lieutenant Wu."

As the other members of the cockpit crew fastened their restraints, Trieka closed her eyes and leaned back in her chair, letting her body go limp. She'd discovered some time ago that, if she held any tension in her body, the hyperspace jump could be uncomfortable, even painful. But, if she relaxed completely, the sensations were actually enjoyable.

Kind of like sex, she thought, not for the first time. The comparison still brought a smile to her mouth.

She peeked out from under an eyelid to see her crew

members settling down. Robin was the only one with eyes still open. Even though the ship followed an automatic sequencing and course setting, the navigator wasn't happy unless she watched the entire process.

The sound of the engines shifted slightly as they entered the jump site. Only a set of stationary red signal buoys marked the spot as unusual. Then, as the nose of the *Starchild* passed the buoys, the universe changed.

The feeling started in the pit of Trieka's stomach, like the initial descent on a roller coaster. She willed herself to relax, letting the sensations take over.

As the ship lumbered on, the sound of the engines changed again in a weird Doppler-like effect. They had entered a rift in space, where the normal three dimensions of human existence twisted into the fourth dimension of time, then into the fifth which was hyperspace.

All exterior viewports blanked out, and would remain blanked until they returned to normal space. Once, on a smaller ship where the viewports were blocked manually, Trieka had looked out a small viewport, only for a second. She'd had to—something in her had needed to face the demon that had killed her father. For days, she'd been disoriented and had fought to hide her condition from her superiors. But it hadn't killed her, and now it no longer frightened her.

Something strange happened in hyperspace—not only a warping of distances, but a convergence of possibilities. Dimensions crossed and mingled within it, time and place undifferentiated. Visually, it was something the human brain simply couldn't process. Trieka still couldn't describe what she'd seen, or how it had felt.

The ship moved on, trembling a little, then settling. Trieka felt dizzy, breathing deeply as a wave of nausea gripped her. That didn't usually happen. Apparently the jump site, while stable, wasn't as smooth as it could have been.

When the ship began to stabilize, Trieka heard it in the sound of the engines. She opened her eyes again to take a peek at the crew. Everyone looked all right, relaxing with closed eyes. Even Robin had given in. Jeff, though, held a blood-soaked cloth to his face. He was the only person Trieka knew who got nosebleeds from hyperspace.

"You all right?"

"Ibe fide," he replied.

"Lieutenant Wu, what's our ETA to the Denahault jump site?"

The navigator still frowned over her terminal, calculating the available probability curves. "Approximately eight days. I can give you an estimate to the minute in about an hour."

"Good enough," said Trieka. She leaned back, closed her eyes and smiled a little. "Steady as she goes."

✳ ✳ ✳

Fairfax pulled at his safety harness, which cut uncomfortably into his neck. The seat of his chair vibrated faintly, and he could hear the rising pitch of the engines. "*Relax,*" the commander had told him. "*Relax, and it'll be over in a few minutes. It really isn't all that bad.*"

The roar of the engines rose louder. A strange enervation passed down Fairfax's limbs. Suddenly he was afraid to stay strapped in the chair. He pulled again at the restraining straps, his fingers weak and uncertain. The engines seemed to scream inside his head. Blood pounded behind his eyes like fingers trying to push his eyeballs forward, out of their sockets. The walls of the small cabin shimmered.

He closed his eyes, panic rising in his chest. The howl of the engines drowned out everything but the sound of his own heartbeat.

"*Harrison...*"

Fairfax gasped in shock, his eyes snapping open. The voice had been impossibly soft, a murmur he shouldn't have been able to hear over the engines. But the sound of it closed a fist around his heart.

"Kathi."

The room was empty. The shimmering had intensified. Looking at the moving walls made him sick. The voice came again, a breath of memory, carrying with it a soft odor of roses.

"*Harrison...*"

Colors came together from the air and suddenly she stood in front of him. Straight black hair framed an oval face. Her eyes were dark, and she smiled. A hard lump rose in Fairfax's throat.

"Kathi..."

"It's all right," she said. She faded, becoming translucent. He tried to reach out, but the webbing held him.

"No."

"Don't stop searching," she said. *"You have to end this. She can help you."*

The lump rose into Fairfax's sinuses, filling his head with thick tears. She had become a wisp of color against the cabin's gray walls. She lifted her hand to her lips and kissed her fingers, then turned her palm toward him.

"I love you." Her lips moved, but he could no longer hear her voice.

"No!" he howled, and tears came behind it. He sagged against the webbing, weeping.

❈ ❈ ❈

They settled nicely into hyperspace, the ship weaving a stable course through folded space. Trieka returned to her cabin to enter her daily log. She was just finishing when her comm panel buzzed.

"Cavendish."

"Captain, it's Commander Anderson."

"What's up, Jeff?"

"Not a lot. I just thought you might like to know that Fairfax called medical right after we stabilized in hyperspace."

Trieka frowned. "Is he all right?"

"I don't know. I assume it's not serious. He was treated in his cabin."

"All right. Thanks."

Trieka broke the connection and considered, tapping her keyboard with a short, blunt fingernail. He was probably fine. If there had been an emergency, she would have been notified by medical. That didn't stop her from worrying, though. Apparently Fairfax had awakened her maternal instincts. Funny—she hadn't thought she had any.

He didn't answer her buzz immediately. She was about to buzz again when she heard the soft click of the door lock disengaging. She pushed the button and the door slid open. With some trepidation, Trieka stepped in.

Fairfax lay on the too-short bed, on his back. He had one arm bent behind his head, the other rested on his stomach. His legs were crossed at the ankles. As Trieka came in, he swiveled his head slightly toward her. His eyes looked dead, as if he hid pain behind them.

"Captain," he said in a voice just as emotionless.

"Mr. Fairfax." Trieka paused, not sure what to say. "I heard you called medical. I just wanted to see how you were doing."

"I'm fine." He almost snapped the words, then his lips pressed tightly together and he blinked rapidly a few times. Trieka waited.

After a moment, he sat up in the bed and looked at her. His eyes were red-rimmed. Startled, Trieka realized he'd been crying.

"I'm sorry," he said, more gently. "The hyperspace jump had some side effects I didn't expect, that's all."

Trieka nodded. "Hallucinations?"

He merely looked at her without answering, then said, "What causes that?"

"Nobody knows. Theory has it that some people are more sensitive to the probability intersections than others. So the hallucinations are actually glimpses into other probabilities."

He absorbed her words in silence. His jaw clenched, a muscle bulging along his jaw line, then relaxing. He looked away from her. "I saw my wife."

"Oh," Trieka said, because she could think of nothing else. She could only imagine what it must have felt like. "I'm sorry."

"The doctor gave me a shot. She said it should make me feel better." There was a bitter twinge in his voice. Trieka moved toward the door.

"If there's anything I can do for you, please let me know—"

He looked at her then, and she froze in the intensity of his gaze. There were too many emotions in his eyes to count: fear, anger, heart-rending sorrow. Then a quick flash across his face: determination, decision.

"There is something you can do for me. No matter what happens, no matter what you find out, I want you to trust me."

Trieka swallowed. Her throat was utterly dry. "I don't understand."

He shook his head once, sharply. "No. Not understanding. Trust." He moistened his lips, still holding her in his gaze. "Will you?"

Her head moved a little to one side, as if in negation. She felt weak with him staring at her, as if she'd lost control of all faculties, mental and physical.

And suddenly she realized she wanted him. More than just casually, or out of curiosity. She wanted to cradle him with her body and make him forget the tears he'd just shed and whatever had caused them. And then she wanted to peel him out of his clothes and crush him naked against the wall by the narrow berth.

Control came back to her only because she fought for it. Still his eyes held her, and somehow she knew something fundamental was about to change. Within her, around her. Outside, hyperspace divided possibilities, probabilities, wide and narrow paths.

Tentatively, Trieka set her feet on one.

"I'll see what I can do."

Chapter Five

The sound of the engines wound down from a scream to a rumbling roar as the *Starchild* eased back into normal space. Trieka closed her eyes and clenched her teeth, then unclenched them, trying to relax. She'd been afraid of this. It didn't always happen, but occasionally reentry from a longer jump, particularly with instabilities at the initial jump site, gave her a howling headache.

"Transfer complete," Robin announced. Her voice was calm and quiet, as always. "Estimated time to Denahault...fifty-three hours, twenty-seven minutes."

"Thank you, Lieutenant," Trieka said. She also spoke quietly, in deference to her pounding head. "Commander, take it from here. I'll be in medical."

Jeff nodded. "Are you all right?"

"I will be." She started toward the door. "I'll be back."

The *Starchild*'s sickbay was only a shade larger than the average cabin, but two beds and a wall full of equipment competed for the tiny space. Trieka stepped into the cramped room, surprised to see she wasn't the only patient. Fairfax sat on one of the beds, shedding a collection of restraining belts. He looked up and started to say something, but Doctor Franklin interrupted.

"Don't get up just yet, Mr. Fairfax. The medication will throw off your equilibrium for at least another thirty minutes. You're better off staying here." The doctor turned to Trieka. "What can I do for you, Captain?"

"Headache," Trieka said.

"All right. Sit down."

Trieka eased onto the other bed. The doctor filled a hypo. Trieka watched her, rolling up her sleeve.

"This should do it," Dr. Franklin said. The sprayer burned against Trieka's skin as medication shot into her arm. "Sit tight for about a half hour. If you don't feel better by then, we'll give you another." On the wall, a light flashed on the communications board. Dr. Franklin grinned wryly. "That'll be Mrs. Gibson losing her lunch. You two take it easy. I'll be back."

Trieka meticulously rolled her sleeve back down, careful not to look at Fairfax. She'd seen little of him during their time in hyperspace. Rattled by their last encounter, she had, quite simply, been avoiding him. He hadn't sought her out, either.

"Headache, huh?" He broke the silence gently.

She looked at him then. Their last conversation seemed surreal now. Especially her sudden surge of...whatever it had been. Lust? No, not quite. Something more alien to her system. Something she'd never quite felt before.

"Yeah," she said. "It happens sometimes on long jumps."

"I decided to take the jump here. It seemed prudent."

"I can't say I blame you."

They fell into an awkward silence. Trieka dredged her brain for something to say, found nothing. Finally Fairfax spoke again.

"Captain?"

She looked hesitantly up at him. He seemed nervous. "Yes?"

"I don't know what kind of...facilities...are available on Denahault, but I wonder if I might take you to dinner?"

"I really don't think it would be appropriate," she said. Or intended to say. What came out was, "There's a restaurant at the embassy."

Fairfax smiled a little. "Is that a yes?"

Trieka couldn't bring herself to say the word. Finally she nodded. "It's probably not appropriate, though."

"Appropriateness has never been my forte. I am, after all, a wealthy eccentric. And my immunity from societal judgment tends to rub off on those around me. In other words, I think we can get away with it at least once. Maybe twice."

Trieka smiled in spite of herself. She wanted to see him in a more normal context, when she could be herself instead of Captain Cavendish. And he was right. They probably could get away with it. As long as she didn't do anything illegal, her off-duty time was pretty much her own.

"All right," she said. "I'm game."

"Good." She noticed that he looked smug, then she noticed her eyes were closing completely against her will.

"Damn," she muttered.

Trieka barely registered Fairfax's look of concern through her eyelashes. "What's wrong?"

"She did it to me again. Gave me something to put me to sleep..." She paused to yawn expansively, covering the unflattering gape with both hands. "Didn't have the decency to tell me." She stretched out on the small bed, vaguely aware of his chuckle as she drifted into sleep.

❀ ❀ ❀

Fairfax's own medication had him a bit wobbly and weak. He watched with amusement as Cavendish fell hard into unconsciousness. She looked peaceful and content, her slow, deep breathing soughing in the small room. Studying the innocence of her sleeping face, Fairfax suddenly felt guilty for what he'd done.

It had been necessary, though, and now, after hacking into and reading her personal logs, he knew she wasn't involved. Or at least he'd found no evidence she was, and his instincts had filled in the rest.

And Kathi—he was nearly certain Kathi had meant Cavendish when she'd said, "She can help you."

His thoughts turned from his vendetta. It had driven him for too long and he knew it. Watching the quietly sleeping woman reminded him of that. He resisted the temptation to reach across the small space separating them to touch her. He wasn't sure he wouldn't have fallen off the bed if he tried, anyway.

Katharine would have liked her. They would have fought

tooth and nail, but in the end they would have been friends. Then he realized what he was thinking, and an icy tendril of fear curled into the pit of his stomach. This was too fast, too soon. He wasn't ready.

It's been seven years, another voice protested.

But he wasn't sure he could let go. Not until all was laid to rest. He had to know the truth, and until he did, he couldn't let anything else matter.

❋ ❋ ❋

The *Starchild* docked cleanly, hooking airlocks with the Denahault station, which in contrast to EarthStar II was barely larger than the ship. Trieka's breath came fast and her heart pounded in her ears as the airlocks meshed. They had arrived.

"Docking complete," Lieutenant Wu announced.

Taking a slow breath to calm herself, Trieka keyed her intercom. "Attention passengers. We have completed docking procedures and will begin disembarking in approximately fifteen minutes. Please prepare your belongings and consult your schedules." Keying off the comm, she turned to her crew and grinned. "We made it."

Disembarking was a long, tedious affair, but Trieka's adrenaline wouldn't stop pumping. High as she was, the endless string of "good-byes" and "good lucks" seemed exciting. Most of the passengers were able to find their own way to the shuttles that would take them planetside. The few who needed help were handled quickly and efficiently by Jeff and Robin.

Fairfax was one of the last to disembark. He looked tired. He'd looked tired through most of the journey, actually. He carried a simple, large suitcase and a shoulder bag for his computer equipment. He shifted the suitcase from his right hand to his left as Trieka extended her hand in farewell.

"How was the trip?" Trieka asked. His hand closed firmly over hers, warm and big.

"Could have been worse," he said, then smiled.

She smiled back. "You're here in one piece, I suppose that's what counts."

Fairfax glanced at Jeff, who was talking to another passenger. "Can I have your contact number?"

She mumbled it to him. He repeated the numbers silently. "When will you be planetside?"

"About fifteen-hundred."

"All right. I'll call you."

She grew warm again, on the verge of a blush. How did he do that to her? It was hard, suddenly, to look into his eyes. She forced herself. Sad eyes, she thought, sad even in their color, the color of the sky before a heavy thunderstorm. He gave her a quiet, tired, sad smile. She swallowed hard.

"I'll be there." Her voice gave her away, as she'd feared it might. He only nodded and turned away, walking down the corridor to board the shuttle that would take him planetside.

She arrived in Denahault Prime at 1445 local time, after a quiet shuttle ride, during which her adrenaline had finally crashed. Jeff had awakened her as they entered the atmosphere, so she could watch the approach. Denahault was blue and green, much like Earth but with more water. Denahault Prime sat on the eastern shore of the largest land mass, situated in the northern hemisphere. The continent was roughly the size of Australia.

As part of her training, Trieka had spent a year on each colony planet. In the end, she'd chosen Denahault as her planet of choice, because it was the newest, least populated and farthest-flung. Even now, with the obvious expansion of Denahault Prime, it felt rugged, untouched.

"We've added a wing to the embassy building," the mayor, Greg Williams, explained as he led them to their temporary lodgings. "It can accommodate special guests now. The rooms are very nice."

"Unlike ours," Trieka commented, smiling.

Williams grinned back. "We can take advantage of you because anything looks good after two weeks shipboard."

"Too true."

The rooms *were* small, but bigger than ship's quarters, and Trieka actually liked the snug comfort they afforded. She unloaded her luggage, then settled down to set up her computer so she could start her planetside log. She would be here for a week, making sure the colonists settled in. If there were any problems, she could take passengers back with her when she left. A few older colonists were already booked on the *Starchild*'s return voyage.

It was nearly 1700 when she realized she'd forgotten to turn on her wrist comm, which she'd had to shut down for the duration of the shuttle trip. She flipped it on and the red message light began to blink. She pressed a button to retrieve her messages. The tiny screen flickered, then displayed Fairfax's face.

"Captain, you're late. Call me when you get in. I'm at the embassy, room six-eleven."

She called. Fairfax looked like he'd just come out of the shower. His hair was wet, and he was shirtless. He also looked more rested. Trieka got a good look at his bare torso before he moved closer to the vidphone, cutting himself off at the nipples. He looked good—lean and trim, his chest carrying a nice thatch of brown hair.

"Hello, Captain," he said. "You finally made it."

Trieka shrugged apologetically. "I've actually been here a couple of hours. I forgot to turn my comm back on."

"Ah. So you're avoiding me."

"Not intentionally."

"Then we're still on?"

"Sure."

"Okay. The bad news is the restaurant is closed for remodeling. The good news is I've got a kitchenette in my room."

"I can't cook."

Fairfax grinned. "Not a problem. I'm cooking."

Trieka weighed that. "All right. Sounds interesting."

"Can you be here at seven-thirty? That's nineteen-thirty for you military types."

She smiled. "I'll be there."

She sat smiling at herself for a few minutes after she broke the connection. He was cooking. Even in this liberated age, Trieka had never had a man cook her dinner. Apparently she'd been seeing all the wrong men. Then she realized the only civvies she'd brought were utilitarian. Well, he couldn't expect an evening gown, so jeans and a sweater would have to do.

The embassy was only a few blocks from Trieka's building, so she elected to walk. The night was cool and crisp, the stars bright. She looked up at the constellations, clear in the dark sky. There were only a few streetlights, not enough to block out the stars. The Great Horn hung to the south, the Starwalker next to it. Alien patterns to remind her she was no longer on Earth. It was easy to forget, here in a city, which, though still small by Earth standards, was modern and comfortable.

The new visitors' wing at the embassy resembled a luxury hotel. She rode the elevator to the sixth floor, knocked at the door marked six-eleven. A moment later, Fairfax opened the door.

He wore jeans and a sweater, too, so that worry was out of the way. The room smelled of garlic and olive oil. Trieka's mouth went moist at the odor.

"Come on in," said Fairfax. "Let me take your coat."

"Something smells good." She shrugged out of her light jacket, trying to avoid his touch as he helped her. His hand brushed her shoulder, though, and she fought the warmth that suffused her at the contact. She was far too aware of him, of the shape of his body beneath his clothes, of the way his hands moved and the subtle odor of his cologne.

"I made spaghetti," he said, shifting her jacket in his hands before hanging it in the small closet. "Not spectacular, I know, but I added some things to the sauce. The main street store actually had fresh garlic."

"They grow it here. It's medicinal."

"I picked up some wine, too. I don't know how good it is. Would you like some?"

"Please."

He brought her a glass, and she sipped while he puttered in the kitchen. Finally he brought a plate of spaghetti and garlic bread. They sat on the floor and ate off the coffee table, talking of Denahault Prime, the outlying colonies and local politics. Then the conversation drifted.

"This is a nice place," Fairfax commented. "I expected something more rugged."

"The settlements are. No electricity, fetch your water from

the river. Forest Walk isn't far from here, and I think they're working on running electricity out there, but funds are tight so it's taking forever."

He smiled a little. "You like it that way, don't you?"

Trieka shrugged. "Somehow it just wouldn't be the same if you could pick up a phone in Forest Walk and call Farhallen."

He studied her, his eyes betraying unexpected warmth. "You're very good at what you do, you know."

"Thank you." She almost stammered. The compliment had come from nowhere.

"It needed to be said. I doubt you hear it often enough."

He fell silent, perusing the depths of his wine glass. For a time his thoughts seemed far away, then they jerked back. "I almost forgot. I bought cheesecake. Do you want some?"

"Oh, absolutely." Fairfax started to get up. Trieka moved, too, waving for him to sit back down. "Let me get it."

"No, that's all right."

"Let me pick up the dishes then."

"Be my guest."

Trieka gathered the dishes and carried them into the little kitchenette. The sink was too small to hold them, so she turned on the faucet and started to rinse the plates.

"Don't bother with that," Fairfax said. "I can get it later."

"It's no trouble, really—"

"I said leave it." There was laughter in his voice as he reached around from behind her to turn off the water. "I'll do it later."

He was standing directly behind her, his right arm extended around her to reach the faucet, practically embracing her. His chest brushed against her back. Gently, Trieka laid the dishes down in the sink. Fairfax let go of the faucet and started to move away. Quite deliberately, Trieka took a step backward, full into him.

They were both still for a long breath. Then Trieka made a small, nestling motion with her body, to make sure he knew the contact hadn't been accidental.

His hands came up and clasped her shoulders. She felt his

breath on her neck, his lips. It seemed the shape of his mouth was branded on her skin. He withdrew, then kissed her again, near her nape, soft lips, his tongue wet against her skin, and finally his teeth as he bit her gently.

She thought she might melt back into his body, suffused by his heat, drowned in his smell. His right hand left her shoulder, reached across in front of her and cupped her left cheek. With his hand on her face, he turned her to face him.

What she saw in his eyes could only be described as raw hunger, but there was something else beneath it, something born of a less animal emotion. She had only a moment to find it before he closed his mouth over hers, crushing her to him.

His mouth felt as good as it looked, soft and hot and demanding. He tasted of garlic and wine and coffee—not the best of combinations, but she was sure she tasted much the same. She put her hands on his waist, thinking to push him away, but instead her fingers found the edge of his sweater and slid under, meeting skin. Before she knew what she was doing, she had her hands on his back, up to his shoulder blades, the sweater bunched up above her wrists and half off him.

He made a low noise in his throat, and suddenly he shifted, easing her to the floor, ducking his head as she pulled his sweater off him. She buried her head in his chest, his hair rough against her eyelids and mouth. He was lean and cleanly made, and the smell of his skin turned her body to water.

His hands slid up her back, under her sweater, returning the favor she'd done him. For a moment she regretted not having worn a bra. She never wore them off-duty, and she hadn't anticipated having her shirt pulled off this evening. But off it came, and she arched into him, his chest hair rough against her bare breasts, the shock of skin against skin warm and glorious.

He pulled back from her, and her left breast disappeared in the curve of his big hand. His mouth was on her throat again, traveling up to her ear and under her chin, devouring her.

"Oh, God..."

Her voice shattered the spell. Fairfax jerked away. On his knees above her, his hand still cupping her breast, he looked down at her and she saw that sadness in his eyes, so profound it struck her like physical pain. She touched his face, tracing his full lower lip with a finger.

"What's wrong?"

His hand flattened against her breast, then withdrew. He shifted to sit next to her, his face sinking into his hands. Trieka sat up as well. Suddenly self-conscious, she pulled her sweater on.

"I'm sorry," he said. "I can't."

"I'm sorry, too," she replied. "But I'm not leaving without my cheesecake."

A smile flickered across his mouth, bitter, as he lifted his head again. "Yeah."

She went back to the couch and sat down, looking at the front door until he returned with dessert. They ate in silence. Maybe the cheesecake hadn't been worth the discomfort.

Then Fairfax spoke. "It's Kathi," he said.

Trieka turned to him. He was staring at the graham cracker crumbs on his plate. His left thumb pushed at his wedding ring, turning it around his finger. Trieka didn't think he was aware he did it.

"It's been—" He broke off, closed his eyes, leaned his head back against the couch. "It's been seven years, and I know there isn't much hope she's alive, but I have to know."

Trieka touched his elbow lightly, and he lifted his head to look at her.

"It's all right," she said. She stood. "Thanks for dinner."

Walking back to her room, she reflected that it was probably best things had turned out this way. As much as she wanted to make love to him, it would be a point of no return for her, and she sensed he felt the same way.

She looked west, into the strange constellations, into a pattern of stars astrogators had dubbed The Lovers.

Next time, Fairfax. Next time you won't get off so easy.

"You," Fairfax said aloud to no one, "are a complete idiot."

She'd taken it well, at least. It hadn't even seemed to occur to her that he might have been rejecting her personally. Which was good, because that wasn't the case at all. He wanted her. It just hadn't been right. Not for him.

At least his strange attraction was reciprocated. That might smooth the road he had to walk, make it easier for her to stomach the betrayals he'd already committed.

Who was he kidding? That she cared for him, that she knew he cared for her, would just make it worse. He would lose her when the truth finally came out. All the more reason to have ended it before something irrevocable happened.

All the more reason to have made love to her while he'd had the chance.

But it was too late for that now. He stretched out on the couch, staring at the ceiling. He could still feel the shape of her breast in his hand. A small breast, barely enough to fill the curve of his palm. Her eyes had been a strange color, almost teal green. And that slim, coltish body had fit under his like it was meant to be there.

What a waste of an opportunity.

He sat up, wondering where he could get a beer at this hour. Outside, there was a stirring in the hallway, then a knock at the door. Fairfax frowned. Who could that be? Cavendish hadn't left anything behind. He went to the door.

Outside stood three men, suited and official-looking. The tallest of the three, soft-featured and graying, stepped forward into the doorway.

"Mr. Fairfax?"

He resisted the obvious attempt to force him back into the room. "May I help you?"

The man produced a military ID from a suit pocket. "I'm Admiral Ford from EarthFed. This is General Preston and General McCloud from the embassy. We'd like you to come with us."

So this was it. His stomach sank in sick fear, but his voice came quiet and level. "I see. I've been expecting you."

He stepped out into the hallway and gently closed the door behind him.

Chapter Six

Trieka woke to the buzzing of her wrist comm. She sat up, blinking. The clock read 0840. She'd overslept. Straightening her hair with one hand, she checked her pajama buttons, then picked up the comm from the bedside table.

"Captain." Jeff's formality, coupled with the deep groove between his blond brows, brought Trieka to instant alertness.

"Commander. What is it?"

"We have a problem."

"A problem?"

"I'm scrambling the line on this end. Can you do the same?"

"Sure." Trieka flipped the appropriate switch. "So what's wrong?"

"We had an in-flight security breach."

For a moment, she couldn't form words for the shock. "A breach? What happened?"

"Someone broke into our security systems and copied a number of files."

She looked away, then back, still wearing what she was certain was a look of complete stupidity. Jeff went on.

"At first we thought it might be one of our people checking the systems, but it wasn't."

"Do you know who it was?"

Jeff's face shifted slightly, rendering it totally unreadable. "Yes, we do. It was Fairfax."

Trieka opened her mouth, then snapped it shut. She quite simply had no idea what to say. Jeff filled the silence. "It was smoothly done, I'll give him that much. Security had a devil of a time tracing it."

"What did he take?"

"Portions of your personal logs, sir. And it appears he hooked his computer into our mainframe to augment his own power, though we're not sure what he did with it."

She felt suddenly sick. "My personal logs?"

"Yes, sir." He hesitated while Trieka absorbed. "Shall I contact the embassy, sir? By all rights we should have him arrested."

Jeff was right. Completely right. But she'd gathered her wits, and out of her composure rose a deep, personal anger. Why her logs? Had he been using her? If so, for what? Had he backed off last night because his conscience had finally caught up to him?

"No," she told Jeff. "Don't call the embassy. Not yet."

She got up and dressed. In uniform, she was calmer, more businesslike. The problem became one of security and the sanctity of her ship, rather than a personal betrayal. She dialed the embassy and requested room six-eleven.

The receptionist tapped keys on her computer, then looked back into the vidphone.

"I'm sorry, ma'am. There's no one registered in room six-eleven."

Trieka blinked. The day was becoming more surreal by the moment. "I was just there last night. It was registered to Harrison Fairfax."

The receptionist consulted her terminal again. "Mr. Fairfax checked in yesterday afternoon, but he checked out again this morning."

"Did he say where he was going?"

"He said something about visiting one of the outer settlements. There were a couple of men waiting for him in the lobby." She paused, frowning delicately. "It's funny, though. I always thought he was taller."

Trieka felt her eyebrows rise and for a moment was certain

they were going to slide right off her head. "Taller? What did he look like?"

"Maybe five-ten. Brown hair."

"I see. Thank you for your help."

Trieka broke the connection and stared at the vidphone. What in the hell was going on?

She folded her hands and rested her chin on them, eyes narrowing as she considered the options. First possibility, he'd set her up. He'd used her ship to get access to classified information, and she'd let herself be blinded by his face and his aura and her obviously mistaken impression that he was attracted to her.

Second possibility, given the strangely shorter version of himself that had left the embassy this morning, something much more dangerous was going on.

She put her face in her hands, trying to gather convoluted thoughts. Had he known this moment would come? He'd asked her to trust him, no matter what might happen. She wanted to do just that. Was that her head talking or her heart?

Facts, she thought. Stick to facts. Fairfax had disappeared, the circumstances strange enough to make her consider the possibility of his innocence. As far as she knew, Fairfax's background was scrupulously clean. Although his wealth had invited the occasional investigation, all his dealings had proven above board. So why would he risk his reputation—even his whole fortune—to trespass into her private logs? It made no sense.

Unless it was part of a bigger picture.

At the taste of blood in her mouth, Trieka realized she'd gnawed off a piece of skin on the inside of her lip. She clenched her teeth to stop the nervous chewing. What was the greater picture? What mattered so much to Fairfax that he'd risk himself?

His wife. In her mind's eye she could see him, rotating the gold ring around his finger. Katharine Maier's disappearance was still a mystery, and Fairfax himself had said last night that he couldn't move on until he knew what had happened to her.

But what in the name of all Trieka considered holy could Katharine Maier's disappearance have to do with her?

Something was definitely afoot, something much bigger than an abortive attempt at an affair. Maybe even bigger than financial investment in a foundering off-world colony. Possibilities began to move through Trieka's head, and she didn't like any of them.

But she had to find out. She was going to the embassy.

Decision made, she pulled on her coat and picked up her room key. She'd had it in her jeans pocket last night, but her uniform didn't provide such accommodations. She started to slide the key into an outside jacket pocket, then changed her mind and put it in the smaller pocket inside the coat.

But the pocket wasn't empty.

Puzzled, Trieka pulled out the contents. Computer disks, two of them, unlabeled, and not military issue.

Under other circumstances, she might have put the disks aside and gone on about her business. But too many strange things had happened over the last twenty-four hours. She flipped on the desktop computer and slid a disk into the drive.

The disk contents were password protected. She sat staring at the flashing cursor, wondering what the password might be. If they were her disks, she'd know the password; she used the same one for everything. Curious, she typed it in, and the computer opened the disk.

The disk held two folders and a file. The folders were labeled "Cavendish Logs" and "Derocher Logs". The file said, "Read Me". She opened it.

Keep these, Captain. You're the only one I trust. HF.

The folders of her own logs dated from a week before the departure from EarthStar II to the day after their entry into hyperspace and held nothing of consequence. He could have left them off the disk. Instead he'd included them, admitting his invasion of her privacy.

She opened Derocher's logs. They were excerpts, from various dates. Skimming through them, she felt a slow, sick, sinking feeling. The room seemed to spin around her. Swallowing a thick lump of emotion, she ejected the disk and put in the other.

This one held three more folders, labeled "Letters", "Orders" and "Intelligence". She skimmed them, and understood.

"My God, Fairfax."

Suddenly the trespass into her logs seemed trivial. Either he'd gone to a great deal of trouble to manufacture an elaborate lie, or her whole world had just changed in the space of a few breaths.

Her hands shook as she picked up the wrist comm to call Jeff.

❋ ❋ ❋

"I'm going to ask one more time, Mr. Fairfax. Where are the disks?"

Fairfax closed his eyes. His mouth hurt and the space behind his lower lip kept filling with blood. They'd tied his wrists and ankles too tight, and that hurt, too.

"I don't know." Which was true, in a sense. He knew where he'd left them, but who knew where Cavendish's jacket might be right now?

"Did you give them to someone?" They'd asked him this question before, too, at least five times.

"Who would I give them to?"

He was tired. By his reckoning, they'd been at this nearly six hours. The same questions, over and over, the same answers, the occasional interlude of physical violence. The beatings hadn't been severe, but he was getting tired of swallowing his own blood.

"You might as well give up," Ford said. "No one knows you're here. As far as anyone back home will know, you went to visit one of the settlements and you were lost in an unfortunate accident."

Fairfax just looked at him, weary, aching and totally unwilling to bend.

General McCloud shook his head. "He's not going to tell us anything."

"That's right," Fairfax said. "So why don't you just kill me now and get it over with?"

McCloud looked at Ford. Ford smiled.

"That would be too easy, wouldn't it, Mr. Fairfax? No, I think it's time to try something different. General McCloud, might we treat Mr. Fairfax to a few of our home movies?"

※ ※ ※

Jeff sat at the terminal, his face as sober as Trieka had ever seen it. Finally he took a deep breath, closed the "Letters" folder and ejected the disk.

"This is unbelievable," he said. "As far as I can tell, all the date and origin stamps on this are completely legitimate."

Trieka nodded. The shock had become so pervasive she could hardly feel it anymore.

Jeff turned to her, unsuccessfully trying to school his features to neutrality. "Have you talked to him about this?"

"No. He's missing."

Jeff leaned back in his chair, blowing out yet another breath. "If he's missing, and all this is true, I'd wager he's in deep shit."

"That's my guess."

She watched in silence as Jeff folded his arms across his chest, his eyes glazing a bit. Finally, he came back to himself and straightened in the chair, still looking at the computer. "My sister's still at MediaNet. She could double check everything with her contacts, make sure we've got real news here and not a hoax. Then, if it is true, she's in a position to do something about it."

"But how do we get the disks to her?"

"We'll have to take them back on the ship. We can't transmit the data—there's too much chance it could be intercepted."

"And what about Fairfax?"

Jeff shook his head. "I don't know. He might have to fend for himself."

"No." The word came quick and short.

Jeff looked at her, comprehension subtly softening his frown. "What's going on?"

"Nothing." But that, too, came too quickly. *It's Jeff*, she reminded herself. Jeff, whom she'd known since academy days. "I just...I've gotten a little attached to him."

"Then I'll go into the embassy and see if I can ferret him out."

Trieka considered the possibility, but only for a moment. "No. I can't ask you to do that. It's too dangerous. I probably shouldn't have involved you this far."

"No, I think you should have. This is too important to let fall to anyone, or to risk having it be lost with you and Fairfax. At least this way there's a chance of it coming to light." He slid the disks almost absently into his pocket. "So, do you have a plan?"

Trieka stared at the pocket. It was quite possible that, once those disks made it to Earth, the whole world would change. "I don't know. I have to find him before they kill him."

Jeff was silent for what seemed a very long time, his long fingers tapping arrhythmically on the desk. Finally, he bent over the computer again, bringing up a communications program.

"I have an idea," he said. "I'm not making any guarantees, but I think it's worth a shot."

"I'm listening."

There was nothing to listen to, though, except for the computer as Jeff logged into a remote system. Trieka tried to figure out what he was doing, but the screens offered little help.

"That software must be older than I am," she muttered almost in Jeff's ear as he waited for a connection.

"It probably is. You saw the colony's supply request. These people would much rather have frozen cow embryos than new computer equipment."

"What are you accessing?"

"Town hall."

"What for?"

She had to wait for the answer until the town hall computer deigned to speak to hers. Jeff logged himself in as a visitor and went into a section called "Building Permits".

"Blueprints of the embassy," he said. "They should be in here somewhere. Here we go." The blueprints appeared on the screen, one of the original structure, then one of the new building. Jeff fell silent again, studying. "There," he said finally.

"What?"

"Here." He pointed at the screen. "These rooms used to be main floor offices. From the new construction blueprints, it looks like they've been cut off from the main corridor and turned into storage areas or something. I'd start there if I were you."

"But that wing's also been changed from level two security to level six."

"Exactly. That's another reason it's a good bet they're holding him there."

"It's also a good bet I can't get in."

"That I really can't help you with."

Trieka studied the map. "Can you download that into my wrist comm?"

He fished around a bit, looking for a connector, and finally produced a cable from behind the computer. "No infrared eye, but this should work."

She watched him fiddle with it, hooking the connector into the side of her wrist comm. After a few minutes and a bit of swearing, the maps were successfully transferred.

"I'll have to wait until tonight. It's not like the place is well guarded. And you already said their technology is out of date, which probably means no retinal scans to get into level six."

Jeff shook his head. "No. It's a magnetic access card. But it looks like they may have pulled the readers out during the last renovation phase, and they haven't put them back yet." He had left the maps and was looking at a "Work Progress" chart. "No, they haven't replaced them. They have guards posted in the hallway twenty-four hours a day to check IDs." He shook his head in disgust. "The security in this place is deplorable."

"But think about it. With the retinal scanners and the card readers down, they can go in and out without leaving a trail. It plays right into their hands. And, fortunately, into ours. With the security this lax, it'll be easy." Which was quite possibly the biggest lie she'd ever heard, much less spoken.

Jeff looked at her, not bothering to disguise his concern. "Do me a favor, Trieka. Wear a gun."

❋ ❋ ❋

Fairfax sat in a small, uncomfortable chair in the middle of a small, dim room. He faced the door and tried not to think.

He hadn't slept since they'd taken him from his room in the embassy. And they'd taken his watch—a Rolex, damn them—so he didn't know how long ago that had been. At least twenty-four hours, though.

Behind him lurked a low bed, but he refused to lie down on it or even to look at it. Russet stains of old blood marbled the single sheet. Katharine's blood.

He'd sat for hours watching the recordings, sheathed in darkness while images flickered in colored light against the opposite wall. At first, his mind had rebelled at what he'd seen, insisting it couldn't be real, that it was a hoax, a trick. But eventually it had become impossible to deny the truth. So he'd watched, though he'd wanted more than anything to close his eyes and stop up his ears. He owed her that much.

The downing of his father-in-law's plane had been no accident. The plane had been brought down by military craft. Katharine and her father had been plucked from the wreckage and taken to an EarthFed garrison. Once there, EarthFed had tried to extract from Katharine's father what he knew. What Fairfax now knew. What Katharine may not have known, but for which she'd suffered and died at the hands of General Ford.

They'd used her to try to get her father to talk. They'd tied him to a chair and tortured her while he watched, and then they'd put a bullet in the back of her head. Her last words, with the cold muzzle of the gun against the nape of her neck, had been, "Go fuck yourself."

That had made Fairfax proud of her.

Her father had never talked. He was dead now, too. And they'd kindly preserved the proceedings on camera, to use against Fairfax. For some reason, they'd thought the recordings would make him talk. But talking wouldn't bring her back. It would only rob her death of all meaning.

So here he was, in this tiny room with only the blood-stained blanket to lie on. He'd rather die than talk. He'd rather die than lie in Katharine's blood. He thought about that final moment, she with the gun at the back of her head and the thin smirk on her lips...

Don't think about it. Tears bit his eyelids, filled up his throat. *Don't think about it.*

So he thought about Cavendish, which did and didn't surprise him. She, after all, had the disks. She also had his trust, and that wasn't easy for him to give. He still wasn't completely certain it hadn't been a mistake. She'd been EarthFed most of her life—she ate, breathed and bled it. There was no way to know for certain which way she would bend when faced with the horror of the truth.

It didn't really matter, though. He'd be dead soon.

He put his face in his hands. He was tired, emotionally exhausted to the point he ached with it. He almost wished they'd kill him now.

As if in answer to his thoughts, he heard a noise outside the door.

Chapter Seven

Sliding a palm-sized medical laser and a military-issue laser with a second, shatterbullet barrel into a holster under her uniform jacket, Trieka felt like she was strapping on her six-guns. The huge yellow moon that met her as she stepped out of the building enhanced her mood. She was off into danger, to rescue the damsel in distress...

Something's wrong with this picture.

The embassy grounds lay silent under the deep bowl of the star-spattered sky. The world seemed to have paused, as if it had taken a breath and was waiting to let it out. Trieka's chest burned and she realized she herself hadn't breathed for several strides. She let her breath out silently. Around her, the world still waited.

The guard at the front door barely acknowledged her as she strode past. Out of the corners of her eyes, she evaluated him. Relaxed, unsuspecting, still potentially dangerous. At the front desk, the receptionist gave her a passing glance, which Trieka returned with a small smile. She felt loose and energized, ready.

Last time she'd come into this building, she'd turned left, toward the hotel. This time, she turned right.

Most of the office doors were closed, probably locked. She ducked into the nearest ladies' room, locked herself in a stall, and turned on her wrist comm to look again at the maps Jeff had downloaded for her. Jeff had also supplied a list of tonight's on-duty personnel. She chose a name, closed her eyes to imprint the map she'd memorized hours earlier, took a deep breath, then let herself back out into the hallway.

She'd been walking with a firm, confident stride before; now she quickened her pace. The high security hallway was just up this corridor and to the left. As she had suspected, a guard stood next to the dismantled electronic ID readers. He wore the gunmetal gray uniform of the colonial MPs.

"Lieutenant!" she said. She didn't have to try to sound out of breath; her own nerves did it for her.

The guard, seeing her captain's insignia and dark blue EarthFed uniform, snapped to attention. "Sir! What is it?"

"It's Captain Dobson. She's in the ladies' room throwing up. Is there someone we can get to go check on her? Any medical personnel on duty?"

The lieutenant looked flustered. He was young. Trieka hoped he wouldn't get court-martialed over this.

"I don't know," he said. "Medical's in the other wing. Their intercoms are under repair."

Trieka stepped forward. "Go find somebody. I'll hold down the fort here."

"Yes, sir."

That was too damn easy, she thought, watching the lieutenant jog down the corridor. Thank God for the military tradition of unquestioningly obeying your superiors. And thank God for slow-moving government renovations, which had left the embassy so ridiculously vulnerable.

As soon as he was out of sight, she ducked into the hallway. There should be six small rooms back here. Yes, six doors. But how to tell which one to check? She didn't have much time. Panic closed her throat. She heard nothing above her own harsh breathing and the slamming of her heart.

Then she realized the spaces under all the doors were dark, except one.

Too easy. Fairfax's captors were either incredibly arrogant, or stupid, or Trieka was walking into a setup. Or maybe they hadn't considered Fairfax might have an ally.

The door was, of course, locked. A square hole in the wall next to it marked where an alarm panel was due to be installed next week. She pulled out the medical laser, set the blade length for two inches, and ran the beam between the door and the jamb, cutting silently through the bolts. Taking a breath, she eased the door open just enough to look in. With her luck, she'd find a pair of admirals holding a meeting.

She didn't, though. She found Fairfax.

He sat on a chair so small she could barely see it beyond the width of his body. He was very still, his head lifted. Trieka had the distinct impression he was holding his breath. His lower lip was split and swollen, his left cheekbone marked by a deep bruise.

Carefully, slowly, she pushed the door open. Raw, naked terror rose in Fairfax's eyes. Trieka swallowed, then slid into the room.

Fairfax's breath came out in a rush. He rose from the chair in a strange, slow lurch. His hand snaked behind him, clamping to the back of the tiny chair.

"Cavendish?" She'd never heard such pure astonishment. She raised a finger to her lips. He said nothing else.

"Is there anything here you want to take with you?" she whispered.

Strangely, he glanced back at the low bed. The sheet was covered with irregular brown stains, like old blood. He looked back at her and shook his head.

"Then come with me. We have to hurry."

She slipped back out of the small room, hearing him follow. Back in the corridor, the guard was still gone. Trieka paused by the guard station and tripped a series of silent alarms. Jeff, never one to leave a stone unturned, had worked out a sequence calculated to cause as much havoc as possible. The guards wouldn't know where to go first.

That distraction established, she led the way down the main hall, toward the back of the building. Fairfax followed without even stopping to ask where they were going. She took a right, heading toward the back exit. He moved right along behind her. No questions, no hesitation. She liked that in a man.

They were nearly to the barred rear exit when he touched her elbow, the slight pressure bringing her to a halt. She turned, eyebrows up, to see him touching his ear. She heard it, too, then. Voices in the hall behind them, coming closer.

His brows were up now, waiting for her instruction. Trieka

swallowed, looking frantically for a place to hide. Fairfax pointed to the office door behind her. She tried the knob. It was unlocked.

Fairfax's hand molded to the curve of her waist as they moved into the room beyond. He closed the door behind them, leaning forward as he did so, his mouth against her ear.

"If they're smart, they'll check the room." The words were moist and warm, barely audible. In the darkness, she made out the shape of a large desk.

"There," she whispered, pointing at the hulking piece of furniture. It was huge, the back going all the way to the floor, the space beneath maybe big enough for the two of them. "You go. I'll lock the door."

He disappeared behind the desk while Trieka peered at the coded door lock. She considered changing the code, then realized she couldn't without the original code. Voices rose in the hallway. There was no more time.

She ducked under the desk. After a quick, silent struggle, they found space with Fairfax on all fours, Trieka curled tight beneath him. For a moment, she heard nothing but his rough breathing in her ear, but even that fell quiet as the voices began to speak just outside the door.

"Check that room. Are you sure you don't know who she was?"

"I don't know." That was the lieutenant's voice, sounding extremely young and a little frightened. "She had on a captain's uniform."

"Stolen, no doubt. Check the room."

Trieka held very still, listening. The doorknob rattled.

"It's locked," the lieutenant said.

"Here. All the door codes are here."

She closed her eyes hard, seeing vague shapes of light and sparks against her eyelids. Fairfax's belly was against her back, barely moving. He was utterly still. Her heart pounded so hard she was sure they must hear it from the doorway.

There was a series of beeps as the lieutenant entered the security code. A pause, then the same series of beeps again. "It's not working."

The other officer grunted. "This is Marsali's office. She changes the code once a week. She must not have recorded the latest change."

Another pause. Trieka bit her lip. The beeps sounded again, then a different series.

"Damn," said the other officer. "I left my override card at the desk. We'll have to check this door on the next pass."

"Should I stay here and watch, just in case?"

No, Trieka prayed. She really didn't want to have to kill anybody.

"No. The other alarms are higher priority. We'll catch this door on the way back. You finish this hallway, then go on to the 'E' aisle. I'm going to the medical wing to see if they saw anything there."

Very slowly, Trieka let out her breath. Above her, Fairfax began to relax. Gradually, she realized he was pressing a little too heavily on her back, and that he was shaking. Still careful to stay silent, she slid out from under him and the desk, then reached behind her to help him maneuver in the darkness.

"Are you all right?" she whispered when he was sitting on the floor behind the desk. She couldn't see his face in the darkness, but the shaking seemed to have quieted.

"I'll be fine," he said. It didn't answer the question, but she let it go.

"We should sit tight for a few minutes, just to let them pass. Then we're out of here."

"To where?"

"I know a place."

Silence again. In the hallway, footsteps retreated, became fainter and fainter. Finally Fairfax spoke, his voice little more than a breath. "I don't know why you did it, but thank you."

"We'll talk about that later." She reached up to cup his face. His cheek was raspy with stubble. Her thumb found his lower lip. Following it, she kissed him gently. "I think they're gone. Let's go."

They slipped out of the office and into the corridor. Distant voices echoed, but the immediate corridors lay silent. Trieka led the way to the rear entrance.

There was no guard, but a heavy bar had been locked into place across the double doors. She looked out cautiously onto a partially completed parking lot. It was dark and empty, the construction equipment blackly still. She trained the medical laser on the bar, absently wondering why they were putting in a parking lot. Last time she'd been to Denahault Prime, there'd only been six cars on the whole planet.

The laser slid through the bar easily. Gently, she pulled the door open and led the way out.

Outside, the crisp chill slapped her across the face, robbing her of the sense of non-reality that had kept her going so far. Her hands shook as she slid the laser back into her pocket.

"This way," she whispered.

"Where are we going?"

She glanced back at him. Fairfax wore jeans and the same sweater she'd pulled off him two nights ago. He'd be uncomfortable as the night chill settled, but they had about four hours of walking ahead of them and the exercise should keep him warm.

"Somewhere safe," she said. "Come on. We don't have much time."

The edge of the largely unnecessary embassy parking lot marked the edge of civilization on Denahault. Of the six settlements on the planet, only Denahault Prime had electricity, and that was a fairly recent development. The rest were true pioneer towns.

In training for her position as a colony ship captain, Trieka had spent a year in Forest Walk, learning the way of life of an interplanetary pioneer. As luck would have it, Forest Walk was the closest settlement to Denahault Prime. She'd become quite close to her host family during her stay. Their politics, like those of most colonists, often differed from what EarthFed would prefer, and they'd jump to support an individual against the government that too often sent them more colonists—or built a parking lot—when they really needed seed corn. Trieka only hoped they hadn't relocated.

She set a rapid pace, wanting to get out of open country and into the woods as quickly as possible. There was a road now from Prime to Forest Walk. There hadn't been when she'd lived here. Back then it had been a rutted trail through barely thinned woods. Though narrow and poorly paved, the road would make it easier for EarthFed to follow them.

But it also helped Trieka navigate the woods. Keeping within sight of the road, they'd not only be less likely to get lost, but they'd know if anyone was coming.

They'd been on the move for about half an hour when Fairfax suddenly lurched forward and grabbed her arm. She turned, taking hold of his arms as he sagged on his feet.

"What's wrong?"

"Can we stop for a minute?" His voice rasped as if he could barely draw air.

She glanced at the road through the trees. There were no lights, but moonlight glinted wetly off the paved surface. The forest brimmed with animal noises. Her ears picked out and identified a few. All small animals, which would have scattered at any motor traffic.

"Yeah, I think it's safe."

Fairfax wilted to the ground in a shaking heap. She knelt next to him, mentally berating herself for not checking his condition earlier. "Are you all right?"

He had his face in his hands and seemed to concentrate on just breathing. After a few minutes, he pressed one hand to his side and looked at her. "I just needed to catch my breath."

He moved as if to get up, but she stopped him with a hand on his shoulder. "How long has it been since you slept?"

"Not since before I saw you last."

Trieka rocked back on her heels, looking at him, part of her appalled at his condition and eager to comfort, the other part quickly reevaluating and modifying their escape plan. Around her, leaves whispered as a breeze picked them up and laid them back down. "Did they hurt you?"

He shook his head, teeth glinting faintly in an odd smile. "No, not really. They just slapped me around a little."

"I'm sorry. I should have asked how you were before I pushed you out here."

"It's all right. We had to get out somehow." He paused, wincing and pressing his hand deeper into his side. "Where are we going?"

"Forest Walk. It's the nearest outer settlement. I know some people there."

"And where do we go from there?"

"We have to hide out for a few weeks. By then, this thing will have blown open back on Earth and we'll be safe."

Even in the darkness, she saw the flash of alarm that rose in his eyes. "What do you mean? How?"

"Jeff has the disks. His sister works for MediaNet."

He studied her for a moment, then asked, "You trust him?"

"Yes."

Fairfax nodded. "That'll have to do." Reaching out to a tree for balance, he pulled himself back to his feet. "Let's go."

❋   ❋   ❋

Forest Walk was dark and sleeping except for six kerosene lanterns hanging from poles along the main street. Trieka closed her eyes and breathed deeply, letting the smell orient her. The green and black odors of vegetation, fresh earth and freshly peeled tree trunks took her back to the last phase of her training. Forest Walk had been smaller then, but the Taylors' house should still be in the same place.

Avoiding the main road, she led the way past the half-dozen shops of Forest Walk's minuscule business district, then through the backyards of the western residential area to a homestead set slightly apart from the main grouping. The dark wooden house still looked the same. And the root cellar door was still unlocked, which was the important part.

She swung the door open, found the kerosene lantern just inside and lit it. Here, too, the smells were thick and evocative: drying herbs, the earthy smell of potatoes and native root vegetables, the bite of kerosene and a suffusing backdrop of garlic. She set the lamp down on the floor. A large wooden chest hulked against the cellar's back wall. Trieka opened it and pulled out blankets and a package of food.

"What's this?" Fairfax said as she handed him a bag of

dried fruit. He looked bemused, but also a little shocky.

"Storm supplies," she replied. "They have monster tornadoes in this area." He was still staring at the food as if he didn't know what it was. Gently, she took him by the shoulders. "Why don't you sit down and eat? You look like you could use it."

He sat down and opened the bag. It was cloth, tied at the top with a cotton drawstring. Inside, the fruit was wrapped in paper. His fingers fumbled, but he managed to free a stack of dried apple slices from the paper. Trieka unfolded a blanket and draped it over his shoulders, then touched his forehead in an instinctive gesture. He looked up at her, a little surprised. He was warm and clammy, but not feverish.

They ate in silence for a time. Trieka, opening her own package of dried fruit, discovered her hands were shaking. *About time.* She'd really been far too calm about this.

She managed to eat a few dried apricots before delayed panic closed her throat. Rummaging in the chest, she found water bottles. She took one and handed another to Fairfax, thinking she should have pulled them out first. He said nothing, but drank half the bottle. She found bread and cheese in the chest and passed those on to him as well.

After a time, Fairfax laid the food aside and stood, shrugging off the blanket. "Do you think it's safe to go out?"

"Why? Where are you going?" She couldn't control the near-smile that pulled her mouth.

Which apparently irritated him. "I have to pee," he snapped. "Do you mind?"

"No, I don't mind at all. Do you need any help?"

That elicited a smile, if a small one. "No, I don't think so."

She watched his jeans pull snug against his buttocks as he climbed the small ladder. "Give a holler if you do."

He was out and back in a matter of moments, and when he closed the door, he did it carefully, in utter silence. His jaw clenched as he sat back down.

"What?" Trieka whispered.

"Cars in the street," he answered in a murmur. "Sounds like they're going door-to-door." He paused. "Will they look in here?"

She shook her head. "Not likely. They'd have to get a warrant. The settlers are very protective of their property."

"How did you know to come here?"

"I stayed with the Taylors as part of my training program. Colony ship captains are required to spend at least a year living in each colony. It helps to have a background when you're helping new colonists acclimate." She paused, chewing the side of her thumb. "A duty which I am, at this moment, shamefully neglecting."

Fairfax studied her, his face leaping with shadows in the dim light of the lantern. "You could be court-martialed for this."

She nodded. "I'll lose my ship, at the very least."

"Why did you do it?"

For a time she said nothing, not certain what he wanted to hear, or if she wanted to answer at all. Finally she said, "The same reason you collected the information in the first place. Because what's going on opposes everything colonization is supposed to be about."

"But you could have just gone back to Earth with the disks. You didn't have to rescue me."

He was right, of course. And she wasn't completely sure she knew the answer. An inexplicable lump rose in her throat. God, but he was beautiful, even with the bruises. The yellow light made shadows and brightness all along the planes of his face. She swallowed.

"They would have killed you."

He nodded, but said nothing else. She closed her eyes, afraid he might read the emotion in her face. When she had gathered herself enough to look at him again, he was asleep.

She woke to the sound of screaming. Adrenaline brought her heart into her throat and sent her instantly to her feet. They'd been found, she knew it, and they were taking Fairfax, maybe even killing him, while she slept...

They were still alone in the warm, redolent cellar. Fairfax lay tangled in his blanket, twitching. He wasn't screaming. The sound coming from him was more like a howl, a low, primal sound of unutterable pain. Her dreams must have translated it to something less frightening. Her stomach twisted at the noise and an equally primal instinct made her want to stop it.

"Fairfax!" The hissing whisper could hardly be called motherly, but it was the first thing that came to her. It also didn't work. She knelt down and touched him. He was still warm and clammy. Gently, she shook his arm. "Fairfax, wake up."

His eyelids tightened shut, then opened. For a moment he blinked as if unsure where he was. Then a sudden, hideous clarity settled onto his face. His body moved in a deep shudder and then, to Trieka's complete bewilderment, he closed his eyes again and started to cry.

"My God." She could barely make out the words between the wrenching sobs. "Kathi..."

Feeling tears spring to her own eyes, she went to him. Hesitant at first, she cupped his shoulder, then gently gathered him to her, holding his face against her chest. He grasped her arm in one hand, his grip almost painful. Trieka just held him. She'd dealt with some difficult situations before, but she didn't think she'd ever seen anyone break down quite so thoroughly. She wondered if he was even completely awake.

She was in tears herself, patting and shushing him because she didn't know what else to do, when he finally took a deep, shuddering breath, swallowed audibly and stopped.

"I'm sorry."

"It's all right." He moved a little in her arms and she instinctively pulled him closer. "Must've been a hell of a dream."

He was silent for a time, then slowly pulled himself to a sitting position. His eyes avoided hers as he wiped at his wet face. Then, quietly and still without looking at her, he explained. Trieka's stomach clenched in shock, then in sickened horror.

"They *recorded* it?" The exclamation came out as a strangled whisper. "My God."

He touched a hand to his mouth, gingerly feeling the swollen place on his lower lip. "So now I have the answer to one question, at least. She's dead."

"Fairfax, I'm so sorry."

He made a small movement, not quite a shrug, as his left

thumb rotated his wedding ring. "I knew it all along. I just didn't want to believe it."

And this wasn't the easiest way to find out. She wanted to say it, but didn't. He'd been through enough—he didn't need her flippancy right now.

He sniffed, staring blankly at the semi-darkness. Trieka had turned the lamp down, but hadn't put it out.

"Is there more water?" he asked finally.

She rummaged in the chest for a bottle and handed it to him. He opened it and drank, then closed his eyes again, leaning his head back against the wall. She felt awkward in his silence, uncertain what to say.

"Is there anything else I can do?" Her hands felt big and useless, her words strained and trite.

He took her hand, then pulled her back against him. His arms closed warm around her, as if he were comforting her instead of the other way around. "No," he said. "There's nothing else you can do."

She sat for a long time listening to him breathe, listening to his heartbeat under her ear, before she fell back to sleep.

❋ ❋ ❋

Light, bright orange and intense against her closed lids, woke her the second time. She opened her eyes, registering the golden rectangle of morning where a closed door had been only hours before, and the shadow of a figure inside the light, barely discernible in the brilliance. Stomach clenching in panic, Trieka flung one hand up against the light. The other jerked toward the gun at her waist, but didn't reach it. Her arm was pinned under Fairfax's body, and he lay limp and unresponsive, half on top of her, snoring faintly.

"It's all right."

A moment after the words were spoken, her eyes found detail in the glaring brightness. She knew the person who stood just inside the door. Slowly, avoiding sudden movements, Grace Taylor closed the door to the root cellar behind her.

Trieka shifted, panic receding. Fairfax tensed suddenly and

opened his eyes, then sat up with a jolt. The sound of a strange voice had apparently jarred him awake when the light hadn't. He looked at Trieka, fear warring with the questions in his eyes.

"It's all right." She echoed Grace's words. "At least, I hope it is." She looked at Grace, raising an eyebrow.

"When they came looking for you last night, I thought you might be here." She paused. "I didn't tell them that, of course." She looked at Fairfax, obviously brimming with questions she was reluctant to ask. "Why don't we go back to the house for some coffee?"

Chapter Eight

The coffee wasn't really coffee, but a hot, bitter concoction made of roasted barley and a native grain. Fairfax drank his black, and it tasted like heaven. Grace also offered sinfully sticky sweet rolls, and hot rolled oats with honey and milk. He ate in silence while Cavendish conversed with her friend.

The small house was cozy in spite of the lack of modern amenities. The kitchen smelled of fresh bread and the herbs that hung drying from the bare rafters. Sunlight poured in through a wide glass window, filling the room with morning. A wood-burning stove radiated heat, taking the bite out of the early chill and keeping more oatmeal warm at the same time.

"Whatever's going on, I don't want to hear about it," was the first thing Grace had said, setting steaming mugs on the table. She was older than Fairfax would have expected a colonist to be, perhaps fifty, with graying dark brown hair and green eyes. She looked like an eighteenth-century farm wife in pants, her hair tied back in a careless knot, hands dry and rough with calluses.

"That's good," said Cavendish, "because I have no intention of telling you. It's too dangerous."

Grace regarded her, not quite smiling. "I should have guessed anything you got involved in would be complicated."

"Complicated isn't the half of it." Cavendish paused, looking at the sweet rolls and finally taking one. "So how are the kids?"

Fairfax tuned them out as they discussed personal news. He felt strange—had felt strange since that embarrassing loss of control early this morning. It was as if he'd suffered phantom pain all these years—the kind of pain an amputee feels when he knows a limb is gone, but can feel the ache in fingers or toes. All this time he'd known Kathi was gone, but a piece of his mind had insisted she was still there. Now his mind had finally admitted her loss. He still felt the pain, but it was deeper, more pervasive. And, at the same time, he felt utterly empty.

"Fairfax?" Cavendish's voice intruded on his thoughts. He looked up to see both women looking at him expectantly. Grace was holding up the coffee pot.

"More coffee?" Grace asked.

"Please," said Fairfax.

"You looked like you were a million miles away," Grace said. The coffee flowed black and steaming from the pot to Fairfax's mug. The hot steam on his face felt good. It was real.

He smiled a small, twisted smile, eyes on his mug. "Not quite. Only about seven years."

Grace gave him a strange look, but said nothing.

Much to his surprise, a hand closed on his under the table. He looked up at Cavendish. She was looking at her sweet roll, but as he moved, her hand tightened on his. He squeezed her hand back. Emotion rose again out of the emptiness. He knew what it was, but it was still as unexpected as a flower in snow. He was in love with her.

She looked at him then, and he wondered if she could see it in his eyes. Her own eyes were gray and tired, her hair a mess of orange frizz. If they'd been alone in the room, he would have kissed her. Hell, maybe he would anyway.

The front door suddenly slammed open, admitting a wide, solid man with lined features and graying hair. His mouth was thin with something approaching anger. He looked directly at Cavendish.

"So you *are* here," he said. "I was afraid of that."

"Why, Jim?" Grace said. She looked worried now, too, turning in her chair, then slowly rising to face her husband.

"They're back. They've got a pile of warrants thick as a bible. You've got about thirty minutes to get the hell out of here."

❄ ❄ ❄

Visiting the Taylors' tool shed was an enlightening experience. Fairfax found it difficult to follow the conversation, distracted as he was by his surroundings. He could honestly say he'd never seen anything quite like it before.

The back wall was a veritable arsenal, with everything from hand-held lasers and stun guns to old-fashioned shotguns and pistols, even a composite bow and a medieval morningstar. Trophies of native animals decorated the side wall: deerlike heads with large, palmate antlers; the mounted head of a horned something that looked like a cross between a rhinoceros and a late-model BMW; a man-sized white pelt.

Fairfax examined the pelt. The fur was thick, a pure white. The shape and angle of the limbs made Fairfax think the animal that had once worn it might have been bipedal.

"I'd take one of the big guns if I were you, Trieka," Jim was saying. He gestured to the huge, horned head on the wall. "There's some nasty stuff out there in the woods."

"Where will we be going?" Cavendish asked.

"Go straight northwest and you'll hit Station Twelve in about three days. The embassy folks should be done searching the place by then."

"Station Twelve?" Fairfax queried.

"It's a smuggler's port," Jim explained. "You'll be able to get off-planet from there. Go to dock three and ask for Lucas. He'll take you back Earthside. He runs out of the Gobi desert, but his operation is pretty sophisticated. You won't get stuck there."

Cavendish smiled a little. "You deal with this guy often?"

"Where do you think I got the guns?" Taylor took one of the big rifles down from the rack and handed it to Cavendish. She looked it over with an experienced eye. Fairfax turned back to the thick, white-furred skin on the wall.

"Did you get a bounty for this pelt?"

It was in many ways a completely irrelevant question, even a waste of time, so he was prepared for the strange look Taylor gave him. He wasn't prepared for the look of sudden interest he received from Cavendish. Surely she couldn't have picked up his line of thought so quickly.

Taylor handed Fairfax a pistol. "Not on this one. I didn't turn it in. EarthFed does offer bounties on those hides, though. The animals are classified hostile."

"Do you see them often?" Fairfax pressed on. "Have you ever witnessed an attack?"

"That one was prowling around the sheep pens one night. I shot it myself."

"What did it look like?"

"Like a big white ape." He shook his head, irritation thinning his mouth. "Look, you two had better get going before the search teams show up."

Cavendish nodded. "He's right." She shouldered the rucksack Grace had filled with travel supplies. They'd supplied her with clothes, as well, and burned her uniform just in case. "Come on, Fairfax. Let's hit the road."

❊ ❊ ❊

They'd been walking not quite half an hour through gradually thickening forest when Cavendish finally asked the question.

"What was that about the pelt? What made you think there'd be a bounty?"

Shifting the rucksack on his shoulder, Fairfax looked at her. Her expression was a little too neutral, as if she was trying not to influence his answer. Birds chirped overhead, and something that sounded like a squirrel with influenza berated them soundly from a tree limb.

"What do you think?" Fairfax said.

She grinned a little. "I think you think they may not be hostile."

Fairfax shrugged again under the rucksack's straps. The left strap kept chafing against his collarbone. "Hostile's not really the issue. I think they might be sentient."

"Sentient?" Cavendish repeated. There was no surprise in her voice, though. It was as if she'd repeated the word just to make it tangible.

He nodded. "Maybe even intelligent."

She shook her head. "I can't believe EarthFed would put a bounty on an intelligent life-form."

He didn't answer. He couldn't convince her, so there was no point trying. She had to make the conclusions on her own or they'd be meaningless.

"Of course, I can't believe EarthFed would terraform over existing ecosystems to make a planet habitable, either, and it's pretty obvious from your information that they did exactly that on Farhallen." She paused, obviously waiting for Fairfax to jump in. He didn't. After a moment, Cavendish added, "Am I talking to myself, here?"

"It's not obvious," Fairfax contributed, "but it's fairly strongly implied."

"I think you and I both know what went on." Her voice was harsh. "And I think your wife knew, too." She opened her mouth to say something else, then closed it with a snap, as if only then realizing what she'd said. Her face went red and she looked away, hunching a little under the weight of her backpack.

He felt the sting of her words, but only dimly. This was hard for her, too. She'd put her future in the hands of EarthFed when she'd first put on her uniform, and now she'd burned that uniform along with several metaphorical bridges. It couldn't be easy to face that kind of upheaval.

"She didn't know," he said quietly, "but her father did."

"I'm sorry," Cavendish said. Her mouth was thin and tight, closed over her anger. "I shouldn't have said that."

Fairfax shrugged. He wasn't going to tell her it was all right, because it wasn't. But he wouldn't torture her with it, either.

They walked in silence for a long time. Fairfax was starting to ache, but he didn't want to admit it. Instead, he admired the landscape.

The trees were huge and he couldn't tell if they were evergreen or deciduous, though the air occasionally bore a piney tang. The ground was littered with fallen foliage, undergrowth and the occasional mass of pale flowers. It was beautiful, severe and wilder than anything he'd ever imagined. A breeze touched his face from time to time, cool but promising iciness after sunset. After last night's cold walk, he was glad for the winter wear the Taylors had supplied.

Though they walked through forest, the going hadn't been difficult. The trees were thick enough to provide camouflage from above, but not so thick as to impede their progress. Cavendish consulted their compass periodically, just to be sure they were on track. Fairfax was relieved when she finally called a halt for lunch. The place she chose was sparse enough they could sit on the ground, but still provided cover.

"Hang tight," Cavendish told him. She dropped her gear on the ground and disappeared into the trees, carrying one of the rifles. Fairfax relieved himself against a tree. By the time Cavendish returned, he had fished a few lunch items out of his pack, and was in the process of downing a jar of water.

"How are you feeling?" Cavendish asked, dipping into her own food supplies. He recognized her captain persona. When she moved into it, the set of her body became almost masculine.

"A little stiff," he said. He meant it innocently; his thighs and back were starting to ache and he had a catch in his right shoulder. But, as the words came out, he realized they were applicable to other parts of his anatomy as well. Especially when Cavendish looked at him from where she stood bent over the backpack, her eyebrows raised in concern.

"How bad is it?" she asked.

"Put it this way—I may not be able to walk in the morning."

Cavendish, far too observant for her own good, gave him a brief downward glance. "As long as you're not telling me that *I* may not be able to walk in the morning."

Surprised at her, Fairfax sat down, both to stretch his sore legs and to make his anatomical challenges less obvious. "I imagine you're in a little better shape than I am, so I doubt you'll have any trouble walking." He paused. "No matter what we do."

He saw the edges of Cavendish's grin past the water bottle as she took another long chug. She settled down to the ground as well. "We could stop for the day. We're far enough off the beaten path that we should be fairly safe, and there's no hurry getting to Station Twelve. In fact, it might be better if we did take longer. The trail will be that much colder."

"They might send out search teams, though. It's probably best to get off-planet as soon as we can."

Cavendish shrugged. "What do you want to do?"

"You're the captain. You tell me."

"Let's finish lunch, then go for a few more hours."

"Aye, aye, sir."

※ ※ ※

A few more hours brought them to nightfall. They found another fairly clear area and Trieka set about putting up their camping equipment. Fairfax disappeared into the trees for a moment, then returned. She could tell by the way he moved that he was both extremely tired and in considerable pain, but he knelt on the ground and began to unload his own gear. She considered telling him to relax and let her do the work, but decided against it. He would undoubtedly be insulted.

The Taylors had supplied them each with lightweight sleeping bags made of material which, though no heavier than a bedsheet, would keep them comfortable in all but the harshest conditions. They'd also supplied a tent of similarly compact design, which took only a few minutes to put up. When it was done, Fairfax sat down on the ground, his legs straight out in front of him, grimacing.

"My feet hurt."

Trieka, sorting through the food, looked up. "Take off your shoes and let's have a look." She put the food aside, rummaging now for the first aid kit.

He untied and pulled off his left boot, then stared at his foot, apparently surprised to see blood on his sock.

"That's what I was afraid of," she said, tossing him the packet of first aid supplies. "There should be something in there to help. And toss it back this way when you're done. I think I'm going to need it."

Judging by the condition of their feet, they'd both been walking on blisters for at least half the day. She wasn't much better off than Fairfax, though she seemed to have avoided the muscle fatigue. Fortunately the first aid kit contained a quick-heal spray that would have them walking painlessly again by morning.

"Thank God for Fairfax Pharmaceuticals," Fairfax said, tossing her the bottle with a grin.

Feet properly treated, they settled down for a meal of travel rations while the cool breeze grew around them.

"How cold do you think it'll get?" Fairfax asked. He sounded bone-tired, as if he barely had enough energy to form the question.

"It'll stay above freezing, but it won't be cozy. Between the tent, the sleeping bag and our own body heat, we should be fairly comfortable."

He wasn't too tired to quirk an eyebrow at her. "Body heat?"

She shrugged. "It's a small tent."

"Then I guess it *will* be cozy." He reached into his bag for another strip of dried meat. "Don't worry, Captain. I'm too tired to try anything."

"More's the pity." Her tone was dry, but she knew—and she suspected he did, too—that there wasn't much she would deny him at this point.

He grinned back. "Well, the spirit is willing, but the flesh is—actually, a good bit of the flesh is willing, but the rest is just plain exhausted."

She finished her ration of water. "Why don't you go to sleep? I'll take the first watch."

Fairfax hesitated. For a moment, Trieka thought he'd try some kind of macho posturing and insist she go to sleep first. But finally he nodded.

"All right. I guess I'll see you in a few hours."

He headed into the tent. Trieka heard rustling as he prepared for bed, then nothing but the profound silence of someone who had fallen instantly asleep.

She was exhausted herself. The breeze had picked up, and her skin was starting to prickle under the insulated hiking gear. She had no intention of spending her watch out here in the cold, with the wind making the trees talk. After making sure the campsite was in order, she crawled into the small tent.

Fairfax was deeply asleep, his breathing a slow, even susurration in the quiet tent. It was a few degrees warmer inside, mostly because the tent blocked the wind. She sat down in the narrow space between Fairfax and the tent wall. He rolled partially toward her as she settled next to him, as if seeking her warmth.

Taken aback, Trieka looked down at him. He'd taken off his shirt, and one arm lay outside the sleeping bag. His hair was tousled, his face dark with three days of stubble. His well-cut mouth moved almost into a pout, then opened as she watched. He'd be drooling on his pillow soon.

She grinned a little at the thought, then sobered. There was something disturbingly intimate about watching him sleep. Only a wife or a lover should see a man drooling in his sleep. She was neither. She was...well, God only knew at this point.

Carefully, she lifted his wrist and moved his arm back inside the sleeping bag. He was warm—a veritable furnace under there. It had been a long time since she'd been close to a sleeping man. She'd forgotten how hot they could get.

There. That was better. He'd get too cold with his arm exposed like that...

He shifted again. As he rolled even closer to her, the other arm flopped out of the sleeping bag and across her lap. Trieka jumped, then relaxed in his inadvertent embrace. Gently, she pushed the dark red-brown hair out of his eyes.

"Sleep tight, Fairfax," she whispered.

❈ ❈ ❈

Fairfax woke with a jolt some hours later, not certain what had brought him to consciousness. To his surprise, he discovered he had his head in Cavendish's lap. She was very still, and at first he thought she might be asleep, too.

He shifted, his cheek rubbing against her thighs. This was far too close for comfort; the feel and the smell of her gave him visions of planting his face right between her legs and—

Her hand came down on top of his head, fingers moving into his hair.

"Are you awake?" Her voice was barely audible.

"Yes," he whispered back. He felt the tension in her then, in her thighs, and in her fingers as they dug into his scalp.

"Can you hear that?"

He listened. He heard something—a rustling, chuffing noise from outside the tent. He nodded.

"What do you think it is?"

"I don't know," Cavendish said. "But I do know I'm taking a gun."

"I'll go." He moved off of her, slowly and quietly, and sat up. He couldn't quite see her expression in the moonlight.

"You just woke up," she protested, her voice barely above a breath.

"Exactly my point. You've been up, what, eighteen hours?"

He picked up the rifle from the floor next to his sleeping bag. She picked up the other rifle and followed as he edged to the front of the tent and peeked past the flap.

"Holy shit," he mumbled.

Moonlight illuminated the campsite, but Fairfax didn't need the light to see the huge, hulking creature now dominating it. Fairfax recognized the head immediately. He'd seen a similar one stuffed and mounted on the Taylors' trophy wall. It was digging in the ground a few yards outside the tent, apparently unaware it had company. The tiny eyes glistened in the bright moonlight. Carefully, feeling his heart speed up, Fairfax eased back into the tent.

"Do you know anything about these things?" he asked Cavendish.

"They're big and ugly," she answered. She paused, and before Fairfax could bristle at her flip reply, he saw the flash of fear in her eyes and heard her swallow thickly. She put her hand behind his neck and pulled his head down so she could whisper directly into his ear. "They're herbivores, but if they feel threatened, they'll kill. They don't see well, and they hunt mostly by smell. We're downwind, or it would know we were here."

She moved away and he nodded, then put his mouth against her ear. "I think we should kill it. I don't want to risk it rushing us. If it did, I don't think we'd have much of a chance." And then, for no reason whatsoever, he sucked her earlobe into his mouth and nipped it gently. "Wish me luck."

"I'll cover you." Grinning a little, she wiped her ear on her shoulder.

Between the few hours of sleep and the heady rush of adrenaline, Fairfax felt incredibly alert. Cavendish's hand touched his back, then fell away as he crept out of the tent and into the moonlight-covered forest.

The creature hunched not five yards away. It was gray and black, with a hide like an elephant's, and stood nearly six feet at the shoulder. Improbably small, cloven hooves dug at the ground like little shovels, sending a spray of dirt under its low belly and out between its hind legs. The low-slung, porcine head bore a long, sharp nasal horn. It looked like a cross between a giant boar and a triceratops.

Fairfax considered, not certain what to do. A shot in the head might kill it, and was certainly less risky than trying to put a bullet between its ribs. If he didn't fell it on the first shot, he'd be in for a showdown. He didn't like that idea very much. He resisted the urge to glance back at Cavendish. There was no telling what the thing might do if he made the wrong move.

Slowly, carefully, he lifted the rifle to his shoulder and lined up the shot. The creature continued digging, snorting and chuffing blissfully. The night breeze stirred his hair. The forest lay deathly silent.

Then, the creature lifted its big blocky head and looked directly at him.

He froze. The space between the creature's eyes was centered in the scope. In what seemed like an eternity, he heard his heart speed up, felt adrenaline soak his blood, heard Cavendish's nearly silent intake of breath behind him. Then the beast charged, and Fairfax pulled the trigger.

It was a clean shot. Blood sprayed from the crater that appeared between the animal's eyes. It should have dropped in its tracks.

It didn't. It kept coming. Fairfax readied his gun for another shot, then realized the thing would be on top of him before he could pull the trigger. He threw himself to one side. The beast came, head down, and slung its nose toward him.

He stumbled, and the head came up under him. With a casual shake of its head, the creature lifted him off his feet and flung him over its shoulder. The horn went into him. He felt it, hard and cold as it ripped through his thigh, toward his groin. Then he was in the air, shock hitting him as he flew over the animal's shoulder. He heard another shot, a howl, and his world became pain as he hit the ground.

Chapter Nine

Trieka's shot went straight through the thing's eye and dropped it like a rock. But too late. She flung the rifle to the ground, grabbed a lantern, and ran to where Fairfax lay on the ground behind the hulking body of the animal. He was dead. She knew it.

"Shit shit shit shit shit," she said, the word a mantra to hold back the tears fighting against her eyes, against the hysteria wedged in her throat. He wasn't dead. He wasn't even unconscious. He moaned as she knelt next to him.

"Hold still," she told him. Her voice sounded remarkably calm to her own ears.

"How bad is it?" he said through clenched teeth.

"I can't tell. Don't move."

She flipped on the lantern. All she could see was blood. His jeans were drenched with it and it was still coming. Femoral artery, she thought. If the artery had even been nicked, she wasn't sure she could stop the flow.

"You're bleeding," she said.

He grimaced. "No kidding."

"Good. Sarcasm. That's a good sign." Through the blood, Trieka found the line of the wound and drove her hand hard into the seam of his groin. Fairfax howled, lurching under her as she fought to hold him down.

"Hold still!" She had to shout over his protests. Finally he subsided, his face chalky. The bleeding seemed to have lessened.

"God, I hope this isn't your idea of foreplay."

She had to laugh. She couldn't help it, but her smile faded quickly. The flow of blood had lessened, but it was still coming, hot under her hand. At least it wasn't spurting. She was fairly certain the artery was intact.

"I have to get this bleeding stopped."

Fairfax closed his eyes, his face tight with pain. "What are you going to do?"

With her free hand, she fumbled through her pockets for the small medical laser. She held it where he could see it. "Cauterize it."

"Do you know how to use that thing?"

"Basic training." Awkwardly, she adjusted the laser's controls with her thumb, her left hand still pressed hard against his pelvis. She felt like the little Dutch boy in the story, holding Fairfax's life inside him with the heel of her hand. "This is going to hurt like hell," she warned.

He bore it stoically as she carefully burned the wound closed. It was longer than she'd thought, running from just above his left knee, up the inside of his thigh nearly to the crease of his groin. Another couple of inches to his right, and the animal would have gelded him. As it was, she wasn't completely sure he'd escaped damage. By the time she reached the top of his thigh, the wound was shallow enough not to need treatment, but she couldn't tell through the blood exactly how high it went.

He was so still when she finished with the laser that she thought he might have finally fainted. As she turned the instrument off, though, he opened his eyes and looked up at the bright sky. In the flood of moonlight, she saw sweat standing in beads on his face.

"How bad is it?" he asked again.

"Pretty bad." She held the lantern closer, making sure the bleeding had stopped. He really needed to be sewn up.

"I feel like I've been castrated."

The weak sound to his voice made her want to reassure him unconditionally, but she couldn't lie to him. "I don't think it caught you that high, but it's hard to tell through the blood. Let me get some water and the med kit, and we'll assess the damage."

He nodded tightly. She went back to the tent to fetch the supplies she needed, doing a quick inventory of the med kit. There were suturing materials and two vials of a local anesthetic as well as a bottle of fairly heavy-duty painkillers. Good.

Fairfax had his eyes closed when she came back. She'd brought his sleeping bag with her as well, and covered him with it. He didn't seem shocky, but it wasn't exactly warm. She would move him into the tent as soon as she attended to his injuries.

"Okay," she said, wetting a cloth with water from one of the bottles. "I'm going to be as careful as possible."

She cleaned the length of the wound as gently as she could, cutting the leg of his jeans back as she did. She would need the cloth out of the way if she was going to sew him up. As she washed the blood away, only a sparse flow came to replace it. It seemed the cauterization had worked.

The wound was a good two inches deep in the fleshy part of his inner thigh. Toward the groin, though, it became shallow. She sliced his jeans open to the waistband, next to the fly, then cut through his briefs and peeled everything back.

He was intact, but the source of his discomfort was immediately obvious. Trieka peered at him. He was staring straight up, his jaw clenched.

"Your balls aren't normally bright purple, are they?"

"Not last I checked."

She looked more closely. These weren't exactly the circumstances under which she'd hoped to investigate this portion of his anatomy, but she supposed it couldn't be helped. "Everything's intact. You're just bruised."

"Are you sure everything's intact?"

"Well, I don't see any sign that anything's ruptured inside." She paused, looking at him. "Do you want to check, or shall I?"

"I think if I try to move, I'm going to pass out."

She shook her head. "I don't know, Fairfax. This is an awfully cheap way for you to get me to feel you up."

He made a strangled sound. Trieka looked at his face. His expression could hardly be called a smile, but it might have been if he hadn't been in so much pain.

"Don't make me laugh," he said weakly. "It hurts."

Trieka smiled. *God, don't let him die. I really, really like him.*

"Okay," she said. "No more jokes."

With the gentleness of a lover, she curled her hand around his scrotum and outlined him with thumb and fingers. "One," she said out loud, then, "Two. And other requisite equipment appears to be intact." She rocked back on her heels. "It looks like you're okay, but we'll want to keep an eye on that bruising, just in case. Actually, you're more than okay, but at the moment that's a moot point."

"I'm glad you approve."

"Now, do you want to hear the bad news?"

He studied her face, as if trying to read what she was about to say. "Get it over with," he finally muttered.

"I'm going to have to close this up," she said, "and that *wasn't* part of basic training." She paused, hearing him swallow hard. "There is, however, some anesthetic in the med kit. I assume it comes with instructions."

"Any other painkillers in there? Morphine, maybe?"

Trieka suddenly realized she'd been stroking his other thigh, again and again, as if she were comforting a child. She looked at his face, at the pain etched there in dark lines, and something filled her throat so she could barely speak.

"Yes. Not morphine, but heavy stuff," she managed. "You won't need it until the anesthetic wears off."

He nodded. "Do what you have to do."

The instructions on the bottle of anesthetic were straightforward, obviously written for someone who didn't know what they were doing. It was also obviously intended for smaller injuries. By Trieka's decidedly iffy calculations, there would barely be enough to numb the length of the wound.

She decided to proceed a few inches at a time. If she numbed the entire area, the anesthetic might wear off before she finished. Trying not to think about the seriousness of what she was doing, she drew the liquid into the hypodermic, readied a bottle of suturing liquid—*not* labeled Fairfax Pharmaceuticals, surprisingly enough—and set to work.

Fairfax stiffened as the hypo sprayed, then he relaxed. Again, Trieka thought he might have fainted, but he still lay conscious, staring stubbornly at the moonlit sky. She shifted the lantern to light her work area more thoroughly.

She'd never performed even minor surgery before, but the suturing liquid was easier to handle than old-fashioned stitches might have been. She didn't know how the stuff worked—something about dissolving and reforming the edges of the wound—but she did know from personal experience that it hurt like hell without an anesthetic.

She didn't dare look at Fairfax's face as she closed the gape of the wound. Her eyes were starting to burn, fatigue catching up as her adrenaline eased off. She blinked back sweat and the grit of sleepiness. She couldn't afford to make a mistake simply because she was tired.

It seemed like hours later—and it may well have been—when she finally finished and rocked back on her heels.

"All done," she announced, and was surprised to hear her voice quiver. "Now let's see about getting you back into the tent before the last of that anesthetic wears off."

She dragged him by the sleeping bag while he levered with his arms and good leg. When they completed the short trek, Fairfax was gray and sweaty, Trieka close to tears with sheer exhaustion. She helped him get settled, then fumbled in the med kit for the painkillers.

"No," he said as she held the pills out to him.

"Why?"

"You need sleep." He closed her hand over the pills. "Save them for the next shift. In the meantime, the pain will keep me awake."

"I can't—"

"You have to."

She hesitated, but finally relented and stretched out in the other sleeping bag. Exhaustion claimed her almost immediately.

Morning sifted through the trees and settled in soft light on the ground, easing into the tent through the seam in the front flap. Trieka opened her eyes and looked at the ceiling. The small space around her smelled of blood and sweat.

"Fairfax?" she said. She didn't look at him. She was afraid to.

He grunted, a low, rumbling, male sound.

"You alive?"

"I suppose I must be, or this wouldn't hurt so bad."

She sat up, handed him the pills and a water bottle. This time he took the painkillers without protest. She closed her eyes again, waiting for his breathing to tell her he was asleep. When he had quieted, she leaned over him for a closer examination.

He looked much the way she'd feared he would—pale, but with a high flush of color in his cheeks. She touched his face; his skin felt hot and papery. Sorting again through the med kit, she found a thermometer and slipped the infrared sensor into his ear: 103 degrees. Not good. The tablets he'd taken should help, but she doubted it would be enough. She doubted anything would be enough.

If she could get him back to Forest Walk, he might have a chance. But, even if she could, EarthFed would find him there and kill him anyway. Just as EarthFed was likely to find them if they stayed here. And if they stayed here and EarthFed didn't find them, he'd undoubtedly die of infection.

She dug through the med kit again and found a few small bottles of antibiotics. They weren't the latest and greatest, they were labeled as samples and a couple of them were out of date, but at least it was something. She'd have to wait until he woke to be sure he wasn't allergic to any of them. In the meantime, all she could do was wait.

Trying not to disturb him, she unzipped the side of his sleeping bag and drew it back. As she'd feared, the wound was red, swollen and hot. No sign of pus, though. At least not yet. Trieka closed her eyes and made a prayer, then zipped him back up.

Fairfax slept for twelve straight hours. When he woke, he asked for water.

"How do you feel?" she asked.

He sipped carefully before answering. "Not good." He took another drink. "Fever isn't a good sign, is it?"

"No. Not really. Are you allergic to any antibiotics?"

"No."

"Good." She pulled out an ampoule. He flinched a little as the hypo sprayed against his skin.

"I think we might not win this round," he said after a time.

Trieka's mouth tightened, but she didn't answer.

※ ※ ※

She told him to take ninety-minute watches during the night, while she took three hours.

"It's not long enough," he protested. "Ninety minutes isn't long enough to get rested."

"I'll deal with it."

"I don't want to trust my safety to someone who's not sleeping."

"Shut up and go to sleep."

He relented, but only after making her promise to wake him in ninety minutes. Three hours later, she poked him in the shoulder.

"Fairfax, wake up. It's your turn."

It took him some time to fight his way back to consciousness. Too long, she thought.

"That was an awfully long hour and a half," Fairfax said finally. His voice came rough, sounding as if it hurt his throat.

"I told you you were going to sleep three hours."

"And I told you to wake me up in an hour and a half." Some of the roughness in his voice came from fatigue, but a good bit of it now was anger.

Trieka knew it was pointless, knew it was far from constructive, but she couldn't help getting angry back. "Who's wearing the captain's uniform?"

Fairfax levered himself on one elbow, pain and exertion blatant on his face. "No one right now, and even if you were, it wouldn't make any difference. I'm not a member of your crew. I never was."

"This is for your own good, Fairfax. You need the sleep more than I do."

"Unless lack of sleep makes you bitchy, in which case you're in dire need of a good long nap."

That one wasn't worth answering. She took a deep breath and swallowed, realized she was near tears. Mostly from frustration, but also from anger and exhaustion.

"Fine," she finally said. "Wake me up when you don't think you can stay awake anymore."

"Fair enough."

She was still angry, but the anger wasn't enough to keep her awake.

"Trieka."

The voice jolted her, not quite awake, but somewhere close.

"Cavendish."

She opened her eyes. Had he called her Trieka, or had she imagined it? Her mouth tasted like dirt. "I'm awake," she muttered, forcing herself to sit up.

"Are there any more antibiotics?"

She blinked, squinting at Fairfax through the dim light. "Some." She could barely see him, but he looked pale and drawn. Reaching out, she touched his forehead and nearly jerked away from the heat. He was shaking.

"I think you'd better give me whatever you have."

She said nothing, but loaded a hypo and gave him another dose of drugs. Then she turned up the lantern and unzipped his sleeping bag.

The swelling was worse, bright red flesh straining and bulging around the sutured line, which had given way in places. Pus oozed from the openings. She remained silent, but apparently Fairfax saw all he needed to see on her face.

"It's bad, isn't it?"

She couldn't lie to him. "Yes, it's bad."

"Is there anything you can do?"

"I'm not a doctor. I could open it back up, drain off the pus, see if I can find any dead tissue and cut that out with the laser, but—"

"But we're out of anesthetic," he finished for her.

"And I don't know if it would help. If it doesn't, then I don't see any option but to..." She stopped, swallowed. "To take the leg before you go into septic shock and die."

He was silent for a long time, chewing on that. Trieka was afraid to look at him.

"How much painkiller do we have?"

"I don't know. A lot." She rubbed her eyes.

"Enough to kill me?"

She blinked. A dead, quiet calm settled in her stomach. "Maybe."

"Give me the bottle."

"No."

"Cavendish—"

"Not yet. I'm not ready to give up."

"But you *are* ready to hack pieces of me out with a laser while I'm fully conscious?"

"At least let me drain it. That might help."

"Yeah. And God himself might come down and carry us to a safe haven."

Stubbornly silent, Trieka rummaged in the med kit for the medical laser and the bottle of painkillers. And something else.

"It's my life, Cavendish."

She looked at him, angry. After a moment, she handed him the bottle of pills. "Fine. But you're no longer my responsibility."

He twisted off the cap. "I never was."

He picked up the water bottle and used it to swallow the first two tablets. Then he put the cap on the pill bottle and lay back in the sleeping bag. "Do what you can. Just promise me one thing."

She could barely breathe past relief. "What?"

"Tell me the truth. If there's no other option but to amputate, I don't want you to lie to me about it."

"All right. I promise." It was only fair.

"And whatever decision I make, you won't interfere."

She nodded.

"Good."

She waited until he indicated the painkillers had kicked in, then descended with the medical laser. The bottle of alcohol she kept hidden behind her. Last time, the anesthetic had dulled the sting when she'd used it. This time she figured it was better if he didn't know what was coming.

The wound, when it came open, was full of pus. She flushed it out with the contents of a water bottle, thinking that that commodity, too, was becoming scarce. When it looked clean, she doused it with the alcohol.

When Fairfax was done screaming, he passed out. Trieka bound the wound tight with strips of sterile gauze from the med kit, then left the tent and hid behind a tree to vomit.

She came out into the clearing, shaking, and sat down outside the tent. The sun was rising, the sky gone pink and mauve behind the treetops. She put her face in her hands and let the tears come.

She tried to keep the sobbing silent, but it went out of her control until she was wailing with it, slamming her head into the tree in an effort to bring herself back. It didn't work.

A small sound across the clearing, though, did.

She gulped her tears in a huge lump, abruptly alert, together and terrified. *EarthFed*, she thought. *They've found us.* She scrabbled in her pocket for the medical laser. A paltry defense, but her gun was in the tent. She cranked the controls to full power and pointed the instrument toward the sound.

"Who's there?"

Maybe it was just an animal. A squirrel, or a deer. But a shadow moved within the trees, man-sized. Trieka levered herself up against the tree behind her.

"Come out now or I'll shoot."

There was another small, barely audible rustle as the

Katriena Knights

shadow came away from the trees and stepped out.
It was a white ape.

Katriena Knights

shadow came away from the trees and stepped out.
It was a white ape.

Chapter Ten

Though not really an ape, Trieka decided as she faced the creature. It stood upright a few yards away. The white pelt was long and lush, covering everything but the face, which was inky black. Eyes glittered beneath prominent ridges. The nose was flat like a gorilla's, but as the creature turned its head to look at the huge carcass on the ground, she saw its lower jaw did not protrude beneath the upper like a gorilla's would. Lantern-jawed, though. Like Fairfax.

Looking at the huge, dead beast, the animal suddenly lifted a hand. Long white hair fell away from black fingers and a thumb. It pointed at the creature, then at Trieka. Then it lifted both hands in a shrug, which obviously indicated a question.

"Oh, my God," Trieka breathed. Her gun hand sagged, lowering the laser. Fairfax had been right. These things were intelligent. And this one was talking to her.

It lowered its hands and waited patiently. She swallowed, then said, "Yes, I killed it."

The creature lifted its hands again, the gesture accompanied by an upward lift of the heavy brow ridges. It didn't understand.

Of course it doesn't understand. You think the thing speaks English? She thought a moment, then stood straight, relinquishing the support of the tree. "Okay, we'll play charades."

Hunching over, Trieka took on the posture and gait of the dead rhino-creature. Then she moved back into herself, hefting a gun and pulling the trigger. Then the creature again, felled by the bullet, falling dead to the ground. The ape watched with great interest. When she finished, it nodded, and the black lips moved in a smile.

It's smiling at me. Overwhelmed, Trieka grabbed backward to clutch the tree again. *My God, we're having a conversation.* But there wasn't time to indulge in intellectual shock. The ape was talking again. She forced herself to pay attention. It pointed at her, then at its hand. With two fingers, it made walking motions. Then it pointed back to her.

Okay, that's me. She nodded. The ape made another person with two fingers of its other hand, then lifted both hands again in an interrogative.

Are you alone? Trieka considered, debated, and finally waved toward the tent. At least it wasn't EarthFed. And if they were intelligent, maybe they could help.

The ape's brow furrowed in concern. It moved toward the tent. Trieka stared, still disoriented. The creature walked fully upright, with a strong, easy gait. It went to the tent and pulled the flap open. She followed.

The creature saw Fairfax and moved immediately to his side, then looked to her with another interrogative gesture. Trieka unzipped the sleeping bag to show Fairfax's bandaged thigh. She pointed to the gauze-swathed leg, then out the tent flap to the dead animal.

The ape creature frowned. With a gentleness Trieka found surprising, it touched Fairfax's face and forehead with the back of its long-fingered hand. Then it rose, turned, and stepped back into the clearing.

What now? The creature—Trieka suddenly found herself thinking of it as male—lifted a hand to his mouth and made a single harsh, echoing bark.

If she'd been surprised before, now she was completely stupefied. Three more white-furred figures emerged from the trees. One was noticeably smaller than the others, with slightly longer hair and a curvature to the body beneath. So she'd been right. The first one was male.

The four apes collected and began to gesture to each other, the first male leading the conversation. The gestures were small and quick, limited mostly to hands and fingers. There was no vocalization at all.

Sign language, she thought. No wonder the male had been so quick to formulate gestures to communicate with her. She shook her head slowly. One amazement after another.

Behind her, a small moan issued from the tent. She ducked under the tent flap.

Fairfax was waking up. His eyes came open slowly, and when they did, they were dull and glassy. She knelt next to him, pushing wet hair back from his damp forehead.

"Fairfax?" she said. He looked at her, his face blank with pain and shock. "Fairfax, the cavalry has arrived."

His brow creased in puzzlement. He'd heard her, at least, and understood what she'd said. "EarthFed?" His voice was barely a breath.

"No. The natives."

"What?" Then his gaze riveted to the tent flap. Trieka took his hand and his fingers closed on hers, almost painfully tight. "What the hell?"

The female had entered alone. She carried a leather shoulder bag, which she set down on the ground next to Fairfax. He could only stare. With delicate, dark gray fingers, the little ape parted the hair on her chest to display a patch of shorter, golden fur. She outlined it with one finger, emphasizing the circular shape. Then she made a series of gestures with one hand and pointed to herself. Trieka looked at her blankly. The female repeated the gestures.

"It's her name," Fairfax said. "Goldspot or something."

"Goldenseal," Trieka said. It was the name of an herb on Earth, and though she doubted the plant grew on Denahault, the name seemed to fit the delicate little ape.

"Good enough," Fairfax said. A feverish lucidity had risen in his eyes. He looked manic, but spoke calmly. He pointed to his own chest. "Harrison," he said.

Trieka gave him an odd look. He'd never invited *her* to call him by his first name. She pointed to herself and said, "Trieka."

Goldenseal only smiled and shook her head a little. She thought a moment, then pointed to Trieka and made a small finger-flaring gesture in front of her forehead. For Fairfax, she ran two fingers down the short bridge of her nose.

Fairfax grunted. "Fire Hair and Big Nose. I'm going back to sleep—I think I'm having a fever-induced hallucination."

Trieka squeezed his hand again. Goldenseal had turned away and was rummaging through her shoulder bag. The pockets inside held numerous capsules, clever little constructs of wax filled with liquids of various colors. She selected a variety and turned back to Fairfax.

Carefully, she began to undo the bandages. Trieka stopped her with a hand on her arm, handed her a pair of scissors from the med kit. The instrument, obviously unfamiliar to Goldenseal, was met with a look of puzzlement followed by a broad grin as she realized what they were and how they were used. The deft little hands adapted to the task quickly.

Trieka watched with interest, still holding Fairfax's hand. He was still awake, and his fingers tightened on hers as the scissors neared the deeper portions of the wound. Goldenseal carefully cut away the gauze, pulling it back. Her frown deepened as more of the wound came into view. She examined it closely, probing with gentle fingers that still made Fairfax flinch and bite his lip.

After a time she leaned back on her heels and looked at his face, then touched his forehead and cheeks. Fairfax opened his eyes. He looked worried. Goldenseal looked at Trieka, her small gray mouth pressed into a thin line, obviously frustrated by her inability to communicate.

Finally, Goldenseal spoke with wide, simplified gestures. She was asking Fairfax's permission to give him something that would put him to sleep.

"That's the best offer I've had all day," Fairfax said, then nodded to Goldenseal. Trieka started to protest, but bit it off. Too late, though. Fairfax had heard the little sputter.

"What?"

"She's an alien. We don't know anything about her body chemistry, or she about ours. What she gives you could kill you."

Fairfax shrugged. "Frankly, I'm willing to risk it." Again, she began to protest, but he cut her off. "It's my decision, Cavendish."

He was right, of course. She had no right to tell him what

to do, no right to say anything beyond what she'd already said. She felt like she did, though. She felt like some part of him belonged to her. She'd saved his life, after all. And she'd nearly made love to him, wished now that she had.

"Just don't die on me," she muttered.

Goldenseal was careful. Bursting the end of a wax capsule with a bone pin, she gave Fairfax only a small amount of the contents. After a few minutes, she checked his eyes, laid her head against his chest, then gave him more. The third dose sent him to sleep. Even then, she waited, checking his eyes and tapping at joints until she found the nerve under his kneecap.

Once Goldenseal was satisfied with Fairfax's condition, she began to work in earnest on the wound. With a dainty knife apparently also made of bone, she cut away pieces of dead flesh. A fine white powder, which she sprinkled over the raw flesh, stopped the oozing of blood. Then she withdrew a delicate bone needle and stretches of gut. Trieka winced, wondering how sterile the equipment was. But there was little choice since the suturing liquid was gone.

Goldenseal's stitches were small and neat, leaving a black trail up the inside of Fairfax's leg. Finished, she rummaged again in her leather bag, extracting what looked like dark gray mud, wrapped tightly in large leaves.

Trieka cringed as Goldenseal smeared the stuff thickly over the sutured wound. Goldenseal noticed her reaction. She placed an open hand above the smear of mud, then lifted the hand away, moving her fingers together. Trieka understood. The mud was meant to draw poisons out of the wound.

When Goldenseal was certain of Trieka's comprehension, she continued her work, wrapping Fairfax's leg in clean cloth bandages. Then she checked his eyes and touched his forehead again, and sat back on her heels to stretch. Trieka watched, filled with questions she couldn't ask.

No longer concentrating on Fairfax's treatment, Trieka found her attention captured by noises outside the tent. Goldenseal smiled and waved her away. Trieka nodded and went to investigate.

The males were busily butchering the dead beast. It was already skinned and gutted, the hind legs removed and dressed. One of the males—Trieka was fairly certain he was the one who'd discovered them—noticed her and left his work. He pointed to the tent and questioned with a shrug. Trieka returned the question.

There was an awkward silence as the male struggled against the language barrier. Trieka smiled, sensing somehow that he was grasping for words of reassurance. She pointed to herself and made the flaring finger gesture in front of her forehead.

The male grinned, understanding. He pointed to himself, then lifted his right foot. Fur fell away to expose six stubby black toes. He showed her the left foot, where there were only five. Six Toes, then. Trieka smiled as Six Toes demonstrated the abbreviated hand gesture that was his name. He pointed then to her. She interpreted as he briefly reenacted her pantomimed account of the creature's death. "You. Beast Killer."

Trieka smiled and shook her head, pointing to the tent, then at herself, then at the partially butchered carcass. Fairfax's shot had been clean—it had been pure bad luck it hadn't been effective.

Six Toes nodded, his smile enigmatic. Another uncomfortable silence fell. Finally Six Toes made an inviting gesture toward the carcass. Trieka shrugged and went with him.

The other two males were Hare Lip and Blue Eye. Blue Eye appeared to be blind in the eye in question. Hare Lip seemed less accepting of her than the others, and sidled away when she squatted next to him, a bone knife in her hand, to help with the butchering. She wasn't surprised. In fact, she was more surprised he was the only one to exhibit such an attitude.

Following Blue Eye's lead, she began to carve pieces out of the bloody haunch. If nothing else, they'd likely have a good meal tonight.

※ ※ ※

Fairfax woke to the smell of roasting meat. His stomach entered a state of confusion, unsure whether to be hungry or nauseated. He opened his eyes. The shadows on the floor and walls told him twilight had fallen.

112

Next to him, the pale shadow of Goldenseal shifted as he looked toward her. She smiled a little, reached out to touch his face. Then she made the flaring gesture at her forehead, meaning Cavendish, and lifted her hands in a question. Fairfax frowned, then nodded. Goldenseal left him. Cavendish appeared a few moments later.

"Hi." She sat down next to him.

"Hi, yourself."

"How do you feel?"

Fairfax considered. It was an interesting question. His leg ached, the pain throbbing into his groin and belly. But he no longer felt as if there were something alive in there, scrabbling to get out. He also felt less woozy, as if his connection to the world had been hooked back up.

"Better, I think," he said finally.

"Are you hungry? I think Goldenseal is getting you some broth."

"That would be good."

Goldenseal returned with a small, steaming bowl. She started to kneel next to Fairfax, then changed her mind, instead giving the bowl to Cavendish. With an odd smile, she left again. He looked at Cavendish, an eyebrow quirked. "Did she just appoint you my mother?"

Cavendish, too, looked a bit uncomfortable. "I'm not sure."

"Why don't you give me the bowl? I can feed myself." But when he tried to sit up, a shower of stars rose behind his vision, pain lancing up his thigh and into his abdomen. He held very still until the urge to faint passed. "Or maybe not."

Cavendish fumbled in her rucksack and retrieved a spoon. "Don't worry about it," she said, spooning the broth between his lips. "You're better off taking it easy."

He felt ridiculous lying there while Cavendish spoon-fed him. She was matter-of-fact about it, though, performing the task without fuss. After only a few spoonfuls, he asked her to stop. An ominous roil had begun in his stomach.

"That needs to settle," he said. Cavendish sat back, studying him.

"Can I ask you a question, Fairfax?"

"Only if I can reserve the right not to answer."

"Fair enough."

She didn't ask right away, though. Instead, she stared into the bowl of broth, her brow furrowed. He wondered what she could possibly ask that would be so difficult for her. She didn't seem like the kind of person who had trouble saying what she felt. He reached out to close his hand around her forearm. She looked up in surprise.

"What is it?" he said.

"If you..." Her eyes looked dark in the dim light, and he wondered what color they were at the moment. Nearly brown, he'd guess, or dark gray-green. She looked tired. "If these people hadn't shown up, and I'd had to amputate, would you have taken the pills?"

He wondered why the question was important to her. "I was less concerned about losing the leg than about dying a horribly painful death. Under the circumstances, I think amputation would have only delayed the inevitable. There's no point dying in pain when you can do it quietly." He paused. "Yes, I probably would have."

"What about now?"

He considered, then let himself smile a little. "If it comes to that, I think our little furry friend has something that would kill me quicker." He saw a small flash of irritation on her face, but she quelled it and said nothing, waiting for his answer. "I'll give her a chance, at least."

She tilted the soup bowl back and forth as if reading his fortune in the sparkle of melted fat that sat on the surface like a tiny oil slick. She blinked a few times, quickly, then looked straight at him. The fierceness in her eyes shot fire down his belly. Had it not been for the pain, his body would have responded.

"I want you to know," she said quietly, "that if you do lose the leg, it won't make any difference."

"Any difference to what?"

"To how I feel."

"And how is that?"

Some of the seriousness faded from her face as her mouth

quirked in a little smile. "I really have no idea. But it won't make any difference."

He smiled. "I'm glad to know that. Thank you."

"More soup?"

"Please."

✳ ✳ ✳

Trieka fed him as much soup as he'd take, then gave him water. Goldenseal had medicated the water, and within minutes of drinking it, Fairfax was asleep again. She felt his forehead, tangling her fingers in the red-brown forelock. He felt cooler, though still warm. She drew the blanket over him and slipped out of the tent.

Outside it was full dark. Her companions sat around the fire where they'd roasted the night's dinner. They'd constructed a tarp of the beast's hide and propped it with sticks over the fire, obscuring the light from anyone who might be searching. Trieka sat next to Goldenseal and accepted a piece of meat. It was still warm, and tasted like a cross between pork and beef.

Goldenseal pointed to the tent and mimed sleep. Trieka nodded. Goldenseal was quiet for a time, then looked at her soberly. She indicated Fairfax, then Trieka, followed by an incomprehensible gesture.

Trieka frowned. Goldenseal tried something else just as cryptic. Finally, obviously frustrated, she leaned close. She glanced up to be certain no one was watching, then made a circle with her left thumb and forefinger. She poked her right forefinger into the circle.

Still baffled, Trieka shook her head. Goldenseal pointed at the tent, then at Trieka, then repeated the gesture, this time moving the finger in and out.

Slowly, it dawned on Trieka she was miming a sexual act. On the heels of that realization came a translation of the question—not, "Have you slept with him?" but, "Is he your lover?" or, "Is he your husband?"

She shook her head. She could think of no way to explain her relationship with Fairfax in hand gestures. Finally she just shook her head again. Goldenseal nodded, seeming to understand.

Forget hand gestures—she wasn't sure she could explain Fairfax in words. She chewed thoughtfully on her meat. Only feelings seemed to hold any truth. She felt like smiling when she thought about him, remembering the way his hair felt between her fingers, or the rasp of his body hair against her breasts. And when she thought about losing him, a piece of her soul began to ache and wail in fear.

It occurred to her she might love him.

When Goldenseal rose to return to the tent, Trieka followed. She watched and helped as the healer removed and replaced the mud poultice and the bandages. The wound seemed less swollen.

When Goldenseal went back to the fire, Trieka stayed. She slid into her own sleeping bag and lay down next to Fairfax. The heat of fever curled off his skin. He was deeply asleep, caught in the web of whatever drug he'd been given. Trieka watched his face for a time, then drifted into sleep.

※ ※ ※

Sounds of activity woke her. Fairfax still slept next to her, though now his eyes roved under his lids as he dreamed. Trieka looked through the tent flap to see what was going on.

Her companions were breaking camp. Seeing Trieka, Six Toes pointed to the tent and made folding motions. Trieka nodded, frowning. What about Fairfax? Her eyes found Goldenseal's. The healer was busy sewing a large piece of the animal hide around two long, straight branches. She gave Trieka a reassuring nod. The stretcher was nearly completed.

When Goldenseal had tied off the last stitch, she waved for Blue Eye to come with her. Trieka ducked back into the tent to see Fairfax rubbing at his eyes.

"What's going on?"

"We're breaking camp."

"Where are we going?"

"I don't know. I assume to the Land of the Furry White

116

People."

"And what will we do there? Dance and sing happy songs?"

She grinned. "You must be feeling better."

"I do. I'm surprised, really. I've just been subjected to the most primitive medicine I've ever seen, and I think I'm going to live through the experience."

Trieka sobered a little, wondering how sarcastic he'd intended to be. "She saved your life. And it looks like she saved your leg, too."

Fairfax, too, sobered. "I know that. I also know she wouldn't have been able to if you hadn't done what you did. And that includes that unfortunate alcohol incident." He paused, looking at her in a way that made her tingle, down into her belly and below. "Thank you."

"You would have done the same."

"I would have tried. I probably would have passed out, though, and you'd've bled to death."

So the moment of seriousness had passed. Just as well. Trieka smiled, and Fairfax smiled back. The tent flaps rustled and Trieka turned to see Goldenseal, Six Toes and Blue Eye behind her.

"I think they're ready for you."

Carefully, the two big males carried Fairfax out of the tent and positioned him in the hide stretcher. In spite of their caution, Fairfax was pale and sweating when they laid him down. Trieka made certain he was all right, then disassembled the tent and packed it away in her rucksack. Six Toes watched with great interest, apparently fascinated that the large tent could fold into such a small package.

Trieka gathered her things, then hefted her rucksack and Fairfax's. Blue Eye obligingly relieved her of one of them. Before full morning had quite settled into the forest, they were on their way.

Trieka walked next to Fairfax, who seemed to be in less discomfort once they started moving. "Are you okay? Should I see if Goldenseal has something for the pain?"

"She gave me some tea or something before we left. It's not too bad. And I don't want her knocking me out again, not just yet."

Six Toes, at the head of the stretcher, looked back at them, frowning a little. Their speaking seemed to discomfit the apes. Trieka refused to be silent just to make them happy, but she did lower her voice. It was probably a reasonable precaution, anyway.

"I can understand that."

"I wonder how far we're going?" Fairfax, too, lowered his voice to a near whisper.

Trieka pondered, wondering how to ask the question. Finally she indicated the sky and the movement of the sun. Blue Eye, nodding in comprehension, indicated sunset, then noon.

"A day and a half," said Trieka, overly pleased with herself.

"Yeah, I got that," Fairfax mumbled. His voice was too low to catch his tone, but the little half-grin told Trieka he was kidding her. She smiled back, more warmly than she'd intended, and fell silent to enjoy the walk.

❊ ❊ ❊

A day and a half later, they arrived. They'd been walking through foothills for the last three-quarters of the journey, and when they stopped, it was near the mouth of a long shallow cave. More of an overhang, really, it ended in a wall about fifteen feet under the jut of stone. The ceiling was only about six feet high. Trieka and the apes could walk under easily, but Fairfax would have to duck when he was able to stand again.

The cave appeared to be a family dwelling, but was empty at the moment. Goldenseal, coming to direct Six Toes and Blue Eye, indicated she lived there. She had Fairfax deposited in a bed near the front of the cave. A half-dozen other low beds occupied the perimeter of the dwelling. Curtains separated two from the rest. In the center of the space was a fire pit where banked coals smoldered. Not much privacy, but it was cozy.

Fairfax grunted a little as he was lowered to the bed. Goldenseal knelt next to him. A simply built but sturdy wooden chest sat next to the bed; Goldenseal opened it and rummaged through an impressive collection of medical supplies. Trieka wavered, not wanting to interfere, but not really wanting to leave Fairfax either.

A hand on her arm made the decision for her. She turned to see Six Toes smiling at her. He moved his head, indicating she should follow him. Reluctantly, she did.

There were fully a dozen cave entrances along the side of the hill, some larger than others. Many were simply deep overhangs, but others seemed to descend into more complex caverns. Other apes—Trieka was beginning to become uncomfortable with calling them that—moved about their daily business, eyeing her with interest and a certain amount of fear as she passed. Six Toes's smiles and relaxed gestures put most of them at ease.

He paused briefly by one cave opening, indicating it belonged to him. A well-polished piece of wood hung next to the door; Six Toes struck it with his hand. A surprisingly bell-like tone sounded from it. It must have been hollow inside, or set over an opening in the rock.

A few moments later a female, taller than Goldenseal and thicker through the waist, appeared at the door. Seeing Six Toes, her face lit with a bright smile. She reached toward him and was rewarded with a warm embrace. Then Six Toes backed away and nodded toward Trieka. The female started, her eager happiness changing to worry. Her hands and fingers began to fly in rapid signs.

Abruptly, Six Toes cut her off. Slowly, so Trieka could follow, he signed Trieka's new name. The name he gave for the female looked to Trieka like "Always Pregnant". However, since she didn't seem to be in that state at the moment, Trieka translated it as "Always Mother", and assumed it to be an honorary title of some sort.

After another exchange with Six Toes, Always Mother seemed to relax. She turned to Trieka with an interrogative gesture and made washing motions over her body with her hands. Trieka nodded emphatically. A bath sounded like heaven.

Six Toes touched Always Mother gently as the two women departed. An intimate relationship existed there, Trieka was certain. Unfortunately, the only sign she could remember to ask about it was the crude one Goldenseal had used, so she decided to refrain from talking for the moment.

Always Mother had no such compunction. As they walked, she pointed to bits and pieces of the landscape, demonstrating the signs for individual items. Grateful someone was finally offering a language lesson, Trieka paid rapt attention.

It wasn't until they had nearly arrived that Trieka heard the sound of running water. A few minutes later, they stopped by a slow-moving river. Along the near side, the bank had been cut away to create a nearly still, quiet pool. The bottom of the pool was lined with large flat stones, some stacked on top of each other to make seats. Always Mother stepped down into the water and gestured for Trieka to follow.

Trieka hesitated. She wanted to wash, but felt suddenly awkward about taking off her clothes. Always Mother had the advantage of fur to cover her anatomy, and Trieka found herself self-conscious about her bare, relatively hairless skin. Finally she decided her clothes could stand a washing, too, took her shoes off, and waded in. Always Mother seemed unconcerned.

The water was considerably cooler than Trieka normally liked her baths, but the slow movement of it against her body was soothing. She dunked her head, soaking her hair to her scalp. Gooseflesh prickled all over her body as she surfaced.

Always Mother eyed her with frank curiosity. Trieka glanced down to see her shirt clinging to her skin, her nipples, tautened by the cold, protruding boldly against the cloth. She must look bizarre to her fur-covered companion. Always Mother herself was drenched to the skin, but even wet, the long white hair concealed the more intimate contours of her body.

Trieka smiled a little, uncomfortable again. Always Mother looked embarrassed to have been caught staring and made a small sign which must have been an apology.

They sat in the water for a time, Trieka on the bank with just her feet wet, hoping the sun might dry her clothes before they went back. They were partially dry when Six Toes approached.

For a moment that edged on panic, Trieka thought he looked grim, then realized he only looked very serious. He gestured for the women to follow him. Always Mother came out of the water and shook herself, flinging water from her fur like a dog. Trieka couldn't suppress a smile. Always Mother returned it, setting Trieka a bit more at ease, even in the face of Six Toes's expression.

Six Toes led the way back through the small village to one of the central caves. The opening was small, so even Trieka ducked automatically for fear of hitting her head. The cave opened out again after perhaps fifteen feet. Trieka straightened and stared, catching her breath.

The narrow passage opened out into a huge cavern. The walls were dented with hundreds of small nooks, each of which housed a burning candle. In the center of the area was a deep fire pit lined with stones, the flames within blazing hot and bright. Smoke from the fire and the candles rose straight up, drawn apparently to an opening somewhere in the cavern's vaulted ceiling.

Beyond the fire rose a low dais, where a large male ape reposed. The male's fur wasn't quite white—more the color of old ivory. Around his neck and wrists hung strings of stone: agate and amber. He sat quietly, looking not at the fire, but through and beyond it. Next to him, on the floor below the dais, sat three young females, each wearing a single strand of amber beads. They, too, were quiet, but engaged in domestic tasks. One was sewing some kind of garment, one wove on a small loom and the other was sorting dried herbs into little leather bags.

Trieka jumped, startled, as Six Toes uttered a trilling hoot. The Elder—for Trieka had decided that was what he was—looked away from the fire to acknowledge Six Toes's presence. Six Toes touched his forehead and breast, then began to speak with his hands, pointing occasionally to Trieka. She recognized the signs for her name, and for Fairfax's unflattering moniker.

After a time, the Elder's gaze moved to her. Hoping she did the right thing, Trieka echoed Six Toes's salute, touching her forehead and breast. The Elder smiled a little. He removed two of the amber necklaces from around his neck. The first he held up, open, and lifted toward her. Trieka bent her head and the Elder dropped the necklace around her neck. As she straightened, he handed her the other strand. "Long Nose," he motioned. Trieka nodded understanding. The Elder smiled.

They were accepted, or so Trieka assumed. Both Six Toes

and Always Mother seemed pleased. The Elder turned away to resume staring at the fire.

Trieka spent the rest of the afternoon in the company of Always Mother, learning word after word and being shown around the small village. When she saw the inhabitants settling down for the evening meal, she asked to be taken to Fairfax.

Goldenseal's cave was full of children. The small furry youngsters ate with exuberance, talking emphatically with their small hands. A male had joined the group and stepped in from time to time to mediate. Goldenseal's mate, Trieka assumed. Goldenseal herself sat next to Fairfax, helping him with his meal.

Trieka was surprised to see Fairfax nearly sitting up, propped with blankets behind his back, and feeding himself. Obviously he was doing better. Smiling, she went to join him. He looked up with a start, his face immediately filling with concern.

"Where have you been? Are you all right?" He sounded almost angry. Her smile fell. She felt like she'd been caught sneaking in at two a.m. after a party. What was it about him that kept making her feel like she was in high school?

"Getting some language lessons for one thing." Her tone was more defensive than she'd intended. Remembering the necklace, she held it out to him. "Put this on. It's from the tribal leader."

Fairfax took it, staring blankly at the rich amber. "What's it for?"

"I think it means he approves of us."

He fingered the smooth orange stones, then put the necklace over his head without looking at her. "I'm sorry," he said.

"For what?"

"For snapping at you. I didn't know what was going on. I was worried."

"It's all right." Trieka looked at Goldenseal. She sat quietly, watching their exchange, but the children had stopped talking and were staring at her and Fairfax. She shifted her attention to them and smiled reassuringly.

"How are you feeling?" she asked Fairfax, still looking at

the children. The smallest of the six returned her smile. The others looked away.

"Better," Fairfax said. Trieka looked back at him. He appeared better, less florid and more coherent. "I think I'm mending."

"Good to hear it. You need to get up so you can go take a bath. They have a lovely little pool."

"I thought something smelled different." Trieka was relieved to see his twitching near-smile. "You were starting to get a little gamy."

"You're reeking a bit yourself. And I expect you'll continue to reek until you can walk down to that pool."

"Not much I can do about it." He returned his attention to his meal. "Have you had anything to eat?"

"No."

Fairfax gestured to Goldenseal. Goldenseal repeated the gesture, correcting his pronunciation, then went to the table and came back with food for Trieka. She settled down next to Fairfax to eat.

"I see you've been getting some education yourself," she said, stirring the bowl of thick, fragrant stew. It was full of meat and unfamiliar vegetables.

"A little. Mostly I've been sleeping. I think our little friend here has been slipping me mickeys."

"Whatever works."

Fairfax grunted acknowledgment around a mouthful of food. Trieka joined his silence for a time, then said, "I'm glad you're feeling better."

He only smiled.

She stayed with him for the rest of the evening, while Goldenseal and her family prepared for bed. The children gathered around their father, who told apparently engrossing stories, his hands moving evocatively in the flickering firelight. Goldenseal looked at Fairfax's wound, then washed it and replaced the wrappings. Trieka excused herself to step outside while Fairfax, with Goldenseal's assistance, relieved himself. It seemed to her that it would bruise his dignity if she stayed. Plus she could stand to answer the call of nature herself.

Finally, she watched as he fell into sleep, helped along by whatever pain-numbing draught Goldenseal had brewed for him. As sleep fell over the cave, Goldenseal's mate, Brown Hands, banked the low fire, then drew the privacy curtains into place. Trieka was left alone next to Fairfax, a small, empty bed waiting for her a few feet away from his.

Her clothes were stiff and uncomfortable after the dunk in the water, so she took them off and laid them out on the floor next to the bed. The blankets, some woven, some cured hides, were warm and heavy as she slid under them. It must get terribly cold in the winter here for furred people to need blankets. She did recall a great deal of snow during her winter on Denahault, but couldn't remember how cold it had been.

With the fire banked, it was nearly pitch black in the cave. Her eyes strained against the darkness and found the darker edge of Fairfax's outline. She had just undressed in front of him. Too bad he'd missed it.

She smiled a little, then her smile faded as her thoughts changed. She thought about undressing in front of him again, this time with him awake. And she wouldn't shed her clothes matter-of-factly, as she had a few minutes ago. She'd do it slowly, languidly, showing herself to him one careful stretch of skin at a time.

She found herself thinking then of the way he'd felt cupped in her palm—the weight of him and his rough hair. She thought about doing that again, too, with different intent. She thought about doing it with her mouth.

It was a long time before she fell asleep.

Chapter Eleven

"Do you want to walk today?" Goldenseal's graceful black fingers formed the words carefully.

Fairfax answered with a silent, emphatic, "Yes."

Fairfax had improved greatly over the past three days. Yesterday, Goldenseal had allowed him to walk as far as the first tree outside the cave entrance, to urinate against it under his own power. A milestone, to be certain, and one which Trieka felt strangely privileged to have participated in. Not that she'd done much more than applaud when he'd finished, but still.

"Where?" Goldenseal asked.

Fairfax hesitated. Trieka jumped in.

"Bath," she said.

"Thanks," said Fairfax aloud, but she saw his lurking smile. Goldenseal nodded approval.

At some point during the last three days—Trieka wasn't sure when—Fairfax had retrieved a spare set of jeans and underwear from his rucksack, which he'd been wearing day and night ever since. They'd originally belonged to Jim Taylor and were too big for him, but the extra size was beneficial in this case. Trieka and Goldenseal helped him up, then he waved them off, moving at his own pace while he rucked up the baggy jeans. Goldenseal hovered, asking him to stop only a dozen feet from the cave.

"I'm all right," he assured her. "No pain."

"Not much, anyway," he added aloud to Trieka. Goldenseal backed off a bit and let him continue.

Trieka could tell by looking at him that he wasn't completely without pain, but his stride loosened as they continued.

"Nice to get some fresh air," he said. He reached almost absently for Trieka, not for support, but just to hold her hand. She wove her fingers through his, feeling warm and happy.

She'd expected Goldenseal to take them to the same pool where Always Mother had taken her, and where she'd gone to bathe nightly since then. Instead, the little healer led the way down another path to a different bend in the river.

Here lay another pool, this one not carved artificially from the riverbank, but formed by a natural curve in the river and an outcropping of rock. The still pool was partially hidden by an overhang, its location obscured by the surrounding trees. Branches hung softly to the water from trees that looked like willows, but bore those strange, almost needlelike leaves prevalent throughout the forest. In the center of the quiet water, the sun shone full and dazzling on the surface.

"Warmer water," Goldenseal explained simply. "And more quiet."

Both of which sounded good to Trieka. She stepped through the trees, toward the pool. Fairfax followed, but Goldenseal did not. The healer smiled a little and, pointing to the sky, indicated she'd be back in two hours.

Fairfax watched her go. "Alone at last," he said, and leered at Trieka shamelessly.

"Watch yourself, gimpy." She was laughing, but his comic tongue-lolling had unaccountably aroused her. She loosed her fingers from his as he reached for a tree. He moved from bole to bole, using them for support until he reached the water's edge, where he carefully lowered himself to the ground.

"How is it?" she asked, sitting down next to him.

"Not bad. Stiff at first, but it seems to be loosening up a little." He paused, moving the injured leg experimentally. "It's going to leave a hell of a scar."

"You can have it repaired when we get home. God knows you've got the money."

"If EarthFed hasn't frozen all my accounts."

She looked at him, sobering. She hadn't thought of that.

126

"That would suck."

"To put it mildly."

Fairfax took his shoes off, not without some difficulty, then shucked his shirt. Trieka, trying not to stare at the clean bones of his back, said, "You don't seem concerned."

He shrugged. "It's only money."

Scooting forward on his buttocks, he put his feet in the water. She took off her shoes and joined him, wondering if, after everything that had happened, he was actually working up the nerve to take off his pants.

"Goldenseal certainly has a houseful, doesn't she?" he said presently.

"That she does. Her children effectively demonstrate one of the advantages of sign language."

Fairfax laughed. "Sometimes I regret not having any kids. What about you?"

Trieka didn't answer right away. She looked down at her hands, and after a moment she felt his gaze on her.

"What's wrong?"

She picked up a rock and tossed it into the pool. "I can't have kids. It's a genetic thing. I'm not put together quite right."

She couldn't look at him. She found another rock and skipped it neatly across the surface of the water. Her greatest secret was out now. She'd given it to him like a gift.

"Well," he said finally. "That makes me feel a little better about not having any condoms at hand."

She looked at him then and he was smiling. Something warm and wonderful and full of power opened up inside her as she understood that, whatever it was she was feeling, he felt it, too. Happy, she snorted. "Last I saw, you were in no condition to be using them."

"I feel much better now."

His tone was completely neutral, and he didn't look at her. Trieka swallowed. "Take your bath, Fairfax."

"I'm going to need help." He still wasn't looking at her, but she could see his mouth twitching. He was insufferable. She repressed an urge to laugh, and another to slap him.

"How much help do you think you'll need?"

"Well, to tell the truth, I'm not entirely sure I can get my pants off by myself."

She nearly cracked another joke, but he finally looked at her. His eyes held a strange mix of emotion, and she sensed that, although the humor of the situation hadn't escaped him, he was still sacrificing a good deal of pride even to ask.

Of course, there was one certain way to turn the tables on him, to save his pride and change the nature of everything they were doing. She was more than willing.

"I guess I'll have to join you," she said, and began to unbutton her shirt.

"Let me," he said. Which was exactly what she'd hoped he'd say. She dropped her hands from the row of buttons and leaned toward him.

He eased the buttons loose, one by one, then slipped the shirt over her shoulders and down her arms. As his hands engulfed her breasts, he bent and closed his mouth on her nipple. She arched against him. She didn't think she'd ever wanted a man so badly in her life.

He smelled horrible, though. Her hands moved to his waist, finding and undoing his fly.

"Lie down," she mumbled, somewhere close to his ear. "I'll get these off you."

He followed instructions, stretching out on the grass. Trieka eased the jeans down his legs, careful not to pull the cloth against the row of black stitches. Goldenseal had removed some of them, where the wound had been shallower, but had left the dozen or so down near his knee. Even there, the flesh looked nearly mended. She forced concern into her face and voice.

"This swelling looks pretty serious."

Fairfax, who had just assumed a particularly languid pose, lying there nearly naked on the grass, opened his eyes in alarm. "What swelling?"

"This swelling in your underwear."

She ran a finger lightly over the swelling in question, and he grinned.

"That's not serious. That's just getting started."

"Maybe I should take a closer look."

"Be my guest."

She peeled down his briefs, letting his erection spring free. Obviously there'd been no lasting damage. Trieka folded his pants and laid them down on the grass. When she looked up, Fairfax was reaching for her with one hand. She walked on her knees toward him and braced him as he sat up. His hands closed around her waist and he held still for a moment, pain creasing his face.

"Are you all right?"

"Yeah. Just a twinge."

His hands moved forward, tracing down her belly. The long, graceful fingers tugged at the button on her jeans, wedging it through the slightly too-small buttonhole, then he slid the zipper down. He peeled her underwear down with the jeans. She was kneeling next to him; he pushed the jeans to the ground and she slid them the rest of the way off, using his shoulder for balance. Leaning toward him, she looked away to pull the jeans over her feet.

The wet heat of his mouth on her breast made her jerk back around to face him. He eased back, his teeth light on her nipple, looking up at her through smiling storm-gray eyes.

"You smell terrible," she said, breathless.

He looked completely unrepentant. "Sorry."

She helped him ease down the bank into the water. It was, as Goldenseal had promised, warmer than the other pool, but still not what Trieka would choose for a bath. Fairfax's erection lost considerable momentum. He stood shivering while she dug a bar of soap from her jeans pocket on the bank. She'd fished it out of her rucksack two days ago, after the first soapless bath had left her feeling greasy.

The floor of the pool was lined with rocks, apparently placed there by the apes. She moved to stand behind Fairfax and began to lather him up.

He had strong, broad shoulders, and she felt each clean line of bone beneath his skin. Her hands scrubbed and kneaded him, moving down his back, over hips and buttocks, around to his belly and chest, up into his armpits. He shuddered under her touch. Every muscle down his back was rock-hard, as if fighting for control. Finally she doused him with water, scooping it with her hands and pouring it over him until the suds were gone. Then he took hold of her arm and pulled her around in front of him.

The smell was mostly gone now, or at least she didn't notice it as he crushed her to him, devouring her mouth with his. She clung to him, digging into his wet, slippery skin. His tongue pushed and demanded, the kiss so fierce their teeth struck sharply.

For a moment, she was almost afraid of what he could do to her, but in the next moment she realized she trusted him completely. Then he made a rough sound in his throat as her thigh brushed his, and she broke away. Still wincing with the pain, he ducked his head to kiss her again, but she put her hand over his mouth.

"Is this going to work?"

"We'll make it work." His voice was rough with need. She shifted a little. This time when he bent his head, she didn't stop him.

He'd collected himself a little, and this kiss was less fierce, though no less passionate. She relaxed and tried not to worry about hurting him. His hands slid to the small of her back, pressing her hard against him, then moved to cup her buttocks.

Trieka melted, wet with more than water, her head echoing with her own heartbeat. She still had the soap in her hand. She worked up more lather and slid fingers and soap down his belly. He made another low, male sound, this one far from pain. She lathered the hair low on his abdomen, then down, until she held the hard, soap-slick length of him in one small hand.

Apparently no longer able to concentrate enough to kiss her, he broke off, pressing his face against her hair, his breath ragged in her ear. Her hand tugged him gently toward her.

"I want you, Fairfax."

She heard him swallow, and his whisper came broken against her ear. "Back up."

Trieka moved carefully backward, wondering what he had in mind. Her calves came up against a hard edge.

"Sit down."

She sat. Rocks had been arranged on a natural shelf along the bank to make a comfortable place to sit. The shelf put her at a height where she could put her legs around his waist.

She did. Her thighs pressed against his hips. He shifted slightly forward, then back, stroking her with his length. The soap slipped from her hands as she gripped his shoulders, his movement bringing ecstasy close to pain. His face, though, told her he wasn't going to last much longer. She moved her hand between them and slipped him inside.

Her position and his length brought him in deep. She put her head against his chest, unable to hold back the small, raw sound that rose in her throat, not from pain, or quite from pleasure, but just the sweet shock of having him inside her. His fingers wove into her hair, cradling her head against him.

"What?" he asked with soft concern.

"Don't stop."

He tucked in close to her, his arms enclosing her until she felt nothing but him, around her and within her, and the soft lap of water against her legs. Driving deep, he took her thoroughly, but only managed four strokes before he stiffened, his body bucking against hers. When he was finished and could breathe again, he put his chin against her hair.

"God, I'm sorry."

"It's all right." He started to move away from her but she stopped him with her calves against his thighs. "Not yet. Stay."

Clinging to him, she pressed her face hard against his chest, holding him as tightly as she could until nature took its course and broke the connection. Still she held him, eyes closed against the drying curls of his hair. She didn't want him to see that she was crying.

She couldn't stop the quiet shaking, though, and they were too close for her to hide it.

"I said I was sorry." He sounded petulant now. She wanted to laugh, but it came out in a sob.

"It's all right, really."

"Then what's wrong?"

She squeezed her eyes shut, feeling the tears well out between her lashes. The hair on his chest curled against her lips. He smelled clean and wet and male. She opened her mouth against his skin and gave him the last secret, her last gift. "I love you."

Gently, he took her head between his hands and turned her face up. She saw his throat struggle for a moment, as if trying to form words that weren't there. Finally he kissed her, slowly and with exquisite tenderness. When he raised his face from hers, he carried tears on his lashes.

"Where's the soap?" he said.

Groping, Trieka found it lying on a nearby rock and pressed it into his hand. Lather rose quickly between his strong, graceful fingers, then he laid hands to her body.

She closed her eyes as his soap-slick hands claimed her, inch by inch. He slid lather over her breasts, down her stomach and back, around and under her buttocks. Her mouth found his and clung as if to life itself, as if to air. Finally his fingers moved to the insides of her thighs, and up, cupping her softly and moving until she moaned into his mouth, clutching at him as fire rushed and pounded in her belly. She shook for a moment, lost in sensation. His hands slid back up her belly and he freed his mouth from hers to kiss her shoulder.

"We should get out of the water," he said after a time. "I'm getting pruny."

She laughed, a small, sated sound as he offered puckered fingertips as evidence. They managed their way up onto the grass, into the sun, and lay down together. Trieka pillowed her head on Fairfax's chest, peering down his lean body and long legs. He fitted his jaw against her head, one arm around her. His other hand strayed across his body to touch her. Carefully, he rolled a little to one side, his free hand slipping over her breast, then down to toy with her damp copper curls.

"At least I've found the answer to one question," he said.

"What's that?"

"You're a real redhead."

She shook her head. "You could have figured that out by looking at my eyebrows."

He smiled. "But that wouldn't have been nearly as fun."

He was right, of course. She closed her eyes as his fingers drifted up again, then opened them when she realized he'd paused, tracing the small scars low on her abdomen.

"Reconstructive surgery," she explained. "It didn't work."

He said nothing, his finger caressing the small, silver lines. Then his hand moved on to another scar.

"Appendectomy?"

"That's right."

Fairfax looked into her face, his hand cupping her stomach, covering the place which should have been a haven for new life, but wasn't.

"It doesn't change anything," he said quietly. "Whatever you are or aren't, I love you."

She felt like she would cry if she didn't break her own mood. "Appendix or no appendix?"

Fairfax smiled a little, then looked down at his hand on her belly. "There's been a dead place in my soul for seven years. I didn't think it would ever come to life again."

Trieka could say nothing to that. She looked down, as well, at his sun-browned hand on her pale, freckled flesh. A flash of red caught the corner of her eye.

"You're bleeding," she said in sudden alarm. Fairfax's hand caught her as she started to sit up.

"It's nothing. I think I just pulled a stitch. I'll have Goldenseal look at it when we get back."

Goldenseal. Trieka looked up at the sky. She was due back in less than half an hour.

"We should probably start thinking about getting you dressed."

Somewhere between getting him into his shirt and getting him into his underwear, Trieka found herself straddling him. He moved deep inside her, stoking the fires anew. She didn't want to leave him, didn't want to separate his flesh from hers. She'd never felt such a need. Moving over him, bringing him into her, she looked into his face, into his autumn-storm eyes, and lost a piece of her soul and took it back again.

He lasted considerably longer this time, and when Goldenseal parted the bushes past the edge of the pool, Trieka was just beginning to ease Fairfax's jeans over his feet. Goldenseal, seeing the blood, made her stop.

"How much pain?" her hands queried.

"Small," Fairfax signed back.

"Less moving," Goldenseal instructed. "More quiet."

Fairfax, looking almost sheepish, agreed.

❋ ❋ ❋

Fairfax watched her that night as they sat around the fire eating Goldenseal's thick, savory stew. Cavendish had settled across the fire from him and sat eating quietly, almost as if she were avoiding him, but every time he looked up, her gaze was fixed to him, sometimes alert and smiling, other times distant and almost glassy.

He wondered what she was thinking. He was almost painfully aware of her presence, her slightest movement drawing his eyes. Goldenseal kept looking at her, too, and at him. Fairfax saw thoughts running behind the healer's eyes, then suddenly she smiled. She hid it behind her bowl of soup, but not before Fairfax saw it.

What had changed? Much was different inside him, to be sure—long-empty places brimful again, long-dead emotions alive and breathing beneath his heart—but what had changed to make Goldenseal aware of it? Ten feet separated him from Cavendish, their only connection the tenuous thread of eye contact. Was it really so obvious from the way they looked at each other that they'd made love? Glancing again at Goldenseal's expression, Fairfax decided it must be.

Later, alone in his narrow bed, he heard Cavendish flop over, her exasperated exhalation kept quiet only by tight control.

"What's wrong?" he asked. The whisper sounded like a howling wail in the silence of the sleeping cave.

"I—" She stopped. "Can I come over there?"

"Please do."

He could barely see her in the faint moonlight. A soft rustle brought her to him, then she sat on the bed next to him. Carefully avoiding contact with his leg, she slid under his blankets and curled up against him. He rolled a little toward her to slip an arm around her small warmth. She wore only a light T-shirt and underwear. Starting to fit her bare legs against his, she hesitated.

"It's all right," he said. "Just don't kick me in the stitches."

She moved a little, pressing the backs of her thighs against the fronts of his. He put his lips against her hair.

"So what's wrong?" This close, they could speak much more quietly.

"We need to talk."

"What about?"

"About what comes next. We're safe here for a while, but I don't think we want to get too comfortable. We have to get back to Earth sooner or later, probably sooner, to be sure the disks are delivered. We have even more information now. We could put EarthFed in a very difficult position, and I think we should."

Fairfax hesitated, strangely relieved. He'd thought she needed to talk about what had happened today, thinking perhaps she thought they'd moved too fast, or that she was having regrets and wanted to reevaluate their relationship. That she only wanted to discuss their possible pursuit and execution, and the unleashing of the biggest government scandal in the history of Earth, calmed him greatly.

"How long do you think we should stay?" he said.

"Until you can walk again. I mean, long distances. We still have a good distance to go to Station Twelve."

"Another week?"

"We'll ask Goldenseal."

She shifted in his arms. She was tense, the muscles in her shoulder hard under his chin. He lifted a hand and rubbed her neck and shoulders, up into her scalp and down her back.

"What do you think will happen?" he said after a time.

"I don't know. I don't want to think about it."

His hands strayed forward and down, cupping her small soft breasts. Her nipples peaked hard against his palms. He wanted her terribly. He was sure she knew it; he'd been prodding her in the back for several minutes now. He closed his eyes, caught between his own mindless desire and the realization of truths too terrible to contemplate.

"Whatever can be done to protect you, I'll do," he murmured into her hair. "I have connections now, and knowledge I didn't have...before." He paused to swallow an unexpected lump, and to stop himself from saying the next words. *I won't lose you like I lost Kathi.*

She shifted, warm and snug against him, and put her hands over his. "I know you'll do whatever you can," she said. "But it's EarthFed."

He started to speak, but bit it off. *I sprung a man from federal prison,* he wanted to say, *a hacker who cost the government ten billion dollars before they caught him.* But it had cost money to do that—a lot of money—and for all Fairfax knew, he might go home to find himself a pauper. It was, after all, EarthFed.

And so was she, he reminded himself, but pushed the thought away.

Her hands moved against his, pushing one down until his fingers met the soft, springy tickle of hair. Her other hand pulled her underwear down, out of the way. As his fingers found her slick heat, she reached behind to take him in her hand, guiding him inside her.

Thoughts and fears fled as he yielded to the timeless flood of sensation, and the knowledge that, at least for the moment, she was entirely his.

Chapter Twelve

A week was, as it turned out, wishful thinking. Within three days, Fairfax was walking fairly well again, but long distances brought the pain back. Trieka could see it in his face even when he refused to admit it.

He insisted on going out every day, walking the length of the village, walking to the bathing pools and back. He would disappear sometimes for hours. She knew he stayed close, but he didn't always follow the same route, and his absences worried her. When he returned, his face was nearly always tight with pain, his limp so pronounced he could barely walk at all.

"You have to stop him," Trieka told Goldenseal one bright, chilly morning.

Nearly two weeks of constant use had brought the language securely into her hands. Fairfax, too, had achieved an impressive fluency. For some reason, this surprised her. She herself had learned six languages as part of her training. The official EarthFed policy stated that those directly involved with colonization should have a strong language ability, in case of encounters with intelligent life. The theory was that knowledge of several foreign languages would make it easier to learn an alien one. Knowing what she knew now, Trieka couldn't help but be angered by the irony.

Goldenseal, carefully spreading freshly gathered herbs on a flat stone in the sun just outside the cave, looked at her calmly.

"He could damage himself permanently," Trieka went on.

Goldenseal spread the last few leaves—green, red and brown—freeing her hands to speak. "He is already damaged permanently. The limp will stay. If he doesn't work the muscles, he may lose the use of them. And you have a long journey ahead." She stopped, adjusted a few leaves. A little smile had grown on her mouth. When she spoke again, the words were small gestures, close to her body. "Does he come home too tired for sex?"

Trieka felt the blush coming and tried to regain her composure. No luck. Her face went hot. "No," she answered.

"I thought not," Goldenseal said, then smiled again. "You two make noisy love."

Trieka couldn't blush any redder. She settled for making a face. "Well, someone should talk to Brown Hands about his grunting."

Goldenseal laughed aloud, a series of short, mirthful barks which caught Trieka by surprise in the midst of the silent conversation. "If Long Nose can make love after his exercise, then let him walk."

Long Nose. Trieka thought about that later, watching Fairfax as he carefully stretched his leg after a two-hour hike. He seemed in less pain than on previous occasions, his face less haggard. Which, in turn, made his nose a bit less prominent. It wasn't small by anyone's standards, though, and to the gorilla-nosed White Fur People, it must look immense.

"How's the leg today?" she asked, meandering over to him.

He glanced up. His hair was wet, and he'd shaved. It had taken a long time to explain to Brown Hands why he felt the need to scrape the hair off his face, but Brown Hands had finally produced a suitable tool. Trieka had found the conversation quite comical.

"Not bad," Fairfax said. "I soaked in the pool halfway through. Seemed to loosen things up." He smiled. She wondered why—it was a smug sort of smile.

"What?" she said.

"What what?"

"You look inordinately pleased with yourself."

"Oh." He grinned again, looking even smugger. "Nothing."

She sat down next to him. "Tell me."

He leaned over his outstretched leg, gently pulling his hamstring taut. She looked at his leg, watching the muscles shift under his jeans.

"A few of the men were at the pool."

"So you had a communal bathing experience?"

"Yes. It was sort of like sitting around the sauna at the club."

"After a good, sweaty game of racquetball?"

"Well, I golf, actually, but I don't use a cart, and it does take some energy to throw clubs as far as I do. Anyway...well, apparently certain...portions of their male anatomy are completely retractable, and since I, well...dangle...they assumed I had another foot or so retracted."

"I presume you corrected that misconception?"

"No. Why should I?" He paused, grinning again. "They were wondering what you did with all of it."

"I won't be doing anything at all with it, ever, if you don't wipe that smirk off your face."

Not only did he not dispose of the smirk, he laughed outright. She couldn't fight her own smile. "So have they changed your name now to Long Schlong?"

Fairfax laughed again. "No, I'm afraid I'm still stuck with Long Nose."

"Well, it could be worse. I mean, they could have come up with any number of names for us."

"Like...Spotty Nose," said Fairfax.

"Naked Butt," she countered.

"Little Boobs."

"Gimpy."

"Would you mind if I called you Trieka?"

Trieka, prepared to deliver another less-than-flattering nickname, snapped her mouth shut.

"Um, well, no, I suppose not." It occurred to her that she hadn't paid much attention to what he did call her. "Captain", a few times, "Cavendish", more often than not. And once, in the middle of the night, when he hadn't been quite awake, he'd called her Kathi.

He seemed almost uncomfortable suddenly. "It's just...I feel a little strange calling you by your last name."

"You mean now that you've had your way with me repeatedly?"

"Well, yes. So would you mind?"

"No. What would you like me to call you?"

"Lord and Master. No? How about Flaming Love God?"

She shook her head. He'd seemed such a quiet, serious thing when she'd first met him. "How about Slithering Serpent of Love?" she suggested.

"That'd be good. Although it reduces me to nothing more than a sex organ."

"Well, it's practically an extra limb as far as your little furry friends know. Besides, I'm just using you to fulfill my womanly needs, so you might as well get used to it."

Finished with his stretching, Fairfax lay back in the grass and smiled at her. He still looked smug.

"And am I performing to your satisfaction, Captain?"

"We'll have to discuss that in your quarterly review."

His smile broadened. She smiled back. He looked about sixteen wearing that smile—young and rotten and randy as hell. She reached out and touched his lip, gently pressing the soft, pillowy flesh. He made a slight move and brought her finger into his mouth, fluttering his tongue against the tip. Imagining the same movement against other parts of her body, she shivered. He closed his teeth gently on her first knuckle, then let her go.

"Why don't you help me finish my walk?" he suggested, and rolled stiffly to his feet.

They'd been walking through the quiet trees for about fifteen minutes when she realized he'd never answered her question.

"Fairfax seems to fit you," she said.

He just shrugged as if the question concerned him not at all.

They hadn't walked far from the village, but the trees were much thicker here. Goldenseal had obligingly identified a few different varieties. The long, needlelike leaves did, indeed, stay through the winter, but the thicker version dropped in the fall. There were flat-leaved trees as well, most of them old with no branches below twenty-five feet. Trieka had found some of the

140

leaves on the ground and they resembled oak, perhaps maple. The trees awed her. She'd seen the California redwoods once, years ago, but these were bigger, older, greener—just *more*.

Fairfax stopped in a wide, grassy space between two huge evergreens, catching her hand as she started to walk past him. Swinging her around to face him, he looked at her for a long time. Trieka wondered what he was thinking, but the stillness of the place silenced her.

Finally he kissed her, deep and slow and long.

"I love you, Trieka," he said, his voice as soft as the whispering of the surrounding leaves.

"I love you, Harrison."

He bore her a little stiffly down to the grass and covered her with his body. Her stomach fluttered in anticipation. His injuries had prevented him from loving her this way before. For some reason, she craved it—wanting to take his weight on her chest, to feel him cover her and press her down. She wanted to feel helpless beneath him.

She got her wish. He moved slowly, mindful of his own limitations, careful of his weight. His hands and mouth coaxed her to wet fire before he finally slid inside her. He seemed bigger, heavier, more powerful this way, with her small body pinned beneath him, skewered to the ground by his sex. She pressed her thighs hard against his hips and bit at his chin, scraping her teeth against his stubble of beard.

There was no way to feel any more complete, she thought, no place where she could be any truer to her own soul. Yet, in a single, simple act, she gave him so much. Too much, maybe. She thought suddenly of Jake. They had this now, and it was pure and beautiful, but what would happen when they went back to the real world? What would he demand of her?

She forced her thoughts aside as he pressed high over her body, riding a crest of fire to his completion, then stroking her with his body and his hands until the waves of fire pounded over her as well. Carefully, he settled on top of her, weaving his bare legs between hers and slipping a hand beneath her shirt to cup her breast. He caressed her for a time, his fingers shaping her contours, then he edged her shirt up and bent down. Eyes closing, Trieka drifted as his mouth closed hot and wet on her breast, drawing in more than her nipple, suckling like a child.

How much like a child? She would never know.

Finally, she came back to herself and wove her fingers into his hair, pressing against the warmth of his scalp. He lifted his head a little, licked her breast and looked up at her.

"I talked to Goldenseal this morning," he said, quiet. "She says in three days the moon will be half dark. That's when we should leave."

"Three days," she repeated. Fairfax nodded. Unconsciously, she clutched at his arms. Walking back into civilization would be like walking to a gallows. She wasn't sure she could do it. His arms came around her, holding her close.

"I'll be with you," he said. "No matter what."

But what will you be able to do? What, besides hold my hand and kiss me good-bye?

❋ ❋ ❋

She woke that night to searing, twisting pain in her abdomen. It felt like someone was wringing her womb like a dishrag. The pain shot down into her legs and up to the points of her shoulder blades. Unable to control herself, she doubled over with it, crying out. Hands grabbed her shoulders, firm and warm in the darkness.

"Trieka, what's wrong?"

Fairfax lay hot and naked against her. Even the brush of his body hair on her back was too much. She tried to move away from him, but another wave of pain took her. His fingers bit into her shoulders, and when he spoke again, there was fear in his voice.

"Trieka, talk to me. What's wrong?"

Across the room, a light sprang up next to Goldenseal's bed. The little healer rolled out of bed, picked up her ever-present bag of medicine vials and hurried to Trieka's side.

"What is it?" she queried. The movements of her hand cast strange, writhing shadows in the wavering light of the candle she carried.

Trieka made barely meaningful signs with one hand,

clutching the pain with the other. She'd forgotten what it was like to go through this. She'd also forgotten to bring her pills when she'd left Denahault Prime. *Stupid, stupid, stupid.*

"You're pregnant?" Goldenseal said. Trieka wasn't sure if it was a question or a diagnosis. She shook her head vehemently, then buried her face in her pillow as another contraction tore through her.

Vaguely, she realized Fairfax was signing hurriedly to Goldenseal. Apparently he'd retained enough presence of mind to figure out what was happening. By the time the pain had paused, Goldenseal's face was lit by understanding, and she pressed a small wax ampoule to Trieka's lips. She swallowed the thick bitter liquid, then blinked back tears as the pain tore through her again. Fairfax's hands came back to her shoulders.

"Can I do anything?"

"No," she managed. "Just...please...don't...touch me."

He obligingly lowered his hands. Goldenseal continued to fuss with her, bringing rags to deal with the blood, obviously surprised when there was none. The blood would come in a few hours, scanty and out of all proportion to the pain. And the pain would last at least three days, maybe four. The pills suppressed the pain but didn't affect the quantity of blood, so that under medicated conditions her period could come and go with little notice.

Goldenseal's medication took effect in a few minutes that seemed like hours. With the worst of the agony gone, Trieka was able to relax enough to explain a few more details to the healer. Goldenseal became quiet and serious as she sorted meaning from Trieka's sometimes hesitant and probably inaccurate signings.

"There have not been many like you among us," she said finally. "I will have to speak with the Elder."

Trieka opened her mouth to speak, then shut it. Goldenseal's expression, combined with the strangeness of her words, had brought her as close to fear as she had been since coming to these people. Between the fear and the pain, she couldn't think to make words with her hands.

Fairfax, though, signed a quick, "What do you mean?"

Goldenseal smiled reassurance, but something in her eyes

left Trieka ill at ease.

"Don't worry," Goldenseal said. She sorted out another vial. "Take a sip of this if the pain is too much. Only a sip at a time until the pain is bearable. Not all at once." She left then, her eyes averted and, to Trieka, she still seemed troubled.

"What the hell's going on?" Fairfax mumbled to Goldenseal's departing form.

"I know as much as you do." She closed her eyes, letting the pain pass over her. It was less, but still harsh. And it was useless pain, the cramps accomplishing nothing.

"What about you?" he said. "Are you going to be all right?"

"I'll be okay."

"Can I do anything?"

She considered. "You could hold me now."

He did, nestling her softly against his body. When she tensed, he pressed his hands against the pain and it seemed to help, though only a little. It was hard to sleep with the hurting, but finally it faded and she dozed, his arms warm around her in the darkness.

Goldenseal touched her awake some hours later. Pale light drifted into the cave from the growing dawn outside. Fairfax still held her, one arm heavy and warm around her waist.

"Are you awake?" Goldenseal's small hand made the abbreviated signs against Trieka's shoulder. Trieka could barely see the movements of the other woman's fingers in the dim dawn, but the motions against her skin told her enough to convey meaning.

"Yes." She answered with a wide, exaggerated movement. Carefully, she slipped from under Fairfax's arm and moved into the light outside, where they could talk.

"The Elder wishes to see you before full light," Goldenseal said. She had picked up Trieka's string of amber from beside her bed and now hung it around Trieka's neck. "He said it's very important."

"What's this about?" Trieka was still bleary, but she had a sense that something important was happening.

"The Elder will explain." Trieka started to speak again, but Goldenseal touched her hands before she could start. "Even if I knew, I couldn't speak of it. It's the Elder's business."

"What's going on?"

Trieka turned. Fairfax's voice was a low, sleepy grumble. His hair was standing up and he limped stiffly as he came out of the cave. He hadn't bothered to dress. The dawn cast gray shadows down his lean body. Trieka's gaze caught on his shapes and shadows, and she felt suddenly strange, as if she might never see him again.

"The Elder's business is with Fire Hair," Goldenseal signed. "You must stay here unless you are called."

Alarm rose in Fairfax's eyes. "No," he signed emphatically. "I want to know what's happening. What does the Elder want?"

Goldenseal looked at him wearily. "If I knew, I couldn't say. The Elder's business is his own. If he calls you, I will come and get you."

"No—" Fairfax started again, but Trieka cut him off.

"It's all right," she signed. "I'm sure it's nothing dangerous." Aloud, she added, "And I *can* take care of myself. I think you know that."

Fairfax's jaw bulged as he clenched his teeth, but he nodded reluctantly. He stood outside the cave, arms crossed over his bare chest, as Trieka let Goldenseal lead her away.

In the wide cave lined with flickering candles, the Elder sat contemplating his fire, as if he hadn't moved since Trieka had last seen him. The women around him, though, had changed. Always Mother sat closest to him, stringing beads of amber and round, blue stones into long necklaces. Another woman, hugely swollen with pregnancy, sat with her, chin on one hand, apparently trying not to doze off. The third woman worked with smaller beads, sewing them to a strip of thin leather.

None of the women looked up as Trieka and Goldenseal entered. Neither did the Elder. Goldenseal sat down by the fire and gestured for Trieka to do the same. She did, her nostrils tingling with the slight smoke and the smell of melting wax.

Silent, Goldenseal took up perusal of the fire. Trieka followed her example, but couldn't resist a quick glance up at the stone-faced Elder. He didn't look away from the fire. Always Mother, though, smiled a little. Some of Trieka's anxiety dissipated.

"You have come." The Elder signed the words without looking up. Trieka wouldn't have seen the gestures at all if she hadn't been looking at Always Mother.

"It seemed I had little choice," she replied.

The Elder looked at her then, somberly, through the faint haze of smoke and the distortion of heat from the fire.

"You had a choice. You have always had a choice."

Trieka swallowed. The Elder's eyes held unquestionable power. "Why was I called here?"

"I had decided to bring you into the tribe, with Long Nose."

Trieka was relieved at first, then the tense of his statement struck her. Aware she may have misinterpreted, she repeated, "*Had* decided?" emphasizing the tense with a slash of her hand.

"Your status makes it impossible."

"My status?"

"Only a whole woman may join the tribe."

Trieka's face went hot, the bottom of her stomach cold. She lifted her hands to speak, feeling her fingers tremble. Goldenseal laid a hand on her arm. Reluctantly, Trieka subsided.

"Let him finish," Goldenseal said.

The Elder watched the exchange impassively. The three attending women had fallen still, watching. Always Mother shifted slightly, pressing the inside of her upper arm against her left breast.

"A woman who cannot bear children is compensated with other gifts. A Never Mother carries clear sight."

"Clear sight?"

The Elder sat forward abruptly, elbows on his knees. Trieka jumped a little, startled by his sudden change in attitude, and by the intensity of his eyes, dark blue and utterly clear.

"You can tell us how it will go with our people. There have been deaths in other tribes. Your Naked People have killed our White Fur People without reason. Will this continue?"

Trieka swallowed, wondering why the subject hadn't come up earlier. She thought of the white pelt in the Taylors' shed. Making the two-finger gesture, which indicated she was gathering her thoughts, Trieka considered her reply.

"Something has begun," she said finally. "It is why Long Nose and I are here. The people who allow the killing of the White Fur People also wish to kill us. We carried information which could..." She paused, searching for words. "Which could hurt them terribly, and end the terrible things they have done to this place and to others. When this has all come to an end, it is my hope that the White Fur People will be able to live in peace together with my people, with no more killings."

Still leaning forward, the Elder studied Trieka closely. "You have done this at great risk to yourself."

"Yes. I carry a...level of authority among my people. It will probably be taken from me because of this."

"Yet, you have done this for us without knowing us. Why?"

"I didn't do it. Long Nose uncovered the truth, which these people were hiding. These people killed his mate. He told me the truth, and I chose to help him. The greatest part of the work has been his."

The Elder nodded. "Look ahead for me. What do you see? How will it end between your people and mine?"

Trieka considered. The Elder wanted a prophetic pronouncement, something she couldn't give him in good faith.

"My sight is not as clear as you might hope, I'm afraid. But I can tell you what I think will happen—what I hope will happen. I hope the evidence, once it arrives back at our home, will bring these people to justice. Once it's known what has happened to your people and to others, it will be ended. Your people and mine will be able to live together in peace."

The Elder studied Trieka closely, as if simply by looking at her he could judge the truth of her words.

"Your sight is clear," he said finally. "You see the truth of us, and you can take that truth to others." He leaned back, approval on his wide face. "It will be as you have said. I hope for that, as well." He looked into the flames, out of habit, or a search for guidance. "I cannot make you a member of the tribe, but if you are mated to a tribe member, you will be of us."

Trieka had a sudden, uncomfortable vision of herself in bed with the Elder. She hoped that wasn't what he meant. "I am mated to Long Nose."

The Elder smiled. Trieka had the distinct feeling he knew what she'd been thinking. "That makes it easier then. He will join the tribe and, as his mate, you will be of the tribe. When you leave us to return to your own people, you will take with you a responsibility to us."

Trieka nodded. "I'm willing to do whatever I can to end what wrong has been done here."

"We will be grateful to you for whatever you can do." His gaze moved again to the fire, becoming distant.

"Wait," Trieka said, hoping he would see the quick gesture. The Elder looked back to her, brows raised. "What happens if, in the future, Long Nose and I are no longer mated?"

The Elder smiled. "My sight is clear, as well, Never Mother. I do not see that it will happen."

He had nothing more to say. He returned to the fire and contemplation.

Chapter Thirteen

Fairfax lay on his back in the narrow bed, staring at the ceiling as it was slowly illuminated by the dawn. He had dressed after Trieka had left, then had paced for a while when he realized there was nothing he could do. He didn't understand the secrecy or the urgency. What could possibly be happening?

Brown Hands and the children had begun to stir when Fairfax heard footsteps outside. He jerked to a sitting position, then lurched to his feet. The damn leg was always stiff in the morning, achy and hard to move.

He forgot the pain when he saw Trieka with Goldenseal and Always Mother. The morning sun glinted off her copper curls. He swallowed the lump of relief that had risen in his throat. It was hard to admit it, but he'd honestly been afraid they'd hurt her. She looked at him as he emerged from the cave, a little smile quirking her mouth.

"What?" he said.

"The Elder wishes you to join the tribe." Always Mother formed the words with her long fingers. Fairfax looked at Trieka.

"You've already joined?" he asked quietly, not matching gestures to words. He wanted to speak only to Trieka.

"No," she said, also without including the others. "Not me. Just you."

"I don't understand."

"I'll try to explain later." This time she did add gestures. Then, without speaking aloud at all, "Always Mother will take you to the place of the ceremony, and will bring you into the tribe. As your mate, I will also have a place, but I can't be brought in by the full ceremony."

"I still don't understand," said Fairfax, still aloud, still stubbornly refusing to translate.

"You will later," Trieka said aloud. "Come on."

He followed them through the growing morning to the pool where they'd first made love. A small, sly look from Goldenseal told him she knew the significance of the place, but she added an additional explanation.

"Occasionally we have reason to bring an adult into the tribe. Usually it is because a member of our tribe has chosen to mate with a member of another. These ceremonies take place here."

Always Mother moved past her to stand in front of Fairfax, taking over with a demeanor of formality. "When a child is birthed, it comes from the waters of the womb and is brought to its mother's breast. The taking of mother's milk makes it one with the rest of the tribe. When the child becomes an adult, we place upon it the mark of our clan." She lifted her left arm, displaying a dark blue tattoo in the nearly hairless patch of skin in the hollow below her armpit. "This is the mark of the People Who Live at the Edge of the Mountain, naming our clan of the White Fur People. What clan do you come from?"

Fairfax was still staring at the tattoo, wondering exactly how it had been applied. His gaze jerked to Always Mother. He cleared his throat, then abruptly made the gesture to indicate he was preparing to speak.

"I am of the People Who Live on the Earth That Shakes, of the Furless Loud-Talking People."

Always Mother nodded approval. "And your mate?"

"She is of the People Who Travel Through the Sky, of the Furless Loud-Talking People."

"Your mate is a Never Mother, she who sees clearly but cannot birth children. Because of this she cannot be rebirthed into the tribe, for she can birth no one else into the tribe with the water of her womb. But she has clear sight and has agreed to use it for the People of the Edge of the Mountain. As your mate, she will be of the tribe, but not in it."

Fairfax looked quizzically at Trieka. Clear sight? What did they think she was? Whatever it meant, Trieka had obviously agreed to it. "I understand," he lied.

"You must come to the water as you came from your birthing," Always Mother continued. "Please, prepare yourself."

Fairfax drew a blank. "Take off your clothes," Trieka whispered into his confusion.

Oh. That made sense. Fumbling a little, he stripped out of his flannel shirt and jeans, boots, socks and underwear, and put them in a pile on the ground. He felt eyes on him and looked up to find Always Mother giving him an interested once-over. He flushed a little, realizing she was the only one in the group who hadn't seen him naked. He must look ridiculous to her with patches of hair in illogical places and his genitals dangling in full view, instead of decently retracted or covered with thick white fur. She smiled at him a little and held out her hand. He took it, and she led him into the pool.

The water wasn't warm. Fairfax shuddered, his teeth clattering, as Always Mother coaxed him in until he was waist-deep. Then she laid a hand on top of his head. With her free hand, she said, "As a child is born from the water of the womb, so you will be taken into and brought forth from the waters of the clan. Hold your breath and go under until I bring you out."

He did as he was told, ducking into the cold pool until he felt water close over his head. Always Mother's hand came down on the back of his neck, holding him under. Recalling an immersion baptism he'd once attended, Fairfax expected her to bring him right back up. But she held him down until he was afraid his lungs would burst with the effort of not breathing.

Involuntarily he moved a little, feeling panic start to swell. At his slight shift, she brought him up. He gasped, dragging air into his lungs. Always Mother still had her hands on his head. She let him breathe a moment, then pulled his head to her breast.

Her thick fur was warm and soft against his face, her breasts swelling against his cheek. He opened his eyes and saw a nipple, pink and inviting. To his surprise, she put a finger under his chin and guided his mouth to it. Reflex made him suck. His action was rewarded by a spurt of hot milk. It tasted strange, like the smell of Always Mother's skin, and like Trieka. He swallowed and drew another mouthful before she pushed him back.

"The milk of the clan makes you a part of the clan, as it

makes a newborn child a part of the clan. You may return to the earth now and be marked."

Chattering from the cold, Fairfax made his way through the water to the shore, where Goldenseal waited with small bone needles and a vial of dark blue pigment.

"Lie down," she said. "Fire Hair, take his right hand."

Trieka's hand closed warm on his as he lay down, naked and shivering, on the grass.

The first few pricks of the needles were excruciating. The small needles felt huge under his skin, and Goldenseal expertly wielded four at a time. There must have been something in the pigment, though, for after the first few minutes of burning pain, he began to feel numb, and to drift. Sweat beaded on his upper lip in spite of the cold.

His eyes found Trieka's face. Her brow was creased with concern as she gestured to Goldenseal. He couldn't see her hands to read her words, nor could he see Goldenseal's reply. Then he could see nothing at all as blackness encroached on his vision.

He hung for a long time, suspended in silent darkness. He was aware of hands on him, Trieka's and Goldenseal's, but nothing else. No sound, no light.

A voice rose. It was faint at first, barely louder than thought, wordless. But he knew it.

"Kathi?" Whether he actually spoke the word, he didn't know, but it formed somewhere in his mind. He struggled to see her face through the enveloping darkness, but there was nothing there. Only the small murmur of her voice.

Then he felt a touch. A long-fingered, delicate hand cupped his body just below his right armpit, sliding down his side, the fingers resting for small moments in the grooves between his ribs. He knew that hand, as well. And then the murmur became words.

"Take care of her."

"Kathi?"

But he was alone again, and this time he knew he would never hear that voice again. She was gone, finally at peace.

As she left him, Fairfax surrendered to the darkness. When

he woke he would be someone else, a man of the White Fur People, a man Kathi had never known. And Trieka, his mate, the Never Mother, would be there to ease his birth.

❋ ❋ ❋

He still hurt when he woke, the dull pain under his arm spreading down into his chest, like an ache in his heart. He heard movement around him, scuffing and muted hums—sounds he'd learned to associate with the conversations of the White Fur People. He listened for a time, his eyes closed, feeling reality slowly return. Then he heard a laugh among the small sounds. A human laugh, soft and silver. Her laugh. He opened his eyes.

"Trieka," he said, his voice barely louder than the soft hums of the White Fur People. He turned his head until he could see her.

She stood only a few feet away, at the mouth of the cave, Goldenseal and Always Mother with her. They spoke to other White Fur People, people Fairfax didn't recognize. Next to Fairfax's bed, on the floor, was a pile of parcels. Trieka had another in her hands. She was still smiling as she turned toward him.

"Excuse me," she signed to their companions, then came to sit on the bed next to him.

"Fairfax," she said aloud. Strange as it seemed for her to call him that, he liked the way it sounded. She leaned toward him, laying a hand on his bare chest. He was still naked, he realized, although someone had pulled a blanket up to his waist. "How do you feel?"

"A little sore." He glanced toward Goldenseal. The two visitors were still with her, looking expectant. "Why are they hovering?"

Trieka followed his gaze. "About half the tribe has been here, bringing gifts to welcome you. I think they want to pass on their good wishes. Feel up to it?"

He looked at the almost eager faces and smiled. "Sure."

Carefully, to avoid dislodging his blanket, he sat up. The

pain under his arm had lessened. Trieka waved his visitors in. Goldenseal came with them while Always Mother stayed at the entrance, receiving another guest who had just arrived.

The male of the pair made a slight bobbing movement with his upper body. "We are Fire Father and Shining Eyes. Welcome, Long Nose, to the Clan of the People who Live at the Edge of the Mountain. And welcome also to your mate, Never Mother. Would you honor us by accepting the gift we offer?"

"Yes. Thank you. I accept for myself and for Fire Hair." He couldn't call her Never Mother, not even here, not even knowing what it meant to these people who'd adopted them. It just didn't seem right.

Trieka had the gift already—a small leather drawstring bag. She gave it to him and he pulled the bag open to look inside. It held about a dozen large, dried mushrooms.

"We hear you are to make a long journey," Shining Eyes said. "These are very good in stews made from dried meat. They also help you gain strength and keep health through a long trip."

"Thank you," Fairfax said again. It was hard to infuse the simple gesture with sincerity, but he did what he could, hoping the sentiment would show on his face. "Your gift is greatly appreciated and will be used well."

Fire Father and Shining Eyes looked pleased. "Our thoughts will go with you on your journey. May the winds carry you safely to your destination."

It was much the same with the next visitor, who brought strips of dried meat. When he had departed, Goldenseal came closer, touching Fairfax's forehead.

"How do you feel?"

"All right," he answered. "Good enough to get up and get dressed."

Goldenseal smiled. "Do that then."

He swung his legs out of the bed, only to find himself ankle-deep in more parcels. Carefully, he pushed them aside. "For us?"

"For you, technically," Trieka said, "which is why I haven't opened them. But everyone was quite generous in including me in the official welcome."

"You are his mate," Goldenseal said, "and because you have clear sight, the clan will hold you in honor even though you can't be truly birthed into it."

"But we aren't of your people," Fairfax said, pulling on his trousers. "Why were we invited to join the clan at all?"

"The Elder has clear sight as well." Always Mother had come to join them. "Since the arrival of the Loud-Talking People, he has foreseen the end of our clan, or at least a great disaster. When you were found in the forest, his seeing changed. He saw a fork in the road. Down one side was the end of the clan. Down the other was a joining of our clan with your people. He chose the second path. Now he sees hope." She looked directly at Fairfax. "Were you granted a sending in your birth sleep?"

Fairfax, buttoning his shirt, was suddenly uncomfortable. "Yes."

"What did you see?"

He shook his head, uncertain what to say, reluctant to share his experience with Always Mother. Trieka's hand slipped over his upper arm, gentle.

"Kathi?" she said aloud. Fairfax nodded.

Always Mother watched the exchange with interest. "It was a personal sending?"

"Yes," Fairfax said. He hesitated, trying to decide if he should tell her more, but she spoke in his hesitation.

"The ceremony, as I told you, is usually performed at adolescence. Often our young people receive visitations from ancestors—grandparents who have died or even earlier generations. Sometimes they receive visions important to all of the clan, but if the sending was only for you, there is no obligation to reveal it."

Relieved, Fairfax turned his attention to the unopened parcels on the floor. He could still feel Always Mother's gaze on him. Suddenly he could taste the hot spurt of her milk, feel the shape of her erect nipple in his mouth. He swallowed, surprised at his own arousal. She wasn't even human.

"What else do we have here?" he asked, forgetting to sign. It didn't matter. Trieka picked up a large package and passed it into his hands.

"This one is from Six Toes."

The package contained a set of bone knives with beautifully carved handles. Fairfax gave a low whistle, turning the largest knife in his hand.

"You're writing the thank you notes," he told Trieka.

The rest of the gifts varied from food items to clothing to small bits of carved bone, which Fairfax assumed were fetishes or talismans of some sort. The quality and quantity of the gifts overwhelmed him. "Is it always like this?" he asked Always Mother.

"Coming into the clan is a great honor and a great change of life. It is proper that it be celebrated." She smiled. "There will be more celebrating tonight. The men have killed grass-game for you."

"I'm honored."

Always Mother laid a hand on his shoulder. "It is we who are honored."

Later, when all the gifts had been opened and nearly every member of the clan had come to give congratulations, Always Mother bade them a formal farewell, and even Goldenseal departed to make sure the women who were cooking had a sufficient supply of herbs. Fairfax, still tired and a little achy, stretched out on the bed.

"Why Fire Father?" he asked Trieka, thinking of the guests who'd been there when he'd awakened. "What does the name mean?"

Trieka was admiring a piece of jewelry, a bit of fine, dark wood carved in the shape of a delicate flower. "Fire Father oversees the making of fires throughout the village. They have rules which have to be enforced, to lessen the risk of fires getting out of control."

Fairfax nodded. Practical. There had been other, obviously titular, names among their visitors. Fairfax had asked for explanation of most of them. Grass Mother directed the growing of crops and herbs, except for the medicinal herbs, which Goldenseal supervised. Flint Father oversaw the supply of flint and other weapons-making materials. Some, though, were less obvious.

"What about Always Mother?" he ventured.

"She always lactates," said Trieka. "My guess is it's some kind of hormonal imbalance." She paused, peering at the small piece of dark, carved wood. One corner of her mouth quirked. "Of course, I don't really need to tell you, since you've experienced her...talents firsthand."

He wasn't completely certain how to read her expression, or her tone. "That didn't...bother you, did it?"

"Maybe a little." She looked up, smiling. "I like the tattoo, though."

Fairfax lifted his arm. He hadn't really looked closely at the work of art Goldenseal had inflicted on him—he'd been too busy trying to ignore the pain. The tattoo was circular, about three inches in diameter. It looked like a mandala, filled with simple, elegant designs of curved lines.

"She did a nice job," Fairfax said. "Too bad it hurt so much."

"Is it still bothering you?"

"It's not bad now." Tentatively, he ran a finger along the outside of the circle. It was really quite well done, rivaling tattoos he'd seen made with modern electric equipment. "How am I going to explain it?"

"Say you got drunk one night and a crazed alien woman did it to you." Trieka reached toward him, sliding her fingers gently down his side. "Who would you have to explain it to?"

"I don't know. The guys at the club?" He put his hand over hers, feeling her small, fragile bones beneath his fingers. She was so small and yet so strong, and he loved her more every time he touched her. His heart and soul were full of her.

She had a strange look right now, almost wary. "Do the guys at the club really matter?"

He smiled, leaning toward her. "No. No, not really." He kissed her, holding her small mouth with his, trapping her for an instant in his arms. Soft and sweet, she yielded completely. He wanted more, but this wasn't the time or place. Reluctant, he drew away. He lifted a hand and spoke in the language of the White Fur People. "I love you, Fire Hair."

"I love you," she answered in kind, then grinned. "Long Schlong."

❋ ❋ ❋

The evening feast lived up to Always Mother's promise. Fairfax wasn't certain what kinds of animals had supplied the meat, but it was wonderful. There were roasts and stews and pastries filled with meat and vegetables. There were roasted tubers and stewed berries, flavorful nut pastes and more pastries sweetened with something much like honey. And there was alcohol—the first Fairfax had tasted among these people. It was the color of ripe peaches, sweet yet bitingly tart at the same time.

He couldn't seem to stop eating. Next to him, Trieka devoured more than anyone her size should eat in a week. As the sweet-tart wine flowed, she laughed more sweetly, and more easily, her hands seeming never to leave him.

Finally, as the fires began to die, the crowd dispersed. Satiated in every way but one, Fairfax led Trieka back to their bed. Her drink-clumsy hands struggled with his clothes, her fingers cold against his skin. He found her body beneath her shirt, sliding his hands up to her breasts. She was warm and soft, and he could think of nothing but having her. She gave herself freely, and he lost himself in her smell and her taste and her slippery heat. As his body overflowed, so did his heart.

In the dark silence afterward, she trailed her hand down his chest. He caught it and held it. A faint light caught the glint of metal on his hand.

"I'm sorry about the ring," he said.

She shifted, looking up at him. Her eyes glistened a little but he couldn't see her expression. "What do you mean?"

"My wedding ring. I should have taken it off a long time ago, especially with us... But I don't want to lose it, and there's not really anyplace else safe to keep it..." He trailed off, seeing the glint of her smile.

"It's okay, Fairfax."

He shook his head a little. "I should have let her go a long time ago."

She lay silent against him for a moment, her fingers combing the hair on his chest. "What was the sending?" she whispered finally. "What did she say to you?"

He swallowed. He hadn't expected her to ask. "She said—" He stopped, unsure.

"You don't have to tell me."

"No, it's all right. She said, 'Take care of her'. And then she left." He paused again, swallowing, afraid of tears, surprised to discover there were none. "I'll never see her again."

Trieka laid her face against his chest. "I'm sorry."

Chapter Fourteen

The day of departure arrived cool and cloudy, with an ominous rumble of distant thunder. It came too soon for Trieka. She'd become used to the silence and simplicity. She'd become comfortable with Fairfax and what they now were to each other. As soon as they moved on, though, everything would change. The world they would return to had little sympathy for romanticism. Watching Fairfax stiffly prepare his rucksack, she already felt as if she'd lost part of him.

Six Toes had volunteered to go with them as a guide, but only as far as the outskirts of Station Twelve. A half-dozen members of the Deep Forest Clan had been killed the year before when they'd wandered too close to one of the docking areas, so his caution was understandable.

Fairfax paused in his work, stretching his still-stiff leg. Trieka harbored doubts about his ability to make the trip, but Goldenseal had assured her he was fit.

"You okay?" she asked him.

"As okay as I'll be without reconstructive surgery," he said. His slight quirk of a grin was lost in a sudden grimace. "What about you?"

She nodded. "I'm fine." The searing cramps had faded under Goldenseal's care—the herbal concoctions had worked as well as the synthetic hormones she'd been taking before. Her short cycle had nearly run its course by now, leaving her, as always, a little tired. In spite of the pain, she'd shown almost no blood at all. As usual, Trieka didn't know whether to be relieved or annoyed by that.

Six Toes looked at them, seeming a little put off by their insistence on verbal speech. Fairfax, noticing his expression, grinned.

"We *are* the Loud-Talking people," he signed. "Get used to it."

Surprisingly, Six Toes grinned.

They started out into the morning, Six Toes leading the way. He'd said it would take them three days to reach the station if they kept a good pace. Looking at Fairfax, Trieka couldn't bring herself to hope for better than five.

They made good progress, though, the first day, despite Fairfax's stiff limp. He seemed to loosen up as the hours passed, only asking to stop once to rest, and that had been after a difficult hike up a steep incline.

"So what'll we do when we get there?" he asked that night after Six Toes had gone to stand the first watch. The pale light of the half moon cast strange shadows on his face, making him look gaunt. He'd spoken in a faint whisper.

"First, we have to find Lucas. Then we'll access MediaNet and find out if anything's going on. We might be able to tell where we stand by the news reports."

"MediaNet here is two weeks old."

"Well, we'll have to make do. We've been holed up nearly eight weeks—there's a good chance something has made it back by now."

He spread out his sleeping bag. "Do you think Commander Anderson went right back to Earth?"

"He was scheduled to. I was supposed to stay here another month, to be sure the newcomers got settled and make arrangements to ship out any passengers. But Jeff was supposed to ship out in a couple of days because he had personal business at home. So he should have been Earthside about eleven days after we landed. He would have handed the disks over to his sister, and she would have taken it from there."

"Who exactly is his sister?"

"Remember the Pasternack scandal two years ago? That was Jenna Anderson. Not just the reporting, mind you. She dug up the story itself. She's very good. This is right up her alley."

161

Fairfax's eyes became distant, and Trieka knew he was thinking of his wife. Katharine Maier, too, had been a well-respected investigative journalist, known for her unquestionable integrity. Jenna was of a similar mold.

"Then what?" he finally asked. He slid into the sleeping bag, stretching out on the ground. She lay down next to him. The fire banished some of the chill, but his body heat was more than welcome.

"We'll have to play it by ear. When it looks like there's some vague chance we might be safe, we head back Earthside." She didn't care to think past that point. Once they returned to Earth, there were a number of possibilities, most of them unpleasant.

"And what then?"

Can't leave it alone, can you, Fairfax? Trieka's chest burned suddenly with anger. Just as suddenly, it subsided, leaving behind tears that pricked her eyes and ached in her nose.

"I don't know, Harrison, and I wish you wouldn't ask."

He rolled toward her, closing his arms around her. *Safe,* she thought. *I'm safe here.* But only for the moment.

"I think," he said quietly, "that everything will be all right." She felt his hands moving slightly against her, shaping the basic forms of the language of the White Fur People. "I think you'll be acquitted, maybe decorated. And then...then I think you'll marry me."

"No," she said. The word slipped out before she could stop it. All she could see was Jake, his dark eyes flashing with anger. *"You said you loved me. Now what's more important? Me or that stupid ship? Make up your mind now or I'm leaving."* And of course he'd left, because Trieka had chosen the *Starchild.* Fairfax would leave, too, because he would force her to a similar choice. That was what men did to her.

She expected anger from him now. Instead, he laughed softly. "It's too late. According to the White Fur People, we're already married."

"Somehow I doubt we'll be filing joint tax returns."

"Tax returns? What's a tax return?"

She shook her head. "You're being awfully flippant."

"Only because I'm scared shitless."

"That makes two of us then."

He held her closer, kissed her temple and said nothing else. She lay quietly in his arms and didn't sleep.

❋ ❋ ❋

Two hours past noon on the fourth day, Six Toes brought them to a halt at the top of a rise.

"There," he said, pointing with one hand while speaking with the other.

Trieka moved to stand beside him, shading her eyes with one hand. The bright sun caught the bleached white of a docking apron in a blinding flash. If she squinted, she could see the outline of one of the small, squat rocket ships favored by smugglers. She wondered what they smuggled off Denahault. Probably local vegetation—EarthFed hadn't found a habitable planet yet that didn't come with hallucinogenic flora. She just hoped no one was smuggling white pelts.

"I will leave you now," Six Toes said, turning toward them. "I will miss you both. I hope to see you again."

"I hope so, too," said Trieka.

"Do you foresee it?"

Trieka smiled a little. "I'm not sure. I think so."

Six Toes closed his hand around hers gently, then addressed Fairfax. "Remember, no matter where you may go, you are always a man of the People who Live at the Edge of the Mountain. Remember this when you speak to your old clan about us."

Fairfax nodded solemnly. "I will remember. Take care, Six Toes."

Six Toes made a last gesture of farewell, then slipped away through the trees. Trieka felt a sudden stab of loss.

"Well, it looks like it's just you and me, Captain," Fairfax said.

She nodded slowly. "We'll see him again."

He gave her an odd look. "I'd say you're taking this clear

sight stuff a little too seriously, but I have the strangest feeling you're right."

Trieka took his hand and squeezed it firmly. "Let's go."

They paused just outside the station gates to assess their appearance.

"You look like hell," she said, wiping a smudge of dirt from his chin. He hadn't shaved since they'd left the clan. The four days of stubble combined with hair grown shaggily past his collar made him look as disreputable as anyone they were likely to meet at the station. He certainly didn't look like billionaire financier Harrison Fairfax.

"You look pretty good," he answered, grinning. Following instructions from Goldenseal, Trieka had for the last two days been washing her hair with a concoction of herbs. Now it was nearly black, the copper curls gone until she let them grow back. She'd dyed her eyebrows, as well, but the stuff hadn't worked well on her lashes. Without a mascara brush, it was nearly impossible to apply.

"Let's just hope it's enough," she said, "in case they're still looking for us."

Fairfax took a breath and reached out to adjust her cap. Trieka suddenly realized he was stalling. She gathered herself, then touched his face, running the back of her hand across the rasp of his stubble.

"Let's go find Lucas."

Guards stood at the gates, dressed in quasi-military khaki uniforms. Somehow this surprised her—she hadn't expected the place to be so well organized.

"Identification?" asked one of the guards. He was young—they both were—with blue eyes and blond hair in a severe crew cut.

"None," said Fairfax. Trieka schooled her expression carefully, finding herself surprised, pleased and even amused at the authority in Fairfax's tone. He hadn't gotten to be a billionaire by letting people walk on him, she supposed. "I was of the understanding that identity wasn't important here."

The guard's mouth quirked. "I didn't say your IDs have to be legitimate. We just need to log your arrival. It's a little easier with a name."

Fairfax nodded. "All right. I'm John Smith and this is Jane."

"You don't have any papers on you?"

"Bill Taylor sent us," Trieka contributed. She hadn't gotten where *she* was by letting people walk on her, either. "We were told to ask for Lucas at Dock Three."

"Bill Taylor, huh?" The guard considered. "All right. Lucas shipped in yesterday. You should find him at the dock." He stepped aside, and the second guard opened the door to let them pass.

The most immediately notable feature of Station Twelve was its smell. The stench of rocket fuel was nearly drowned out by the reek of garbage. Trieka, eyes watering, involuntarily covered her nose and mouth.

"Lovely, isn't it?" Fairfax mumbled.

"Most appetizing."

Traffic on the narrow, dirt-packed roads was minimal, but proceeded at speeds Trieka was certain were unsafe. The breeze from a passing aircar dislodged her hat and splashed water on her pants. Fairfax retrieved the hat, brushed it off and handed it to her. Ironic, she thought, that there were probably more vehicles in this small, illegal port than on the rest of the planet.

"He must have learned to drive in New Jersey," Fairfax said, nodding toward the departing aircar.

"Well, at least I'm not too wet." Trieka peered at the buildings lining the narrow street. Representing a wide variety of styles, colors and materials, they were also surprisingly clean. Even the road seemed well maintained. The smell seemed out of character, and she wondered what caused it. "See any numbers on any of these buildings?"

Fairfax shook his head. "What I'd really like is a big arrow that says, 'This way to Dock Three'."

"That would be too easy."

Eventually they did see a large sign, but it didn't say, "This way to Dock Three". It said, "Booze. Food. Live 32-Hour Stage Show".

Fairfax turned to Trieka. "How much money do we have?"

"I don't know. Do we have any?"

"I have a cash chit worth a grand or so. I had it hidden in the waistband of my jeans, so they didn't find it when they abducted me. Do you have any on you?"

"I don't normally carry cash. I just use my military chit."

"Which, of course, we can't use here, any more than I can use my credit cards. If I had them, that is, which I don't." He set his rucksack down on the ground and dug through it, finally surfacing with a plastic card. "Hmm. Thirteen hundred." He slid the card into an inside jacket pocket. "Let's hope this is enough to get supplies. The White Fur People were more than generous, but that won't get us all the way home."

Trieka puffed her cheeks, then let the air out in a sharp hiss. "Details. I was never good at civvie details."

He slipped a protective arm around her shoulders. "Come on. Let's see what we can find out."

The small tavern was crowded and hazy with smoke. Trieka smelled not only tobacco, but winder-weed, an illegal substance she'd thought was only grown on Farhallen. She pinched her nostrils shut.

"We'd better get out of here before I start dancing naked on the tables."

"You'd be in interesting company." Fairfax gestured toward the opposite side of the room. On a well-lit stage, two intriguingly clad—or more accurately, unclad—couples performed. Trieka felt herself blushing. Fairfax looked at her, obviously interested in her reaction.

"Don't get any ideas," he said.

"Don't worry. Leather's way too pricey these days." She paused, watching as the performance took an interesting, and particularly lewd, turn. "You could learn to do that, though."

He quirked an eyebrow. "If you ever see me doing that, call a chiropractor." He cupped a hand under her elbow, drawing her to the back.

The woman behind the bar with her towel-wrapped hand in a glass was even smaller than Trieka, with white-blonde hair. The color was natural, too—her eyebrows and lashes were barely visible. She smiled a little as they approached the bar, the expression more patronizing than friendly. Trieka met her gaze evenly, sizing her up and offering a mild challenge. The woman responded with a slight movement of her eyebrow, then turned her attention to Fairfax.

"Haven't seen you around here before," she said as Fairfax settled onto a stool. Trieka sat next to him, trying to maintain her poise as she hoisted herself onto the tall stool. The woman's eyes, she noted, were pale gold.

Fairfax smiled at her, that disarming grin that made him look barely pubescent. Even the scruffy growth of beard only minimally diminished its power. "We just arrived, actually."

"Welcome to Station Twelve. I'm Riva."

"Nice to meet you. We're looking for Dock Three."

"Keep going straight down the main road. You'll see a green archway. That's Dock Three. Lucas came in last night, so he'll be there." She paused. "What's your business here, that you don't even know where you're going?"

"We're looking for work."

Riva smiled again, lewdly. "I've got some openings in the show."

Fairfax returned her leer. Trieka gritted her teeth. He seemed to be enjoying this a little too much. "No, thanks," Fairfax said. "Bad back."

"What about the lady?" Riva looked directly at Trieka, the earlier challenge echoed on her face.

"Sorry," said Trieka. "No boobs." She touched Fairfax's shoulder. "Shall we move on?"

He nodded, but hesitated long enough to give Riva a warm smile—too warm, in Trieka's opinion. "Thanks very much for your help, Riva," he said, then followed Trieka back out to the street.

"What was that all about?" She was unable to keep the annoyance out of her voice.

"What was what all about?" Fairfax looked perfectly innocent, but the usual mischief glinted in his eyes.

"'Thanks very much for your help, Riva'," she quoted, batting her eyelids, her voice dripping with exaggerated sincerity.

He made an obvious effort to suppress a grin, but failed. "My, my. You didn't tell me you were the jealous type."

She pressed her lips together, trying to look angry while holding back her own sudden mirth. Abruptly, Fairfax sobered.

"She's the kind who notices every single person who passes through her establishment. She could come in handy later. It never hurts to have people on your side. Or at least leaning that way."

"So you think your masculine charms were enough to win her over?"

"One can always hope."

They kept walking. Four days on foot had loosened Fairfax's leg quite a bit, but he still moved stiffly, and not as fast as Trieka would have liked. She found herself moving ahead of him from time to time, her edginess driving her pace. Once he reached forward and took her by the elbow, drawing her back to him. His touch calmed her. When he let go of her elbow, she slid her hand down his arm, tangling her fingers in his. He squeezed her hand tight, but said nothing.

Perhaps a quarter mile down the road, they found the dark green concrete archway. The stench which covered the entire station was stronger here, as if more concentrated.

The archway led into a covered walkway, which opened into a large, bowl-shaped area, all lined with concrete. The surface of the bowl was charred and pockmarked with the tracks of previous liftoffs and landings. Currently, a small, shuttlelike craft sat in the bowl. The shuttle, intended for earth-to-orbit deliveries of equipment and personnel, had been modified and refitted with heavier engines and a hyperspace drive.

Fairfax hesitated at the entrance to the bowl, studying the place.

"Over there," Trieka said, pointing. Along the upper edge of the bowl was a wide walkway. Doors led into what she guessed were maintenance areas and workshops, but one door carried a green and white sign proclaiming, "Lounge."

Fairfax nodded. A flight of stairs to their left led up to the walkway. He went first, stiffly negotiating the concrete stairs.

The lounge was even smaller than Riva's compact tavern. There was a bar, but no floor show. In a corner above the bar, a miniature 3D set showed a movie Trieka remembered seeing back home about five years ago. Only a few of the dozen or so patrons were watching.

Even they lost interest in the movie as Trieka and Fairfax came in. Trieka squared her shoulders, prickling a little at the sudden attention. One of the men, a tall, wiry black man of about thirty, pushed out of his chair and came across the small room toward them.

"Can I help you?"

"We're looking for Lucas," said Fairfax.

The man chewed thoughtfully, sizing them up. Trieka caught a faint whiff of spearmint. Finally, the man shifted his gum to the other side of his mouth and said, "I'm Lucas." His gaze went to Trieka. "What can I do for you?"

"Bill Taylor sent us," Trieka said. "Can we talk somewhere in private?"

"Of course. Follow me."

He led the way to a small office in the back of the lounge. An older model computer sat on the desk amid a clutter of ledgers, receipts and manifests. Lucas sat, indicating two empty chairs with a sweep of his hand. He folded his hands on the desktop as Trieka and Fairfax sat down.

"So," Lucas said. "You know the Taylors?" He glanced at Fairfax, but his attention returned immediately to Trieka and stayed there.

"I've known the Taylors for a few years," she said.

"What exactly is it you're after?"

"Passage Earthside."

Lucas shrugged. "Go to Prime."

"If I wanted to leave from Prime, I would have done it already."

"So there's a warrant out for you?"

"Probably."

"What can you pay?"

"Not a great deal. But we can get more money to you once we reach Earth."

"How much?"

"As much as you want," Fairfax said. Lucas looked at him levelly.

"I don't normally take passengers," he said finally. "Especially passengers with no money. But for Bill Taylor, I'll do it. He's about the only man left on this planet with a paid tab. When do you want to leave?"

"As soon as possible," Trieka said.

Lucas rubbed his chin, snapping his gum. "I've got a shipment going out tomorrow. We land in the Gobi desert in nine days, then it's a two-day trip to the nearest airport by prop plane. From there you can catch a Trans-Pacific flight to New SanFran or LA. It's not a quick trip, but it'll get you there incommunicado. Which I assume is why you didn't leave from Prime?"

"Something like that." Trieka calculated silently. "So we'll need about three weeks' worth of supplies?"

"I'd get four, just to be safe."

Her stomach sank. They had enough food for two weeks, thanks to the White Fur People, but there was no way they could pay Lucas and get sufficient additional supplies with Fairfax's cash chit.

"Let me guess," said Lucas. "You're short on cash."

"Very." She was reluctant to admit it, but realized there was no advantage to lying.

"Do you think the Taylors would cover you?"

"They might."

Lucas nodded. "All right. I've never known the Taylors to get involved in anything that wasn't basically justified, legal or not. Plus, I owe Bill one." He paused, apparently debating whether he should go into details. Finally he shrugged. "A big one. Anyway, you use whatever money you've got to get supplies, and I'll settle up with you and with the Taylors later."

"Thank you. Now, where can we get supplies?"

"Riva will give you the best prices. She's back down the road."

Fairfax smiled. "Yes, we met Riva. Do you have an uplink to MediaNet?"

Lucas blinked at the change of subject, then shifted his gum again, grinning. "Want to see how hot things are at home?"

The slight twitch of Fairfax's mouth was probably invisible

to Lucas, but Trieka saw it. "Something like that."

"The answer to your question is no, we don't. There's too much paperwork and too much traceability involved in a legal MediaNet connection. But we do hack in. Unfortunately, my computer man has the day off. He hasn't seen his wife and kids in six months."

"Can you log me on?"

"Sure. But I'm not a hacker."

"That's all right. I am." Fairfax turned to Trieka, taking her hand in his for a warm moment. She had a sudden, strange urge to lace her fingers through his and cling to his big, long-fingered grip. But his hand slipped away. "Why don't you head to Riva's and see what you can arrange for supplies? I'll stay here and try to hack onto MediaNet and get some information. I'll hold onto the money—you negotiate the deal, then I'll go pay for it. That way there'll be two of us to carry everything back and less chance of getting our pockets picked."

"All right." Trieka slid from her chair. "Sounds like a plan." She let her hand slide across his shoulder gently, aware of Lucas's eyes on them. "I'll be back in a few."

Stepping back out into the traffic of the station, Trieka decided she'd come to rely far too heavily on Fairfax. She felt exposed, alone, and paranoia began to stir. Suddenly, it seemed like everyone was looking at her, and everyone was an EarthFed agent in disguise. She let her hair fall forward into her face, to remind herself it was black, not red. It had been eight weeks since their disappearance from Prime. Surely EarthFed had abandoned the search on Denahault by now.

Still, the hairs on the back of her neck prickled as she slipped into the dim smokiness of Riva's. The woman caught sight of her as she came in and met her at the bar.

"Come back to apply for a job?" Riva asked, smiling.

Trieka laughed a little, her nervousness assuaged somewhat by Riva's friendly demeanor. "No. I'm looking to buy some supplies. How much for a months' worth of rations and water?"

They discussed and haggled for a time, until Trieka felt she'd negotiated the best deal she could under the circumstances.

"Can you be back with the money in an hour?" Riva asked.

"Shouldn't be a problem."

"Then it's a deal." As they shook hands, Riva glanced absently over Trieka's shoulder, toward the stage. "On your way out, you might try to grab a look at the black-haired man in the green coat. He's been watching you awfully closely."

Trieka's stomach went cold. "For how long?"

"Since you walked in the door."

"Do you know who he is?"

"No, but I've seen him in here before."

"When?"

"A few times. I saw him the first time...about eight weeks ago, I think."

Trieka's teeth ground hard together. The icy fear in the pit of her stomach quietly resolved into a steely calm. She straightened her shirt, touching the holster just under her jacket where her double-barreled gun was concealed, then turned and walked to the door as if nothing were out of the ordinary.

As she passed the man in the green coat, she looked toward him, eyes down a little, trying to get a glimpse without his being aware of her scrutiny. He was staring soberly into his drink. A long, white scar ran from temple to jaw line on the side facing her. His harsh profile burned itself into her mind.

Then he looked at her. Right at her with eyes the color of gunmetal. He smiled.

Her heart rose to choke her. She pushed against the front door, forgetting it was automatic. As it slid open, squeaking against her hands, she sensed rather than saw the man get up and follow her out.

On the unlikely chance it might have been her imagination, she headed up the street and paused by a parked vehicle, making a convincing show of sorting through her pockets. In the midst of frisking herself, she glanced in the vehicle's rearview mirror. He was there, reflected in the glass. He'd paused in front of a door fifty feet or so behind her to light a cigarette.

Archaic way to kill yourself, she thought, feeling sharp and alert, like a well-honed blade. She'd give him a fight, kill him if she could. *Let's see if we can dispose of you in a more modern fashion.* She slipped her hand under her jacket, deactivating the safety on the gun. It was a nasty little weapon, which fired a shatterbullet and a small, intense laser beam at the same time. Trieka had no qualms about using it.

First, though, she'd try a non-violent approach. Acting as if she'd found what she was looking for in her pockets, she continued down the street, setting a fast pace, moving with the quick, easy confidence of someone who knew exactly where she was going. Too bad she didn't.

She had to assume that, the wider the roadway, the more likely it was to lead to something other than a dead end. Following that assumption, she turned right, onto a wide, paved road. Surreptitious checking showed the man following her. No mistake, then.

She ducked to the left, into something that looked like a reputable street. It opened back out into the main drag, and she had no choice but to follow. Damn. She'd come around in a circle. Now her pursuers knew she was aware of them. What to do now? Dock Three was a good fifteen-minute walk, even if she pressed herself. Running was out of the question. She decided to head straight back to the dock, as quickly as possible without attracting unnecessary attention.

She'd noticed the bum in the street on her first trip by, but he'd been occupied accosting other passersby and she'd managed to slip by him. Now he sat unoccupied, and he pushed himself up from the sidewalk as she approached. He was stationed near the opening of an alleyway. Probably lived back there. No time to stop; no money to be charitable with, anyway. Trieka focused her attention stonily on the sidewalk in front of her. *Pretend he's not there. Keep going. Don't let him stop you.*

But he did stop her. A grip of surprising strength closed over her arm as she tried to pass, pulling her to a halt.

"Spare some change?" the man wheezed. He smelled like an outhouse, worse than the general effluvium of the station.

"I don't have any money on me," Trieka said. "Now let me go. I've got business to attend to."

The tone of voice which brooked no argument shipboard apparently made no impression on this man at all.

"C'mon, lady. Just some change." His fingers closed brutally on her arm. His other hand was in his dingy coat pocket. "Surely a starship captain like yourself can spare a handful of change." He wrenched her arm, pulling her into the alley. At the same time, another hand closed on her shoulder, helping her along with more force than strictly necessary. The man in the green coat had caught up with her.

"What the hell is this?" Trieka demanded. Her mind raced, trying to figure out how she could get to her gun before the bum pulled the weapon undoubtedly concealed in his coat.

"What do you think it is?" said a harsh voice behind her. "You're in deep trouble, Captain Cavendish."

"I think you've mistaken me for someone else," she protested. Her arm was starting to ache, her fingers tingling as the bum's grip cut off circulation. She couldn't fight either of them—she was too small. If she could just get to the gun...

"I don't think so." Green Coat's voice was a growl.

"I have ID." Trieka was hardly aware of what she was saying, her mouth running without her brain engaged. Fortunately, it seemed to be saying reasonable things. She reached for her hip pocket, under the edge of her jacket. "My name's Cathy Marshall. I can prove it." She turned as her hand closed on the gun. Green Coat, behind her, laughed.

"As if any ID you could produce would be legitimate—" He stopped, staring, as she freed the gun and pulled the trigger. Blood blossomed just below the blackened, laser-burned hole in his chest.

Trieka never saw him fall. Something struck the back of her head with a sharp thud, and she wilted forward into blackness.

Chapter Fifteen

"Got it."

Fairfax leaned back in his chair as the familiar access page of MediaNet appeared on the computer screen. He'd only had to fiddle for a few minutes to find the paths Lucas's hacker had already established. Any news he could access would be at least two weeks old, but it was better than nothing.

He clicked himself into the archives and requested clips from a month ago, about the time news of his disappearance would have reached Earth. A search for his name and Trieka's produced a list of articles. Fairfax chose the earliest.

Billionaire Fairfax Reported Missing, read the headline. The report of his disappearance coincided with Commander Anderson's arrival back on Earth. An afterthought at the end of the article said, "Also missing is Captain Trieka Cavendish of the *Starchild,* the ship which brought Fairfax to Denahault. Authorities are currently investigating the possibility that the two events are connected."

The next headline read: *Billionaire Investor Kidnapped?*

"Yes, he was," Fairfax muttered. But the article didn't implicate EarthFed. Instead, it discussed a convoluted theory of Trieka spiriting him off into the wilds of Denahault to protest privatization of the colonies. Well, at least they'd gotten the spiriting off part right.

"Find anything?" Lucas looked up from the stack of manifests he'd been perusing.

"Yeah," Fairfax said. "Not quite everything I'm looking for, though."

Another article reported himself and Trieka still missing. He skipped it, but eyed the next article with considerably more interest.

Investigation Launched Into EarthFed. Information from an "unknown source" has led President Schumann to authorize a full-scale investigation into the colonization arm of EarthFed.

"Thank you, Commander Anderson," Fairfax muttered.

"What's up?" Lucas asked.

Fairfax skimmed the remaining headlines, saw nothing else of interest and logged off. "Nothing much," he told Lucas. "Possibly something good." He studied Lucas's face, wondering exactly how far he could trust the other man. Probably not very. "How long before the news is updated again?"

"Prime should get an archived transmission in a couple of days. We'll be able to access it within twelve hours or so, depending on how long it takes them to get it downloaded and unzipped."

"Two days," Fairfax muttered. "Maybe we should delay departure until I can find out what's happening Earthside."

Lucas shook his head. "I don't know. I'm not in the habit of rearranging my schedule for passengers, particularly non-paying ones."

Irked, Fairfax merely shrugged. "Doesn't matter. I need to check with my partner first, anyway."

Lucas grinned. "I had a feeling she was running the show."

Fairfax kept his face carefully sober, aware Lucas was trying to bait him. "She's a bit more experienced than I am."

"Ex-military?"

"Something like that."

"Speaking of your...partner. Shouldn't she be back by now?"

Fairfax looked at the computer terminal, reading the internal clock display. He'd been hacking and reading articles for nearly an hour. Lucas was right—Trieka should have been back by now.

He stood, rubbing suddenly clammy palms on his jeans. Still staring at the computer, he said, "Has anything unusual happened here lately?"

Lucas shrugged. "Just the garbage converters malfunctioning, but I'm sure you can smell that." He paused, thinking. "About eight weeks ago, a rumor went around that EarthFed was searching the place. For what, or whom, I don't know. No arrests were made and, as far as I know, they left shortly thereafter and they haven't come back." He hesitated, popping his gum. Fairfax was beginning to find the habit supremely annoying. "Is EarthFed after you two? I mean, technically, EarthFed is after everybody in this station, but is this something special?"

Fairfax's jaw clenched. Most of his anger was based in fear for Trieka, but that didn't make it any easier to quell. His voice was clipped, a little too sharp. "You may or may not have a need to know. If you do, I'll tell you." He stopped, dragging his composure back. "In the meantime, would you care to accompany me to Riva's?"

Fairfax trudged in silence behind Lucas. Nothing struck him as blatantly different about the traffic or the people. There'd been a bum by the tool repair shop, sitting in front of the opening to the alley. He was gone now. Probably moved on to another post, or perhaps he'd retired to a box or a sleeping bag in the alley. A car was parked on the next block, the driver squatting on the sidewalk, adjusting the hydraulics on the front passenger side. Nothing unusual about that. And no sign of Trieka.

Lucas led the way into Riva's. Fairfax hunched his shoulders, as if he could hide down the neck of his coat. The floorshow was still going strong; Fairfax forced his eyes away from the writhing, naked bodies.

Behind the bar, Riva saw him, looked at Lucas, and an expression of alarm crossed her face. She hastily dispensed with the tray of drinks she carried and met them as they sat down at the bar. "She didn't come back?"

"No," said Fairfax. "I gather she made it here."

Riva nodded. "There was a man watching her. He left right after she did."

She frowned a little, her eyes going distant. Fairfax sensed she was seeing the scene again in her mind's eye, reconstructing the details. "It was strange. It was like—maybe he knew her. Or she knew him." Her focus came back, and she shook her head.

Fairfax's jaw clenched shut. "Why didn't she stay here and call me?"

Unless...if she *had* known the man. If he'd been EarthFed and had coaxed her away on some pretext. If he'd tried to convince her she'd be safe with him, and then had taken her.

Or turned her.

Fairfax looked at his hand on the counter. It had clenched into a fist and he realized then he could feel the blunt edges of his fingernails like tiny blades in his palm. He tried to rein in his imagination but it was off and running—Trieka kidnapped, tortured...dead. Trieka betraying him, going back to EarthFed, handing him over in exchange for her own freedom—

He looked at Riva, fighting for steadiness. "Did she say anything to him? Did he talk to her?"

Riva shook her head, her pale brows drawn tight above her pale eyes as she studied his face. Fairfax held himself impassive, determined to betray nothing.

"I don't think so," she said. "He looked at her, he smiled. I think she was looking back." She shrugged. "I don't know. How do you read something like that across a room?"

How, indeed? He eased his hand open, surprised to see no blood. Lucas touched his shoulder.

"What are you thinking?" Lucas asked quietly.

"I don't know. Dammit, I just don't know." He looked again at Riva. "Did *you* recognize the man?"

She shook her head. "I'd seen him here before, but I don't know who he is. He's been in off and on over the past couple of months." She picked up a napkin and a pen from the bar and began to sketch. "He's a big man with dark hair, wearing a green coat. He was one of those who sat close to the floorshow, then tried to ignore it."

She pushed the napkin across the bar. She'd drawn a simple but remarkably lifelike full-face portrait of a man with a wide jaw, small eyes and dark hair. "He had a scar...here." She drew a line from temple to chin on the right side of the face, then looked up at Lucas, sparing Fairfax a glance. "Do you recognize him?"

Fairfax took the napkin, studying the picture. The man looked familiar only in the sense that he looked like any number of thugs he'd encountered. But, if he saw him in reality, he'd know him. And he'd kill him, for whatever his part had been in whatever had happened.

"How long ago did she leave?" he asked, his voice strangely calm even to his own ears. *Had* she run back into the arms of EarthFed? He couldn't imagine it, but he couldn't have imagined most of the last seven years of his life.

"About a half hour."

"Do you have any idea where this guy went at night?"

"No. One night he stayed until closing, though, and I saw him heading toward the docks."

"That's where we'll start looking then," said Lucas. "C'mon. We'd better make a quick sweep before the trail gets cold."

Fairfax held up a hand. His brain had finally kicked into gear. "Wait. Down the road. The tool repair shop. There was a vagrant there earlier. He's gone now. Is he usually there?"

Riva considered. "No. In fact, we don't usually see vagrants around here."

Fairfax felt his jaw clench tight. Carefully, he folded the napkin, closing the paper over the blunt face. He slid the napkin into his breast pocket.

"Thank you." He turned and strode back toward the door, leaving Lucas to follow. He heard the other man's quick footsteps behind him, catching up, then Lucas was again at his elbow.

"You think the vagrant had something to do with it?"

"If the guy in the green coat lured her out, he and the bum might have been working together. If that's the case, we may find some evidence in the alley."

The dark, narrow alley would have been the perfect place for an ambush. And Station Twelve itself was the perfect place to abduct a woman, then imprison her God-knew-where while you got ready to ship her back to Earth. Too many illicit things went on here for one more to be given any special attention.

It was also the perfect place to cross back over the line—a nameless, faceless place where anything could be forgiven and forgotten.

He shook his head sharply, not certain which possibility hurt more.

"What are we looking for?" Lucas asked.

Fairfax didn't answer. He scanned the width and length of the alleyway. There was no way out other than to go back onto the street.

A glint toward the back wall caught his eye. He went to see what it was, and his heart twisted as he bent to pick it up. It was a small gun, double-barreled for both bullets and laser fire. He turned it in his hand.

"That's a military issue weapon," Lucas observed.

Fairfax nodded.

"That kind of gun isn't easy to come by, but they do sell them here. We could trace back a buyer—"

"It's Trieka's," said Fairfax. His hand tightened on the small grip. It was still warm from a recent discharge. There was a moment of relief—she wouldn't have fired the gun at someone she considered an ally—then fear filled him.

"Trieka's..." Lucas repeated, then he took a sharp breath. Only then did Fairfax realize what he'd given away. He looked straight at Lucas and watched as the pieces fell into place behind his eyes.

"Trieka Cavendish," Lucas said, his voice barely above a whisper. "And you're—"

Fairfax closed a hand around Lucas's arm and steered him back toward the street.

"Let's go back to the dock. We need to discuss this in private."

* * *

The first thing Trieka noticed when she woke was that she couldn't see. The second thing she noticed was that she was folded in half, so she couldn't move her legs without hitting herself in the chin with a knee. Her wrists were tied behind her back. She felt hard metal walls on all four sides. Apparently, she'd been stuffed in a locker.

Quelling a surge of panic, she closed her eyes to shut out the darkness. She quoted Shakespeare and King James scripture to herself until the panic faded.

You can handle this, Cavendish. You've done it before.

In training, she'd spent twenty-four hours alone in an emergency evacuation capsule on three separate occasions. On one, the capsule had been completely dark, and there'd been no communication from anyone outside. The exercise was meant to simulate an emergency escape in-flight, and the breakdown of the escape vehicle's internal systems. They'd been encouraged to recite poetry or sing to themselves. Trieka had memorized huge sections of *Hamlet* and *Macbeth*, just because she liked them, and twenty or so psalms because of the positive content.

Trouble was, she doubted her current captors would hold to the twenty-four hour time limit. Plus she'd had sanitary facilities in the simulated escape pod.

A sound outside her cramped prison jarred her out of her thoughts. She opened her mouth to shout, then closed it. Might it be to her advantage to let them think she was still unconscious? After a moment's thought, she opened her mouth again and shouted, "Hey!" The worst they could do was take her out and torture her, and even then she'd at least get some fresh air.

Light speared into the small, dark space around her. Trieka recoiled, squeezing her eyes shut.

"You awake, Cavendish?" a voice asked from outside.

Carefully, she eased one eye partially open. She could see four narrow strips of bright light, just above eye level. She'd been right, then—it was a locker.

"No, I'm talking in my sleep," she replied, her voice remarkably calm and amiable. "What the hell's going on?"

"We want to know where the disk is."

"What disk?"

Something slammed into the locker door. She flinched at the almost painful echo. "You know what disk. The one Fairfax gave you."

"Fairfax? You mean that skinny, big-nosed, conceited,

181

overbearing, rich idiot? He never gave me anything but a strong urge to pop him in the face."

There was a pause, and the light blinked out. "We'll be back later. Hit the door twice if you want to talk before then."

"With what? My head?"

There was no answer. She leaned back against the back of the locker and closed her eyes.

"This is unbelievable." Lucas had shot up out of his chair five minutes into Fairfax's story, and was still pacing the small room, arms crossed tight over his chest, snapping his gum in time to his rapid strides. "Absolutely unbelievable."

"And completely true." Fairfax maintained his usual deadpan calm, though he had a strong urge to pin Lucas to the floor and pry the gum out of his mouth.

Lucas stopped pacing, shaking his head. The look of incredulous excitement on his face hadn't wavered for at least fifteen minutes. "We had our suspicions about the natives. We thought they were maybe gorilla level intelligence or a little higher. But this... When this gets back to Earth, God only knows what'll hit the fan."

"It's already gotten back to Earth. That's what I was looking for on MediaNet. An investigation is already underway."

"Then we've got to get you back. They'll want you to testify."

Fairfax shook his head slowly. "I'm not going back without Trieka."

"But if EarthFed has her, or if she's turned you in—"

"I don't care." His voice barely changed pitch, and changed volume not at all. But Lucas's expression suddenly shifted, becoming deadly serious.

"Then we'd better find her."

"'The Lord is my shepherd, I shall not want. He maketh me to lie down in green pastures, he leadeth me beside the still waters—'"

The entire locker shook as someone slammed it, hard, from outside. Trieka swallowed the dryness in her mouth.

"Where's the disk?" a voice shouted.

"'He restoreth my soul. He preparest a table before me in the presence of mine enemies—'"

"We know he gave it to you. Where is it?"

"'He anointeth my head with oil—'"

"You can talk or you can stay in there until you rot."

"'Yea, though I walk through the valley of the shadow of death, I shall not fear, for thou art with me—'"

"You want water, Cavendish? You want food? Tell me where the disk is!"

"'Thy rod and thy staff, they comfort me—'"

"I'll give you a rod and a staff!" The voice was becoming irate. "Where the hell is the disk?"

"'Surely goodness and mercy shall follow me all the days of my life and I shall dwell in the house of the Lord forever.'"

The slamming came again, for a few, unmeasureable minutes, then she was alone again, in the silence and the darkness.

Fairfax, she thought. *Where are you? I rescued you, now get your hairy ass over here and rescue me.*

She closed her eyes. Her throat was parched and sore, her stomach gnawing hungrily on nothing. She had no way of knowing how long she'd been imprisoned. The guards kept coming, shouting, demanding. She ignored them, quoting her quotes and fighting the urge to tell them, just so they'd give her a glass of water or a cracker.

The darkness closed silently around her. In it, she felt Fairfax's hands on her, comforting, caressing.

He'll come. He'll come.

Katriena Knights

Fairfax rubbed his burning eyes with thumb and forefinger, slumping into the chair behind Lucas's desk. The piece of paper with the line drawing of Scarface dangled from his other hand. After a moment, eyes watering hard enough to quench the burn, he laid the paper on the table.

They'd scanned Riva's napkin drawing into the computer, then printed copies. Fairfax and Lucas had then walked the streets of Station Twelve, looking for anyone who'd admit to knowing the man.

After eighteen straight hours of querying, Fairfax had come back empty-handed and exhausted. Any number of people recognized the man—apparently he'd been keeping a watch at various points around the station for at least six weeks—but no one knew who he was or where he went when he left. Fairfax closed his eyes. He kept seeing Trieka with a gun pressed to the nape of her neck.

"Fairfax?"

He jumped, looking up. He must have drifted into sleep for a minute, as he hadn't heard Lucas come in. For a change, the black man wasn't chewing gum, but he carried two steaming mugs that emitted an odor that made Fairfax's mouth water.

"My God," he said. "Is that real coffee?"

"Kona blend," Lucas replied with a grin. "Special from my contacts on Oahu. It ain't cheap, but you look like you need it."

Fairfax nodded agreement at Lucas's diagnosis and took the coffee. He let the fragrant steam caress his face and fill his nostrils before he carefully sipped the rich brew. Lucas sipped at his own mug, waiting for him to finish his ritual before asking, "Any luck?"

He shook his head. "Plenty of people have seen him, but nobody knows who he is or where he's hiding." He took another drink. He hadn't had real coffee since Mabel's on EarthStar II. "You?"

"Yes and no." Fairfax looked up, one eyebrow slightly lifted, waiting. Lucas put his coffee mug down on the desk and sat in the free chair. "I actually found him. He was pulled out of a garbage dumpster behind Eddie's Bar at two this morning, which was just about the time I showed up there. He'd been

184

shot in the chest with a double-barreled, military issue handgun. The body had been stripped—no clothes, no ID, no nothing. Except..." Lucas drew a small silver key out of his breast pocket.

Fairfax stared at the little piece of metal, despair sinking through his gut like hot lead. Now he knew which alternative was worse. If she'd betrayed him, at least he could have been fairly certain she was still alive. If she'd killed an EarthFed agent— "And exactly what good does that do us?"

Lucas laid the key down on the desk next to his coffee. "It's a locker key. Only five docks at the station still use keyed lockers. The rest have all been converted to thumb print access."

Fairfax felt a small bubble of hope. "If the guy was stripped, where exactly was this key?"

"You do *not* want to know. But, for him to have been keeping it there, it must have been damned important."

"So what do we do now?"

"*You*, my friend, get some sleep. My hacker's due back in two hours. I'll get him working on accessing the station records."

"I could get started—"

"It's a little more esoteric than hacking into MediaNet." Lucas stood, picked up the key and dropped it back in his pocket. "Don't worry about it. Cain's always prompt and he's about as good as they come. We'll wake you up when we get some information."

Fairfax wanted to argue, but his body fought on the side of common sense. "All right. Show me to a mattress and I'll get out of your hair."

Chapter Sixteen

"She won't talk."

The voice jarred Trieka awake. How she'd fallen asleep, she didn't know, but she'd been dreaming. She'd been making love to Fairfax, but somehow her right leg had gotten impossibly twisted between them. It hurt and was going numb, but she couldn't get Fairfax to shift enough for her to get free. In wakefulness, the leg felt exactly the same, wedged between her own body and the locker door.

"Let her starve then." The second voice was deeper, unfamiliar.

"We can't do that. If we can't get the information out of her in twenty-four hours, it may be too late."

There was a pause. Someone took a deep breath, almost like a sigh. "It may already be too late." Another pause, then the voice came again, muted, as if the speaker was retreating. "Let her out."

The locker door rattled and banged, and finally came open. Unable to do anything else, Trieka fell forward into the waiting arms of an EarthFed agent. She wanted very much to hurt him, but her legs were useless, her hands bound behind her. She could barely see for the glare of perfectly normal indoor fluorescent light.

"If you don't talk, he's going to kill you," the man muttered to her.

She managed a glare. "Let him try," she croaked.

The agent shook his head and practically carried her out of the locker room.

Circulation began to return to her legs halfway down the hallway. Fighting tears, she forced herself to follow her captor. As if sensing her discomfort, the man leaned closer, taking more of her weight against him. How he could stand her smell, she didn't know.

She was led to a small room that looked like crew's quarters for dry-docked ships. Smaller even than her cabin on the *Starchild*, it looked like a suite at the Hilton to Trieka. And there was a bathroom.

"Not unless you talk," said her captor, seeing the direction of her glance, and probably the hunger in it as well. "Sit down."

She sat in a metal folding chair by the tiny table. The EarthFed man sat across from her.

"My name's Garrison," he said. "I've been instructed to inform you that it'll be better for you if you tell us everything you know."

"I only know what I'm told," Trieka shot back, "and, from the looks of things, I haven't been told anything."

"We had Fairfax in custody. Why did you release him?"

She looked him squarely in the eyes. "I don't know anything about that."

"What about the disk?"

She shook her head. The neutral expression on her face felt like one of Fairfax's.

Garrison nodded. "All right. If that's the way you want it. But I really wish you'd talk. I'd hate to have to kill you."

❋ ❋ ❋

"Fairfax, wake up."

"Wha...?" Fairfax mumbled. Sleep had claimed him thoroughly, mercilessly, and didn't want to let him go.

"Wake up, Fairfax. We've got an upload from MediaNet."

That meant something, he was certain, but he was still disoriented and muzzy. He wasn't even certain who was talking to him. He managed to lever an arm against the bed to push himself up. The face of the man addressing him resolved into dark detail. Lucas.

"MediaNet?" Fairfax said.

"Yes. It's in a little early, and the original broadcast date is only nine days ago. Cain says they put a Priority One on the uplink to Prime. I think you should come look at it."

Bits and pieces finally began to click together in Fairfax's head. "How long have I been asleep?"

Lucas shrugged. "I'm not really sure. A long time."

"Got any more of that coffee?"

Lucas laughed. "I think I could scrounge up a cup."

✳ ✳ ✳

Whatever vestige of sleep still clung to Fairfax's conscious fled as soon as he saw the MediaNet headline: Derocher and Six Others Arrested in EarthFed Scandal.

The admiral and six high-ranking EarthFed officers had been taken into custody on Earth ten days ago. Some charges were still pending, waiting for evaluation of the available evidence, but so far they'd been charged with misappropriation of federal funds, extortion and gross dereliction of duty.

"Add kidnapping, murder and genocide, and you'll just about have it," Fairfax mumbled.

"If our EarthFed friends see this," Lucas said over his shoulder, "what will that mean for Cavendish?"

"I don't know. But I do know it doesn't mean we can stop looking for her."

"Well, that's a given. And it leads me to my next bit of news. Cain's accessed station records, and we've narrowed down the possible sources of that key."

"Let's see what he's got."

Cain looked less like a computer geek than a football player, with broad shoulders and a thick neck in strange contrast to long, graceful hands that played the keyboard like a piano. He flicked through docking permissions, maps and manifests, finally settling on an outline of the layout of the entire station.

"These five docks are the ones that haven't been converted from key-entry lockers," he told Fairfax. "These two are currently registered to legal users—or at least as legal as it gets around here. These three are officially empty. However—" Here he changed screens to a database which was completely incomprehensible to Fairfax. "According to these surface scans, two of those three are occupied. That's not strictly unusual. Station security turns a blind eye if they're passed enough cash. But one of these two has seen a liftoff in the past three weeks. The other hasn't shown any ground-to-space activity for at least a month. Which would be very unusual for any of the smuggling operations around here."

"That would be the one, then," said Fairfax.

"It would seem like a good bet, anyway."

"So when do we start?"

"Who has the disk?"

Trieka swallowed. Her throat was dry again from saying, "I don't know", nearly a hundred times. She didn't bother this time.

Hayes, the EarthFed agent who'd been interrogating her for the last however-many hours, eyed her as placidly as ever. His hands were folded on the table. He had short, stubby fingers with nails chewed back so far there was hardly anything left. She'd been looking at them for a long time. She shifted her gaze from his hands to his face. Hayes was one of the uglier men she'd ever seen. He looked like a warthog.

"Were the disks sent to Earth?"

She didn't answer.

"Who on Earth has the disks? Who did you send them to?"

Trieka stared at him, waiting for him to look away. He did, but only because Garrison came into the room just then. He bent close to Hayes and said something in his ear. Hayes pushed his chair back from the table and stood, then planted his fists on the table, leaning down toward her.

"You think about recovering your memory," he said. "I'll be

189

back."

Garrison stood, tapping his fingers on the table for a few minutes, until Hayes returned. He now looked like a poker-playing warthog who'd just filled an inside straight. He sat back down, nodding dismissal to Garrison.

"Well," Hayes said. "That changes things."

She remained silent, refusing to rise to his bait. Her recalcitrance did nothing to dampen his smugness.

"One of my associates just returned from a little trip downtown. He didn't come back alone."

He let silence fill the small room again. Trieka held herself very still. She wouldn't play his games. But her stomach suddenly felt empty and twisted. She knew what he was going to say. With a thin smile, he said it. "We have Fairfax."

She forced herself to quiet calm, kept her face a mask.

Hayes folded his hands on the table, fingers laced together, thumbs straight up in the air. "Perhaps you'd like to answer our questions now? I don't suppose I need to mention that, if you continue as you have, we'll kill him."

Trieka swallowed. When she was certain she could keep her voice steady, she looked directly into Hayes's eyes. "Before we start, I'd like you to ask him a question for me."

Hayes's eyes narrowed only a fraction, but enough. "And what might that be?"

"I want you to ask him what Goldenseal named him."

Hayes's face went hard, expressionless. Trieka swallowed elation, matching his expression with her own steady mask. She'd called his bluff. Hayes gave Garrison a sidelong glance.

"Take her back to the locker room."

She managed to maintain her calm while Garrison led her out of the room, and while two other EarthFed goons pulled her arms behind her and fastened handcuffs to her wrists. On the way back down the hallway, she moved with careful dignity, not speaking, not looking at her escorts. But when they opened the locker door, something snapped.

Even fighting, she maintained silence. Everything blurred together; she felt like a berserker, consumed by blood lust. Strangely, there was no fear. One of the men put a hand over her face. She bit and her mouth filled up with blood. Finally, an arm pressed against her windpipe. She gagged, and fought and sank into blackness.

She dreamed again, or perhaps it was a vision. In the strange world between unconsciousness and sleep, images formed and faded. She saw the green and blue sphere of Earth from space, growing larger, then the familiar skyline of New SanFran. She saw a huge house, with wide windows, a huge double door in front with a stained glass rosette window above it. The entryway seemed gilded, full of golden wood and light. A spiral staircase wound out of the middle of the room, disappearing into infinity.

Fairfax stood at the foot of it, leaning casually against the stair rail. Bathed in gold light, he was clean-shaven and handsome. She was drawn toward him. A moment later, she was in his arms, held close. She could almost feel his breath against her ear, could almost smell him.

Then, suddenly, she was pushed away. She seemed to fly backward across the huge room. Fairfax diminished in the distance, his face no longer calm and handsome, but ugly with anger. And she continued backward, as if propelled by an engine, until she once again hung in space above the distant Earth. And even that faded before her as she moved farther and farther away—

Trieka jerked into wakefulness. A chasm opened in her soul, and she wept.

"I don't like putting it off this long."

Lucas straightened over the map he'd spread out on his desk. Cain and Olsen, another of Lucas's crew, also looked up at Fairfax. He stood tense and stiff next to Lucas.

"I know you don't," Lucas said, his voice calm in spite of

Fairfax's brusque interruption. "But we stand the best chance of getting her out if we go in after dark."

"That's still five hours away," Fairfax protested. He felt helpless. He wanted to hit someone. "God only knows what they'll have done to her by then."

Lucas started to speak, but closed his mouth as Cain reached for Fairfax, laying a big, gentle hand on his shoulder.

"They're not going to hurt her," he said, "not if they have any sense at all. They're in a very weird position here. Their superiors are being indicted all over the place. If they hurt Cavendish, they'll end up cutting their own throats."

Fairfax was in no mood to be reassured. He shrugged Cain's touch sharply off. "If they *do* kill her, that's one less witness against them."

"We can't just rush them in broad daylight," Lucas put in. "We'll all end up dead then, and there won't be any witnesses at all."

Fairfax took a breath, closing his eyes. "She's been in there two days." His voice was raw.

"And she'll be coming out tonight." Lucas gestured at the map, directing everyone's attention back to it. "Let's go over this again."

They went over it again, and one more time, then Lucas dismissed Cain and Olsen.

"Get some rest," he told them. "We'll need it tonight."

Fairfax sat down behind the computer, rubbing his eyes. He felt sick and angry. He hadn't been able to eat anything substantial for at least twenty-four hours. Lucas's coffee had kept him going, but he was starting to feel a backlash from the caffeine. His head hurt in a hot band behind his eyes. And Trieka was still gone. Still a prisoner. Or dead. Fairfax swallowed hard. Five more hours...

Lucas sat in the chair on the other side of the desk, opening a fresh package of gum. Fairfax was too numb to be irritated as Lucas unwrapped a stick and began to chew.

"You didn't tell me she was your lover."

Fairfax looked up. Lucas's attention was focused on the package of gum as he tidied up the torn edges of the paper.

"I didn't think it was any of your business," said Fairfax. Lucas looked up then, a smile quirking a corner of his mouth.

"You're right. It probably isn't. Except your emotional involvement just might jeopardize her rescue. You need to get a hold of yourself."

Fairfax clenched his teeth. "Those people murdered my wife. I'm not losing Trieka, too."

"I'm sorry," said Lucas. "I didn't know that."

"Besides, she rescued me. The least I can do is return the favor." He leaned back in the chair, looking at the ceiling. His head ached abominably. "She's saved my life twice already."

Lucas was silent a moment, lips pressed together, not even chewing his gum. Fairfax closed his eyes. For the first time in hours, he felt tired, almost like he could sleep.

"I don't think they'll kill her," Lucas finally said, "unless she answers their questions, and I don't think she'll answer squat. She's military trained, Fairfax. She can take care of herself."

"I'm not so sure about that."

Lucas gave a laugh nearly devoid of amusement. "Tell that to the stiff they pulled out of Eddie's dumpster."

Fairfax felt a smile twist his own mouth. Lucas was right, to some extent. Trieka *could* take care of herself. But no one could defend themselves against what a troop of EarthFed goons could dish out.

"You need some sleep," Lucas said, "and probably some food, too."

"I can't sleep."

"Take a pill. And eat a sandwich. And no more coffee. We need you alert and clear-headed tonight. That's an order."

Fairfax nodded, conceding to common sense. "All right."

Fairfax adjusted his infrared binoculars, bringing into focus the pair of guards outside the archway leading to Dock Eighteen. They weren't huge men, but they were big enough. In top condition, Fairfax figured he could hold his own with one of them. With his leg the way it was, he was glad to have the advantage of Cain, Lucas and Olsen. He lowered the binoculars and squinted through the darkness at the top of the archway. There was a spark of light, then another. Looking through the binoculars again, Fairfax could barely make out Lucas's outline, squatting on top of the archway above the two guards.

"That's it," Cain mumbled next to him. "Are you ready?"

"Yeah," said Fairfax. Olsen's reply was so quiet Fairfax never heard it.

"Then let's go," said Cain.

Fairfax quickly strapped the binoculars onto his face and readied his gun. Cain and Olsen made their own preparations, finishing in a matter of seconds. Then Cain looked at Fairfax and nodded.

They rushed the guards with a hideous, wailing howl. Fairfax would have pissed himself, hearing that coming at him in the dark. The two guards were sufficiently taken aback, eyes gone wide, hands just a shade too slow to ready their weapons in time.

Fairfax's first shot glanced off the interior curve of the archway, the second struck the left-hand guard in the upper thigh. Two more reports were shots from Cain and Olsen. Then Lucas fell from the air onto the guards, and the other three held fire.

Fairfax rammed the gun into the holster at his waist and grabbed the guard he'd shot. The man fought in spite of his injury, landing a fist in Fairfax's face and dislodging the binoculars. Faced again with darkness, Fairfax kicked blindly at the man's legs. The guard howled. Fairfax kicked again and the man dropped.

Fairfax scrabbled the binoculars back into place. Cain and Olsen straightened from the inert body of the other guard. Cain had a stun gun in his hand. He knelt next to Fairfax's victim.

"He's out," Cain said, still keeping his voice low. "Nice job, kicking him in a bullet wound. That must've hurt."

Fairfax winced. Cain stunned the already unconscious man, ensuring he'd be out for a good long time.

"Where's Lucas?" Fairfax hissed.

"Went to find the power generator," said Olsen. He turned to look at Fairfax and his slight form bent a little, as if in pain.

"You all right?" said Fairfax.

Olsen grimaced, pressing a hand to his side "Yeah. Bastard caught me a good one, though."

Lucas reappeared then, seeming almost to pop into existence out of the night. "Power's out," he said. "Let's go."

They slipped single file under the archway and into the bowl of Dock Eighteen, Lucas leading, Fairfax in the rear. The docking area was empty—no ships, no vehicles of any sort. They would have left from Prime, Fairfax guessed, if they'd managed to catch all their prey. A light flickered from the lounge area, halfway across the bowl.

"There they are," said Lucas.

They moved quickly along the walkway. Fairfax's breath came too hard and he fought to keep it steady. Fear had a hand clenched around his stomach. *What if she's dead? What if she's dead?* He couldn't stop the thought, and it pounded through his head like his heartbeat.

They reached the lounge and ducked to the ground, staying below the level of the windows. The faint light from inside looked like the output of a weak backup generator. Lucas pulled his binoculars down around his neck and popped up for a look in the window. Back down against the ground again, he closed his eyes. His mouth moved, forming silent words as he squeezed his eyelids tight, then he popped up again and took one shot through the window. The light went out.

"Go," he said.

Cain was first through the door, Fairfax close behind him. There were three men in the room, all gaping into the darkness.

"Everybody down!" Cain shouted. His voice was huge in the blackness. Two of the men dropped, but the other pulled a gun from his belt and fired off a shot toward Cain. Cain jerked, grunting. Fairfax leveled his weapon and shot the EarthFed man in the knee. He went down.

"You okay?" Fairfax shouted to Cain.

"No, you frigging idiot, I just got shot!"

Olsen went to Cain while Lucas covered the two men on the

floor. Fairfax grabbed his own victim, dragging the man up against him with an arm against his throat.

"You can't see us, but we can see you," Lucas said. "So I'd advise you all not to move. I'll kill you if I have to." He turned to Olsen. "How is he?"

"Flesh wound," Olsen reported. "Went clear through. May have nicked a rib."

Fairfax tightened his arm against his prisoner's windpipe. The man choked, clawed at his arm. He pressed the muzzle of his gun against the back of the man's ear. "Where is she? Still in the locker room, or did they move her?"

"I don't—"

He jerked the man's head back, hard. "Tell me where she is or I'll blow your fucking head off!"

The man flailed like a fish on a boat deck. His voice gagged in his throat, forming incoherent sounds.

"She's still in the locker room," one of the other men said. Fairfax looked at Lucas. Lucas motioned with his gun.

"Back of the bowl, behind the crew's quarters. Olsen, go with him."

Fairfax was out the door almost before Olsen could catch up with him. Olsen grabbed his elbow from behind. "Follow me."

Fairfax fell back and followed the other man's slight form down the walkway. There was no sign of EarthFed until they reached the crew's quarters. One guard stood in front of the door, gun in one hand, comm unit in the other, flashlight under his arm. The wan light did little to dispel the dark.

"Foster, this is Carter," he said. "Are you there? What's going on?"

Olsen waved Fairfax back. He slipped up to Carter, avoiding the small circle of light from the flashlight.

"Foster, this is Carter." The comm unit fell from his hand as Olsen kicked him in the stomach. Fairfax had never seen a man move so fast. Olsen dispatched the guard with two quick chops to the neck, then signaled Fairfax forward.

"Nice job," said Fairfax.

Olsen grinned.

They found the door to the locker room. There were no more guards. Apparently the power loss had disoriented everyone as much as Lucas had hoped. The guard they'd just dispatched had probably been assigned to watch the locker room, but the darkness had lured him away. Now all they had to do was find Trieka.

Olsen led the way. Fairfax scanned the room anxiously, but no sign of her.

"Check the lockers," Olsen said.

God. Fairfax's stomach twisted. What had they done to her? He passed down the rows of lockers. There weren't many—the place was designed to handle crews of no more than thirty. Fairfax forced his breathing to quiet. Still, he heard nothing but his own and Olsen's footsteps.

Then, suddenly, a locker door rattled and a scream cut the air.

"Trieka!" Fairfax ran to the sound. Olsen was pulling at a locker door, trying to force it open. Pieces of cardboard were taped to the outside of the door, covering the air slots at top and bottom.

"It's locked," Olsen told Fairfax. "Key didn't work—must be for another locker." He gave the door one last wrench with no result. "I'm going to have to cut the lock out."

"Leave me alone, you son of a bitch!" Her voice screamed from inside the locker. "I'm not telling you anything, you half-assed mother-fu—"

"Trieka!" Fairfax was grinning. "Trieka, it's me!"

The voice fell silent. Then, "Harrison?" The word was almost a sob.

"Yes, it's me. Are you all right?" He glanced at Olsen, who'd produced a palm-sized laser and was adjusting the size of the beam.

"What did Goldenseal name you?"

"Long Nose. Trieka, I've got one of Lucas's guys here. He's got to cut the lock. We need you to hold still."

He heard sobbing now, barely controlled. "You're here on your own? They didn't get you, too?"

"No, honey, this is strictly a rescue mission."

Silence. Olsen, laser adjusted, looked at Fairfax. Gently, Fairfax tapped the locker door. "Trieka?"

"I'm holding still." Her voice was steadier now. Fairfax gave Olsen a nod.

With utmost care, Olsen cut a circle around the lock. When it had detached, he pressed his hands against the door, holding it closed.

"Be ready for her. She might fall out."

Fairfax moved next to the other man. Olsen opened the door.

Trieka tumbled out, bringing with her an amazingly hideous stench. Fairfax caught her before she hit the ground, closing her tight in his arms.

"Oh, God," she said. "Oh God, oh God—" The words disappeared into sobbing.

"Shh." Fairfax stroked her hair. Trieka's hands were cuffed behind her. He motioned for Olsen to slice the cuffs off. When they came loose, her arms went weakly around him. Her legs shook against his. "Can you walk?"

"I don't think so."

He bent and picked her up. She was slight and trembling in his arms, like a little red bird dyed black. He bent his head over her, holding her close, and kissed her hair. "Did they hurt you?"

"No."

"Let's go," said Olsen.

※ ※ ※

In the lounge, Lucas and Cain had cuffed or bound the three EarthFed men. Both were now on the floor, Lucas kneeling next to Cain, who sat with his left arm lifted while Lucas examined the bullet wound. It was hard to make out details through the infrared binoculars, but Cain looked like he was in pain.

Lucas looked up as Fairfax and Olsen came in.

"She all right?"

"I'm okay," Trieka said. Her breath was hot and moist

against Fairfax's chest. He pulled her a little closer. It had to be difficult for her, dealing with all this in the pitch darkness.

"Good," said Lucas. "I'm going to go turn the lights back on. Then we can try to find out what that key is for."

"Want down?" Fairfax asked Trieka.

"Yeah. I think I have some circulation in my legs again."

He eased her to the ground. She stood for a second, then sat down on the floor, clinging to his hand. He sat down next to her.

"What's going on?" she said. "I can't see a damn thing."

Fairfax slipped the binoculars off his face and was immediately plunged into blackness. He hadn't realized how dark it really was. Groping for Trieka, he found her and managed to get the binoculars into her hand.

"Put these on," he said. "I can do without them for a while."

"I like these," she said a minute later. "Why didn't you bring me a pair?"

"We brought every pair we had," said Cain, the pain obvious in his disembodied voice.

"Who are you?" Trieka asked.

"Cain. I'm Lucas's computer specialist."

"Ah. The hacker."

"That would be me."

"You take a bullet?"

"Flesh wound. Hurts like hell, though."

"I'm sure it does."

Just then the lights came on, blindingly bright. Fairfax saw color and detail where he'd seen little more than outlines before—the filth on Trieka's clothes, the blood on Cain's shirt. Trieka took the binoculars off and gave them back. Her face was drawn and haggard. He wondered if she'd been in the locker for the entire two days. At least he didn't see any bruises, but she'd said they hadn't hurt her.

He caught her hand as he took the binoculars from her. He couldn't find words. She smiled, and he saw the tears she'd been diffusing with her own flippancy. His hand tightened on hers.

"I love you," he whispered, and leaned forward and kissed her, unmindful of the smell, or of Cain watching from across the room.

"All right, let there be light." Lucas breezed back into the room. "Now we can see about this key." He rubbed his hands together briskly. "Fairfax, why don't you take Captain Cavendish back? I'm sure she could use some rest. Cain, go with them. Have Riley look at that bullet wound. Olsen, come with me."

Fairfax pushed himself to his feet, holding a hand down to Trieka. "You heard the man. Let's go."

Trieka took his hand and stood. "You told him who we are?" she whispered.

"It seemed prudent, under the circumstances." Cain was already at the door, waiting for them to follow. "Let's go. I'll explain everything later."

Chapter Seventeen

Trieka thought she'd gotten the use of her legs back with the return of circulation, but only a few blocks from Dock Eighteen, they buckled under her without warning. Somehow Fairfax caught her before she hit the ground. He gathered her up in his arms and carried her for a block, then alternated carrying and supporting her all the way back to Dock Three.

Cain showed them to an unused crew's quarters before departing to have his wound checked. There'd be food available in the lounge, he said, in a couple of hours. In the meantime, there were emergency rations in the small room.

Trieka found these right away and ripped the foil off one of the candy bar-sized packages. Inside was a highly nutritious but bland bar. She devoured it. It tasted like heaven.

"Hungry?" Fairfax asked as she ripped open another.

"I haven't had anything at all in the last forty-eight hours." She forced herself to eat the second bar a bit more slowly. The rations were designed for quick and easy digestion, and theoretically they should give her no problem even on a two-days-empty stomach, but there was no point pressing her luck. Plus they tasted like a handful of straw stuck together with peanut butter. Now that she'd gotten the edge off her hunger, taste was more of a factor.

"Now," she said, tossing the metallic wrappers on the narrow bed. "Shower."

She pulled off her shirt and pants, leaving them in a pile on the floor. She hated to think what she looked like. Her skin felt stiff with sweat and old filth. She spared a glance over her shoulder at Fairfax. He was looking at her, but his eyes had glazed over. The telltale muscle in his jaw line bunched. His thoughts came back to his eyes. Trieka flinched at the raw anger there.

"Burn those," she said, pointing to the clothes. Then, quietly, she slipped into the bathroom.

The bathroom was so small she could barely lift both arms out to her sides without touching both walls. The shower occupied one corner, blocked off by an opaque glass door. The walls of the room seemed too close, too confining. Her heart sped up, pattering hard against her breastbone. She opened the shower door and stepped inside.

She froze before she could turn the water on. The walls closed in on her, trapping her in their tiny domain. Feeling her breath tearing out of her in rapid gasps of panic, she shoved the stall door open. Before she quite realized what she was doing, she'd backed out the bathroom door to stand panting in the small bedroom. It was small, but there was air here, at least, and room to move.

"What's wrong?" said Fairfax.

She wheeled. In her mindless panic, she'd nearly forgotten he was there. He took a step toward her, stopped, concern etched deep on his face.

"I can't go in the shower," Trieka choked. "It's too small—" Her hands came up over her face, to stop the raw, uncontrolled voice, the manic panting.

Fairfax's face tightened. He was angry, she knew, but not at her. He unbuttoned his shirt and shrugged it off, then dropped his pants and underwear to the floor.

"Come on," he said. "We'll go together."

He went into the shower first and adjusted the water temperature. When the mirror above the sink started to fog up, he waved at her to come in.

She hesitated, then took a step. He held the shower door open, waiting for her to make that final step. Trieka stood in indecision and fear for another breath, then stepped forward.

It's just a shower. Nobody's going to shove you in and turn the lights off.

She moved into the water, let it sluice down her body. There wasn't enough room for her to move without touching

202

Fairfax. She let the comfort of his body soak into her through her skin. He made lather from a small bar of soap, picked up a washcloth and began to scrub her down.

The movement of his big, sure hands brought reality back. This shower had nothing in common with the locker she'd just escaped. The door wasn't locked, and the lights were on. And Fairfax was here, with his arms around her and his hands full of lather, making her human again.

His hands on her shoulders turned her around gently so she faced him. His face was expressionless except for a small furrow between his brows. His body spoke to her, though, with the steely erection trapped between them. And which he seemed, for the moment, to be ignoring.

He slid a hand behind her nape and eased her head back, fingers in her hair, so the flow of water drenched her scalp. Then he brought her head back up and scrubbed shampoo into her hair from a little bottle he'd picked up off the small shelf in the corner. She closed her eyes, no longer afraid, losing herself in the movement of his hands and the feel of his body against hers. His fingers in her hair were almost rough, scrubbing the shampoo down to her scalp. Finally he bent her head back again to rinse the suds from her hair.

When he drew her up straight, she opened her eyes. The furrow in his forehead had deepened, and a strange mix of emotion had come into his eyes. She wasn't sure if it was fear, or anger, or something else.

"Are you all right?" he said. She could barely hear him over the thunder of the shower.

She nodded. "I am now. Thank you."

"It shouldn't have happened," he said. "I shouldn't have let it happen."

"You can't protect me from everything. As much as we both might wish you could..." She trailed off as his hands came up to close her face between them. Her throat filled with tears, and the words struggled through them. "You can't protect me from what'll happen when we go back to Earth. There won't be a damn thing you can do about it."

His face hardened, the sensuous line of his mouth harsh. Then, hands tight on either side of her head, he turned her away from the flow of water and pushed her against the wall. His mouth came down on hers hard enough to bruise.

She flattened her hands against his chest, letting him overcome her, accepting his rough assertion of possession. For a time she'd thought never to taste his mouth again, and now she could taste nothing else. His body pinned hers to the wall. She couldn't have fought him if she tried. She had no desire to try.

He drew back and she closed her mouth, tasting the soft bruises he'd left behind. His arousal was hard and wet between them. His hands slid from her face to cover her breasts. He pressed closer to her and her thighs opened, loose and liquid, ready for him.

He pressed against her, then his whole body slid down as he went to his knees. Trieka clutched at the wall, eyes closed again, as he buried his face between her open thighs. With fingers and tongue, he took her with rough insistence. Sensation filled her body with fire, walking that delicate line which nearly crossed into pain, then rose and crested into ecstasy. Her hands twisted into his hair.

When finally she sagged over him, he rocked back on his heels, peering up at her. She felt herself shaking, soft aftershocks jolting inside her.

"Finish it," she whispered.

Fairfax rose to his feet, hands slipping a little on the wet walls as he levered himself up. Trieka looked down at her hands, at his red brown hair twined in her fingers. She raised her hands to let the water wash the strands away.

Fairfax, still with that strange anger lurking in his eyes, came hard up against her. His hands closed on her waist, then slid down under her buttocks and lifted her off the floor. With absolute trust, she wrapped herself around him. The embrace of her legs around his waist drew him close; a slight shift drew him inside. She opened her mouth against his wet throat, feeling his flesh against her lips and teeth. He felt huge inside her, a weapon sheathed. He drew back and impaled her as her body opened to him. It burned, and hurt for a moment as he drove deeper than she'd ever felt before.

Trieka lifted her head. His face was still set, his eyes closed, mouth a hard line. He opened his eyes as she looked at him, and she held his gaze, letting his fear and his anger and his pain flood into her.

And, suddenly, she possessed him as he possessed her, as he shuddered against her and emptied within her. His eyes closed again, his mouth opened on a silent cry. Then, still holding her hard against the wet ceramic wall, he buried his face in her shoulder and wept.

＊ ＊ ＊

They had barely dried and dressed when Lucas came pounding at the door.

"You decent?"

Fairfax, giving Trieka a wry look, went to open the door. Lucas stood outside, wearing his gum-chewing grin. "We matched the key," he said. "Get yourselves together and come to my office. You're going to want to see this."

＊ ＊ ＊

"The key opened a foot locker in one of the crew's quarters. Inside the locker was this."

Lucas held up a computer disk. Trieka edged closer to Fairfax, pressing her shoulder against his arm. He lifted his arm around her, and pulled her close.

"So what's on it?" she asked.

Lucas slid the disk into the drive. "Well, that's the interesting part."

Nervous, Trieka chewed a thumbnail as Lucas pulled up the contents of the disk. She could feel Fairfax's heartbeat against her shoulder. Due to the lack of chairs in Lucas's office, they stood behind Lucas, who was seated at the terminal. Trieka wished she had a chair—her legs still didn't feel quite right, and she ached from Fairfax's less than gentle lovemaking. Still, it had been therapeutic. She felt like a human being again.

"All right," Lucas said. "Here's the good stuff." He pulled up a file, which looked like a series of email messages. "These were sent to him in batches, all encrypted. Fortunately, Cain has a certain ability with decryption. I can't tell who sent the messages—the routing information has all been deleted, and the sender just signs himself, 'The General'. But he addressed our scar-faced friend as General also. Which is interesting, because his friends—who are tied up in one of the spare rooms, by the way—refer to him as Sergeant Austin."

"He was a plant," Trieka said. The remembered face loomed before her, the harsh features and the ragged scar.

"That's right." Lucas clicked open another file. "A plant carrying some very specific orders. First of all, under no circumstances was he to allow you or Fairfax to leave Denahault alive. Second, if something happened to disrupt the Grand Scheme—the general's words, not mine—he was to eliminate the entire team, including himself. Third, he was not to disclose any of the above to the rest of the team. So, you see—" Lucas leaned back in his chair "—if you hadn't killed him, we'd have nothing and nobody to take back to Earth to pound the last few nails into EarthFed's coffin."

✻ ✻ ✻

They went on to discuss details of escorting their prisoners back Earthside. Only a few minutes into the discussion, Trieka excused herself to return to the room.

"Will you be okay by yourself?" Fairfax asked, holding on to her fingers as if reluctant to let her go.

"I think so."

"All right. I'll see you in a bit."

In the room, she stripped and slid naked into the bed, comforted by the feel of clean sheets against clean skin in a wide bed. She spread across the mattress, taking up as much space as possible just because she could. She left the lights on.

It was quite some time later when she woke. Fairfax stood at the foot of the bed, pulling off his shirt. Trieka blinked up at him. He had bite marks on his shoulder. Her teeth, she assumed. She doubted Lucas had snacked on him.

"Go back to sleep," he whispered. "I'll be there in a minute."

She closed her eyes, but she was still awake when he tucked in beside her, moving her arms and legs to make room for himself. She curled up a little and backed toward him. His arms came around her and he spooned his body against her back.

"So they arrested Derocher," she said softly.

Fairfax squeezed her a little closer. "Derocher and a half-dozen others. We did good, Trieka. We're going to win."

"This round, at least." She fell silent. His hands moved over her, absently, then with obvious intent.

"Are you asleep?" he whispered.

"No," she said. "And I'm game, but you'll have to take it easy."

His hands stopped moving. "Did I hurt you before?"

"Yes."

He shifted, levering himself up on one elbow. She turned to face him. He looked distressed. "Trieka, I'm sorry—"

She touched his lips, stopping anything else he might have said. "Harrison, if you'd been hurting me enough to matter, I would have asked you to stop."

"But—"

"No buts. It happens. I'll be fine in the morning. But, in the meantime—"

He silenced her with his mouth. The kiss was soft and tender, careful. "I was so afraid I'd lost you." His voice was little more than a breath. "I had no intention of hurting you."

"I know."

"What would you like me to do?"

"Kiss it and make it better?"

He did, softly and thoroughly, bringing the pulse of fire to her not once, but three times before he lifted himself over her body. This time, when he came inside her, it was easy and slow, and even his own jolting release seemed to come in slow motion. When he was done, he rolled her carefully to her side and tucked her against his chest.

"I love you," he said. She fell asleep before she could answer.

Chapter Eighteen

"*This* is the great plan you came up with while I was sleeping?" Trieka looked at Lucas, incredulous.

"It'll work," Dr. Riley assured her. "They used to do it all the time to ship indentured servants to Cutter's Star."

"I think the key phrase there is 'used to'." Trieka wasn't sure why she was reacting so strongly, but she couldn't help it. Even Fairfax's steadying hand on her elbow did nothing to cool her down. "These are human beings we're talking about."

"That's debatable," Cain muttered from across the room.

Riley waved him to silence. "The procedure will cause no lasting effects to any of the prisoners. I use the tranquilizers on Cain on a regular basis. This will just be for a longer period of time. And as far as 'used to', it was the indentured servitude that was outlawed, not the method of transport."

"Plus it's the only way to get everybody onto the ship. And we won't have to worry about security," Lucas added.

Trieka shrugged. She finally realized why she'd protested in the first place. These people were EarthFed officers. As a military officer, she'd been conditioned to her last cell to respect and obey her superiors. Now she was talking about drugging them and stacking them like firewood in a cargo hold. Never mind who they'd killed, or who they'd had orders to kill. It didn't seem right.

"It's your ship," she finally said to Lucas. "Far be it from me to try to tell you how to run it."

Lucas shifted his gum and smiled a little. "I'm afraid you're going to have to put your military brainwashing aside for a while."

"Thanks for the advice."

Cain bristled at her dry sarcasm, but Lucas only grinned. "C'mon, Riley," he said. "Let's get the gear together."

Launch was scheduled for that afternoon, and preparations went smoothly. By one o'clock, Riley was rolling the EarthFed men up the cargo ramp on gurneys. Trieka watched in grim silence, then followed him into the ship to see what exactly was going on.

It wasn't as bad as she'd feared. The cargo hold was bigger than she'd imagined, and there was plenty of room for the men to be laid out on mats where they'd be secured with safety netting. The tranquilizer had been administered in a time-release patch. As satisfied as it was possible for her to get, Trieka retreated and left Riley to his work.

"They'll be okay," Fairfax assured her on the way back to their small cabin.

She sat down on the bed. "I don't know if I want them okay or dead."

He didn't smile, but the lines around his eyes softened a little. "Then you'll have to settle for okay."

At two, all the crew brought their gear onto the ship. Seeing her shipboard quarters, Trieka nearly had another panic attack. The prisoners in the cargo bay had more room—the place was little more than a closet. She laid her rucksack down on the minuscule bunk.

"This is a room?" Her voice wasn't as steady as she'd hoped.

Fairfax had been assigned separate quarters, but he'd come with her to help her settle. Now he paused by the door.

"You want me to stay?"

"Where would I put you?"

"You've never had trouble fitting me into small places before." He tossed his own rucksack on the floor, leaving himself with barely enough room to stand. "I'll stay until takeoff."

Takeoff had her worried. Used to the stately and careful maneuvers of the *Starchild*, blasting out of the atmosphere into a tiny and poorly charted jump site seemed to her like flirting with suicide. Lucas had reassured her that they did it all the time. It was much simpler and more fuel efficient to lift off into a jump site within the atmosphere than to break completely free of the planet, then travel to a larger site. Plus the opportunities for discovery were smaller. Trieka wasn't looking forward to the experience.

Finally she heard the engines rev. Riley came by to give Fairfax a tranquilizer, and made sure they were both strapped in. Trieka took the chair by the bed. It seemed sensible to let Fairfax have the bed, since he was going to be unconscious anyway. The tranquilizer had seemed the best option for him, considering his past experience with hyperspace sickness and the additional stress he was likely to experience with this kind of jump.

When the engines were prepared, the launch scaffolds in the docking bay rose, moving the ship to a vertical position. She found herself flat on her back, feet in the air as she shifted uncomfortably in the chair. Fairfax, drifting into oblivion, said muzzily, "Hey...neat."

He was completely under by liftoff. Even though he was unconscious, she still found his presence comforting. As soon as the ship had stabilized in hyperspace, Riley would come wake him up.

Trieka had never experienced this kind of hyperspace jump before. Academy instructors strongly advised against it—one of hers had even said it was impossible. She and Jeff had argued about it once.

"If you know what you're doing, there's no reason it should be any more dangerous than any other hyperspace jump," he'd insisted. Hyperspace navigational theory had been their last class of the day, and they'd always celebrated with cappuccino afterward.

"How can you say that?" Trieka's head already hurt just from sitting through the class. Jeff's arguments threatened to make it a migraine. "It's hard enough to gauge the stability of a regular route jump site—how can it possibly be safe to blast through a low-altitude splice barely a city block long?"

Jeff shrugged. "You have to know what you're doing. The only reason they talk against them is the only people who use them are black marketeers."

It was one of the few times she'd been on the conservative side of an argument with Jeff. Soon enough, she'd find out if he'd been right.

She felt it when they hit the jump site, just a split second before she heard it. The ship jolted hard to one side, with a scream like tearing metal. Her fingers drove into the arms of the chair. They'd misjudged the size or location of the splice, and left part of the hull behind in normal space. She poised her thumb above the release for the oxygen mask, expecting any minute to hear Lucas's voice over the intercom reporting their imminent demise.

There was nothing. The ship shuddered a bit more, and the engines settled into a particularly hideous wail. Then, gradually, the shuddering and wailing diminished.

Trieka's hands relaxed a little on the chair. They weren't dead yet, which was a good sign. Then again, maybe the pilot's compartment had been ripped away, and they were floating directionless through hyperspace or the upper atmosphere...

The intercom crackled.

"Well, folks," Lucas's voice announced, "that's about it. Unbuckle if you dare."

Letting out a sigh of relief, she loosened her restraining straps and leaned over to check Fairfax. He still slept soundly. Gently, she touched his face, digging the tips of her fingers into his beard. She'd been surprised at how fast it had grown. He'd gone from untidy to fully bearded in a matter of days. She didn't particularly like the way it looked on him, but she liked the way it felt sometimes.

The door buzzed just then, and she jumped. "Come in."

It was Riley. "How's the ride so far?"

"Okay, I guess. What was that noise?"

Riley grinned. "That was the ship being ripped apart."

"Pardon me?"

Riley laid his medical bag down on the bed at Fairfax's feet and snapped it open. "Any time a ship goes through a hyperspace jump point, there's a chance it'll get shredded in the process. We just happened to be close enough to that probability arc we could hear it. It happens a lot in these small splices."

"Well, I can't say it's pleasant." She folded her arms across her chest, watching intently as Riley sprayed a hypo against the inside of Fairfax's right elbow. "How is he?"

"He'll be fine. He'd wake up on his own in about an hour and a half, but this will cut that to about fifteen minutes." Finished with Fairfax, he turned to Trieka.

"I'm fine," she protested. "I'm used to this."

"I know, but the dynamics of this jump are a little different. It never hurts to check."

He checked her pulse and looked in her eyes with a penlight, then tested her reflexes.

"You seem to be all right," he concluded. "I'm going to leave a bottle of pills for Mr. Fairfax. He should take two as soon as he wakes up, then one in eight hours. After that, only if he experiences any nausea. If you feel nauseated, take one." He handed her a small amber bottle with a white cap. Twenty-five or so little white pills rattled inside it. "Call if you need me."

Fairfax drifted awake ten minutes later. Trieka got the pills into him almost before he woke up. He blinked at her, woozy. "Did we make it?"

Trieka smiled. "Only twelve days to go."

❋   ❋   ❋

Twelve days in the tiny ship wasn't as bad as two days in a locker in the dark, but it wasn't an experience Trieka cared to repeat. She was left with nothing to do but watch her hair turn red again. This infuriated her, accustomed as she was to having more shipboard duties than she could handle.

Fairfax seemed content to play games on the computer in the tiny lounge, but Trieka found the games annoying. Sex was, of course, an available option, but there was hardly any room in the tiny cabins. There wasn't enough room for them to sleep together, but she found it difficult to sleep without him. The tiny berth was barely comfortable, and she missed his warm bulk beside her.

Finally, they jolted out of hyperspace. Trieka was surprised to discover they'd used a legal jump site—in fact, the same one the *Starchild* had used on the way out from Earth. The small splices were practically impossible to hit on reentry, Lucas explained. The only tricky part of using a legal jump site was not getting caught.

"So where do we go from here?" she asked Lucas. He'd invited them to the cockpit to watch as they approached Earth. She stared blankly at it. Yes, it was beautiful, but it also held a good many questions she was afraid to hear the answers to.

"I have some legitimate docking permissions at New SanFran spaceport," Lucas said. Because of their cargo, they'd decided against his usual stop in the Gobi desert. "I think it'll be easier if we drop off there. I can't stay, though."

"Understood." Trieka looked at the green-blue planet with its shredded garment of clouds. "I want to thank you for all you've done, Lucas."

He looked at her sidelong. "I only wish I could do more."

"You could testify."

He chewed thoughtfully. "I don't think I want to endanger myself that way, but I'll think about it. For you."

She watched the Earth for a few more minutes, then Fairfax's voice on the intercom interrupted her reverie.

"You gotta see this, guys."

"What is it?" asked Trieka.

"MediaNet. We're getting Earth news like crazy."

※　※　※

"My God." Trieka breathed the words through the trembling in her stomach. She couldn't quite encompass the realization that she and Fairfax had brought this into being.

Eight more highly ranked officials in EarthFed, as well as two from the State Department and another half dozen from the FBI and CIA, had either been arrested or were under investigation. Another investigation was examining the role of the presidential cabinet and President Schumann himself.

So far no evidence had come to light indicting the president. Schumann indicated in interviews that he was solidly behind all proceedings and in favor of prosecuting everyone involved to the fullest extent of the law. Jenna Anderson had revealed her involvement in the investigation, but not her sources. Most shocking of all, the entire colonization wing of EarthFed had been placed under the control of an independent government committee pending evaluation. Editorials fielded rumors that the entire organization would be privatized.

One article from the New SanFran office speculated on the whereabouts of Harrison Fairfax. Another, briefer article from Chicago mentioned Trieka's continued absence.

She looked at Fairfax. He was grinning broadly, but there was a feral thinness to his mouth.

"Those bastards are gonna pay," he said. "They're gonna pay."

But Trieka couldn't stop thinking about one line in the Chicago article, a quote from her new commanding officer, Admiral Carlisle.

"Wherever Captain Cavendish is right now, I'm afraid we have no choice but to consider her AWOL."

Her hand found Fairfax's and squeezed it hard. He looked at her, grin fading. She was afraid to look back. Her day of reckoning was only a few hours away.

Eighteen hours to be exact. It would take that long to travel from the jump site. Once they landed, Lucas would turn over the prisoners and then disappear. As Trieka understood it, he had allies among the local police who would prevent the seizure of his ship. He planned to be off planet within eight hours.

Shipboard night was declared an hour early to prepare for the adjustment to Pacific Time. Trieka's body, though, refused to adjust. She lay down for a few minutes with her eyes closed, to no avail. Finally she flung back the blanket, got up and crossed the narrow passageway to Fairfax's room.

He was a moment answering the door, and the slight bleariness in his eyes confirmed her suspicion that he'd been sleeping. He was wearing a bathrobe.

"Trieka," he said, not sounding particularly surprised.

"I can't sleep."

"Come in."

214

He moved aside to let her in, then closed the door behind her. "What's wrong?"

She sat on his bed, folding her arms across her chest. "I'm scared."

He eased down next to her, resting an arm across her shoulders. Trieka almost wanted him to lie to her, to tell her everything was going to be all right. Instead, he drew her close, pressing her face against his chest. She found solace in his heartbeat. After a time, her hands strayed and found their way past his robe to his skin.

His warm skin and rough hair ignited her, and she bore him back onto the narrow bed with a ferocity that surprised even herself. He moved with her, letting her use him as she would. With him deep inside her, and his arms around her, she felt almost invulnerable.

When she finally relaxed against him, she let the feeling soak into her. Perhaps she could make it last.

A pity she couldn't make it reality.

They landed precisely on schedule in dock fourteen of the New SanFran spaceport. Trieka gathered the last of her belongings into her rucksack. The fear had faded into a stony, calm acceptance. Fairfax came to fetch her and she took his arm, walking close to him as they left the small ship.

Amazingly, there was no sign of any law enforcement personnel anywhere in the docking area. Assisted by a handful of the spaceport's ground crew, Lucas and Riley brought the EarthFed prisoners into a security holding area just outside the dock. A port doctor was waiting. Riley conferred with him for a few minutes, then went back to the ship.

Exactly thirty minutes after landing, Lucas and crew were gone, headed for their usual dock in the Gobi desert. Fifteen minutes after that, the dock was swarming with military police. The EarthFed prisoners were waking up by then. They'd all been cuffed at wrist and ankle, though, so they posed no danger to the doctor. Nevertheless, Trieka and Fairfax lingered in the room along with port security, just in case.

One of the MPs, apparently the highest ranked of the bunch, assessed the situation, barked a few orders, then turned to Trieka. His companions headed for the prisoners and began to take information and confiscate IDs.

The MP spared a glance for Fairfax, but most of his attention was on Trieka. He was a big man, not as tall as Fairfax, but broader. His black eyes seemed to hold no expression at all, but his mobile mouth betrayed something that flickered from amusement to anger and back.

"Captain Cavendish?" he said. She nodded. "I'm Corporal Neumann. Could you tell me what's going on here?"

She felt her posture shift automatically. "Corporal, these men have all been taken into custody on numerous charges, including kidnapping, endangering the life of a military officer and possible involvement in the murder of a State Department official and a civilian. They've also been directly involved in the planned genocide of the native peoples of Denahault."

Neumann's eyes widened fractionally before he regained control and nodded. "All right. We'll get them processed and shipped to a local facility pending formal charges." Neumann reached behind him, unfastening a pair of handcuffs from his belt. "And you'll come with me." He took her arm, turning her around. Trieka clamped her teeth together, hard, as the cuffs closed around her wrists.

"What the hell is this?"

Trieka looked up at Fairfax, wondering if he honestly didn't know. He did, though. She could see it in his eyes. But she loved him for making the protest.

The MP eyed him with a little flicker of anger. "May I ask who you are, sir?"

"Harrison Fairfax."

Neumann gave him a quick once-over, obviously doubting that this bedraggled man could be Billionaire Financier Harrison Fairfax. "Mr. Fairfax, we've been under standing orders to arrest Captain Cavendish on charges of desertion, dereliction of duty and possible kidnapping."

Fairfax straightened, giving Neumann a look that would have made lesser men shrivel into their basic carbon components. Neumann didn't even flinch.

"Pending formal charges, of course," he added. He took Trieka's elbow. Fairfax stopped them both with a hand on Trieka's shoulder. When he spoke, though, the words were directed at Neumann.

"You'll be hearing from my lawyer."

He squeezed Trieka's shoulder firmly, then let her go. She let Neumann lead her across the dock to his waiting aircar. She looked back once, to see Fairfax watching her. His mouth was tight, his fists clenched at his sides. Blinking back tears, Trieka let Neumann put her into the back seat of the vehicle.

Whoever your lawyer is, Fairfax, I hope to God he's a good one.

Chapter Nineteen

Fairfax took a cab home. His neighborhood was one of the few which had survived the quake. He and Kathi had bought the house shortly after their marriage. Like most of his life, it held far too many memories, but he'd seen no reason to let it go. He liked the relatively secure, affluent neighborhood, and he'd sunk a lot of money into the sweeping, two-acre lawn.

Secure neighborhood or not, there appeared to have been some vandalism in his absence—the stained glass rosette window above the six-foot-wide double doors had lost about half its panels. The empty spaces had been covered with cardboard. Fairfax squinted up at the ruined window. There was a good hundred grand down the toilet.

The security system still appeared to be working, though. A small red light blinked under the retinal scanner. Fairfax looked into the scanner as he entered his personal security code into the keypad. The system hummed a moment.

"Good afternoon, Mr. Fairfax." The voice came from a speaker just above the door, a tinny, male voice with very little inflection.

"Yeah, whatever," said Fairfax, and pushed open the right-hand side of the now unlocked double door.

He took his shoes off in the entryway. The slate floor was cold even through his socks. In fact, the whole house was cold. Fairfax shouldered his rucksack and trudged across the width of the foyer to the thermostat. He'd made it halfway across the room when he heard a loud scrabbling on the staircase.

"Hey!" a voice shouted from the shadows above. Fairfax stopped, looking up. A man barreled down the wide stairs. He wore a flannel shirt and jeans with no knees. His face was partially obscured by a tangle of dirty-blond hair. "One more step and I'm calling the cops."

Fairfax lifted a hand in a casual wave. "Nice to see you, too, Madison."

Madison skidded to a stop, nearly losing his footing on the stairs. "Fairfax, is that you?"

"Yeah, it's me."

"You scared me to death. What's with the beard?"

"It's a long story." Fairfax finished his trek to the thermostat. It was set at sixty-five. He turned it up to sixty-eight, then shrugged and pushed it to seventy. What the hell— he could afford it. At least, he hoped he could.

"Do me a favor, Madison," he said.

"Yeah, sure."

"Call Felicity. Tell her to meet me here at eight tonight. I have a case for her."

Madison pushed his hair out of his face. "Yeah, so, uh, what are you going to do?"

"Take a nap. I'll explain everything when I get up."

Fairfax hadn't realized how exhausted he was until his feet hit his own floor, and his body hit his own bed. In spite of the anger and fear, and the recurring image of Trieka, cuffed, he fell into a deep and sudden sleep.

The clock by the bed read seven-thirty when he woke. He lay still for a time. The huge silences of the house bore down on him. He'd slept alone in this bed for seven years. He'd gotten used to it. Now, it felt lonely.

Finally he rolled out of bed and headed downstairs to the kitchen, following the impatient demands of his stomach.

The kitchen seemed too big, too bright, too uncluttered. He couldn't help thinking of the Taylors' small, homey kitchen with herbs on strings and the wood burning stove. This sleek, modern room was a world away, literally and figuratively.

Madison sat at the big oak table amidst a sprawl of papers and books. He'd started a legitimate freelance business a few months after Fairfax had sprung him from jail. In return for upkeep of the house while he was gone, Fairfax let him use the computer equipment and live in the house full-time for a ridiculously low rent. It was worth it to Fairfax to know someone reliable was watching his property. And Madison, in addition to being preternaturally good with computers, had turned out to be a better than fair gardener.

"Big job?" Fairfax said, indicating the mess on the table with a wave of his hand.

"Huge. The writer lady down the street is working on some huge romantic epic. She wants me to do her online research for her and write a database to organize it." He turned toward Fairfax, who had opened the refrigerator and was peering inside. "I made sandwiches. There's a couple extra in there for you."

"Thanks," Fairfax said. He pulled out the plate of sandwiches and a beer. Madison moved a few paper piles aside to make room for him at the table. "She paying you well?"

"Not as well as the Feds used to."

"The advantage, of course, being that she realizes she's paying you and isn't too likely to demand you return it."

"True."

Madison was silent for a time while Fairfax industriously took the edge off his hunger. The sandwiches Madison had left for him were roast beef with lettuce and tomato and enough horseradish to make Fairfax's eyes water. In short, his favorite. He devoured one, then stopped to blow his nose.

"So how was your trip?"

He eyed Madison, trying to judge his sincerity. There was no way a hacker like Madison wouldn't have been following MediaNet over the last couple of months.

"Well, let's see." He took a bite from the second sandwich and chewed thoughtfully. "I was kidnapped, beaten, rescued, adopted into an alien tribe, tattooed and brought back several EarthFed officials who are, even now, being brought up on charges."

"You got a tattoo? Wild."

Fairfax laughed and went back to his sandwich. As he ate, though, his thoughts sobered. He finished the sandwich and took a long swig from the beer can. "I found out what happened to Kathi."

Madison looked up, any remaining levity fading from his face. "What happened?"

"They killed her. Her father, too."

"I'm sorry."

Fairfax shrugged. He picked up the beer can and turned it in his hand, waiting for the pain to return to the place he'd made for it, back behind his heart. After a moment, Madison cleared his throat.

"That alien tribe part—you were kidding, right?"

Fairfax shook his head. Madison, eyes widening, opened his mouth. The sound of the front doorbell came out. Madison snapped his mouth shut.

"That would be Felicity," Fairfax said. "She's early."

"I'll get it," said Madison. "Finish your beer."

"Thanks. Take her to the library."

Felicity Barrett was arguably the most respected defense attorney in the country. Rumor had it she was descended from Thurgood Marshall. Her father had been the youngest four-star general in the history of the US Army. In addition, she and Fairfax had a history.

They'd met in college, unfortunately before Fairfax had developed his theories regarding intimidating women. They'd become friends, though, and Felicity had defended him in a series of lawsuits. Although she'd lacked experience, Fairfax had hired her as his regular attorney. After Kathi's disappearance, she'd dealt with the complexities of settling the estate.

And, a few years later, she and Fairfax had teetered on the edge of an affair. They'd gotten as far as meeting at a hotel, then Fairfax had backed out. He still wasn't completely sure why.

Looking at her now, as she sat in his mahogany and velvet library, he felt, as usual, that small pang of regret. She smiled when he came in, and he reached out to take her hand. She was tall and elegant and beautiful, with café au lait skin and straight, dark brown hair. Her hand was warm and welcome in his.

"Good to see you," he said.

"Good to see you," she replied, with no little emotion. "I was beginning to wonder if we'd ever hear from you again."

He sat down across from her in a velvet-upholstered wingback chair. "Let's just say it was an interesting trip."

Madison came in then, carrying a pot of water for the coffee machine on the table by Fairfax's chair. He also had a bag of coffee. By the smell, he'd just ground it.

"Thought you two might like some of this," he said. He put the requisite pieces together and turned on the machine. Felicity smiled at him.

"Quite a change in career, eh, Madison?"

Madison grinned. "Hey, I get good food and a great place to live. And Fairfax always keeps his computer equipment updated. It's geek Nirvana."

"Just so he doesn't trust you with a modem."

Madison just laughed. Satisfied the coffee was progressing properly, he started toward the door.

"Why don't you stay?" Fairfax said. "You might be interested in hearing this story."

Madison shrugged and sat down.

Fairfax told Felicity everything—or at least everything that wouldn't get him arrested. She listened raptly, as did Madison, occasionally shaking her head or making a small hum of sympathy or amazement. Finally, Fairfax leaned back in his chair, drained. "So that's it. They arrested her, and I'm not going to sit by and watch her be railroaded. Or worse."

Felicity shook her head slowly. "Well, thanks to Dad, I've had some military experience. I'll do what I can, but I have to tell you, I'm in the middle of a pretty high-profile case right now."

Fairfax scratched at his beard. "Nothing to do with the EarthFed scandals, I hope?"

"No. It's a Hollywood case." She waved it off, making a delicately annoyed face. Fairfax knew she didn't like the publicity or the pressure of celebrity lawyering, but she was consummately good at it, and in great demand.

"Whatever you can do, Felicity, it's enough, and it's appreciated." He hesitated. "What—honestly—what do you think will happen?"

Felicity shrugged. "I don't know. She had noble and reasonable motives for what she did. But it's a military issue, and they use different rules. With the political maelstrom surrounding this case, though, I doubt she'll end up in jail."

Fairfax nodded. "Let's hope you're right."

It was late by the time they finished. Fairfax saw Felicity to the door. She turned to face him on the front step as he stood in the doorway, letting the night come in.

"I'm sure they'll want you to testify," she said. "Let me know what they want and I'll advise you when the time comes."

"Thank you."

She started to turn, then hesitated, turned back. "One more thing. However this turns out, I'm really glad you found her. It's obvious she's been good for you."

Fairfax wasn't entirely sure what she meant, so he only smiled and said good-bye.

※ ※ ※

Trieka woke at 0500, as did everyone else in the military holding facility. The wake-up call blared through the intercom in the corridor outside her cell. The raucous wail made her head ache.

She sat up in bed, rubbing her eyes. Looking out the front of her cell, she saw only a blank wall. They had put her in a cell by herself at the end of the block. The EarthFed thugs they'd brought from Denahault were also in the facility, and the MPs had decided it would be best if Trieka was out of eyeshot.

Thank God for small favors. There were worse places she could spend the next few years, she supposed. At least there was room to walk, and a toilet, and light to see by.

The MPs brought breakfast. It wasn't the most appetizing fare, but she ate it. She supposed if she'd been in an ordinary prison, they probably would have escorted her straight out for exercise or to the work rooms. But this was just a holding facility, albeit a large one, so they woke her up at 0500, fed her breakfast and left her to her own devices.

At 0700, one of the guards was decent enough to bring her a book. It was, however, a courtroom drama, and she had no desire to read it. Finally, she got up and started doing calisthenics in the middle of the small cell.

It was nearly 0800, and she'd worked up a respectable sweat, when the guard returned. This time she was carrying a security card and slid it through the reader of Trieka's cell.

"There's someone here to see you," the guard said.

Trieka wiped her face on a sweat-soaked shirtsleeve. "Who?" Fairfax, she hoped.

"A lawyer."

Trieka nodded. Fairfax's lawyer, then. She wondered what Fairfax was doing. Probably sleeping, lucky man.

The guard swung the cell door open and led her out.

"Or perhaps I should say *the* lawyer," she added, giving Trieka the slightest quirk of a smile.

Trieka frowned. "Who is it?"

"You'll see." The guard turned left down a hallway. A bright red "Exit" sign hung above the door. So far, every cell they'd passed had been empty. "Let's just say you must have some pretty interesting connections."

Through the exit door was another small hallway with three doors on either wall. The door at the end of the hallway bore another Exit sign and a huge locking mechanism complete with a facemask for retinal ID verification. The guard unlocked the second door on the right and let Trieka in.

In spite of the guard's comments, Trieka was surprised to see a familiar face. She'd certainly never met Felicity Barrett in person, but she'd seen her on TV and over MediaNet enough to recognize her.

Two years ago, Barrett had handled a murder case in which the suspect was a well-known actor. The trial had gone on for ages, most of it televised. Jeff had been addicted. Trieka had been offended by the hype around the trial, but impressed by

Barrett herself. She'd proven her client innocent without any of the usual histrionics or focusing the case on discrediting the prosecution's witnesses. Trieka still wasn't a hundred percent sure the suspect hadn't committed the crime, but she'd been amazed at Barrett's integrity and her charisma.

That charisma hit her in a wave as she entered the room. Felicity Barrett stood and extended a hand across the small conference table. She was smaller than Trieka had imagined, about Trieka's own height, her handshake firm as a man's. Her straight brown-black hair was pulled back in a simple ponytail, her café au lait skin only minimally enhanced by cosmetics. Amber-brown eyes held reassurance, and she smiled a little.

"Captain Cavendish," she said. "I'm Felicity Barrett."

"Yes, I know. Did Fairfax send you?"

Felicity's smile widened. "Mr. Fairfax and I go back a long way. I knew him in college."

"Really?" Trieka released Felicity's hand and sat down. The attorney settled across from her. "I'll bet you're still charging him a mint."

Felicity shrugged. "What's a few dollars here and there between friends?"

Trieka felt herself stiffening. She appreciated Fairfax's gesture, but she didn't want to be dependent on him. She loved him, but she didn't want to need him. Not this way.

"I don't think I really need your help or his. I'm being represented by a military lawyer. I hear he's a good one."

"Not as good as me." She wasn't bragging. She stated a plain fact. She opened her briefcase, removing a computer pad. "I'm planning a bargaining proposal with the prosecutors handling the EarthFed officers." Felicity smiled. "I think we'll be able to work something out."

Trieka considered. She'd be an idiot to turn it down. She needed all the help she could get. On the other hand, what would the media make of all this? They'd probably have a field day.

Since when did she care about the media? They'd have a field day no matter what. If she was really that concerned about the media, she should never have gotten involved with Fairfax in the first place.

"All right," she said. "I appreciate whatever you can do for me."

"That's good. I think I can do a lot." Felicity laid her briefcase on the table and opened it. "Now, Harrison told me his story. Why don't you tell me yours, and we'll go from there?"

※ ※ ※

It was nearly ten when Trieka finally returned to the small cell. Felicity had left a few books more to Trieka's taste—a science fiction epic and a short biography of Vedder Farhallen. She spent the afternoon reading, then started into another exercise routine an hour or so before dinner. She had a feeling she'd be turning in early tonight.

Just after dinner, Felicity returned.

"Good news and bad news," she told Trieka. "The good news is I think we're going to pull together a good deal. Bad news—we won't know for sure until some time tomorrow."

"So I'm stuck here for another night."

"That's right." She picked her briefcase up off the floor and laid it on the table. "Want more books?"

"No, I'm fine, thanks."

"Anything else I can get or do for you?"

Trieka hesitated, looking at her hands on the table. They looked so small and helpless. Always before she'd thought of them as able, maybe even strong.

"Why haven't I heard from Fairfax?" The quaver in her voice surprised her.

Felicity reached across the table and laid her hand on Trieka's. Trieka's looked pale, almost ethereal, against her darker skin. "He's trying not to attract undue attention to you. He hasn't officially announced his return yet, although there are rumors flying everywhere. He's afraid even a phone call might bring the media swarming in here."

"And sending you doesn't attract attention?"

"It's a little easier for me. I have official business and, when I'm on official business, I demand professionalism. Everyone knows that. Plus I've been sneaking in and out." She grinned. "Don't worry—Harrison has been calling for updates nearly every hour. If things work out, you should be seeing him some time tomorrow."

Trieka let out a breath, unaware until then she'd been holding it. What had she been afraid of?

"I want to thank you for all you've done," she said, turning her hand over to grasp Felicity's.

"No need," Felicity said. "I'm glad to help."

※ ※ ※

She slept well that night, thanks to the exercise, and when she was awakened at five the next morning, she felt rested and alert. And then there was nothing to do but wait.

A guard came for her at ten, but instead of taking her to the conference room, he led her to the bank of private phones down the next hallway. Three of the half-dozen booths were in use—by lawyers, it appeared—but one of the empty booths held a vidphone off the hook. The picture had faded to gray, with a message that read, "Press button to resume picture transmission". The guard opened the booth door and gestured for her to enter.

"One thing I'll say is," the guard said, "you get the most interesting visitors."

With a wry smile, Trieka closed the door behind her and was instantly cocooned in silence. She pressed the button to resume the picture. The gray screen resolved into a slightly blurred color image of Fairfax. He'd shaved, cut his hair and was wearing a dark blue sweater.

"Hey," he said.

Tears pricked her eyes. "Hey. You clean up nice."

And he did look good. She'd become so accustomed to seeing him filthy and scruffy, she'd forgotten what he looked like clean and shaved. He lifted his hands into the picture and spoke in the language of the White Fur People.

"When you get out of there, I'm going to strip you naked and make you forget you've ever had another man."

Trieka smiled, a little weak in the belly. "I forgot a long time ago." The shapes of the words came easily to her, even after weeks of neglect. To her surprise, he continued the conversation with his hands.

"Are they treating you well?"

"Well enough. I'm bored, though."

"I talked to..." He paused, then said with a slight grin, "Light Brown Law Woman. She's working on a deal. It'll be good for you and for all of us. I can't say anything now, but she'll tell you." He hesitated. "I love you, Fire Hair."

"I love you," she replied, and one of the tears fell.

"Take care of yourself," he said aloud. "I'll see you soon."

"Thank you, Harrison," she said. He smiled a little, and the picture clicked off.

Trieka sat for a moment, looking at the glass screen, then opened the booth door and slid out. The guard gave her an odd look.

"I didn't know he was deaf."

Trieka carefully daubed a tear from her eye, trying to make it look like just an itch. "He's not."

With another odd look, the guard led her back to her cell.

Chapter Twenty

It was 1800 hours, and Trieka had given up on hearing anything from anyone when the guard arrived again. Trieka stood, too quickly. Her head went light and her dinner sank hard into the base of her stomach, making her suddenly sick.

"Good news," said the guard, and smiled a little, but said nothing else as she led Trieka to the conference rooms. Trieka felt her stomach subside, but she didn't press for more information.

Expecting to see Felicity Barrett, she couldn't suppress a small "Oh!" of surprise when Fairfax stood up behind the conference table. The guard gave him a smile and left them alone.

She moved quickly around the table and into his arms, clutching him tightly against her. He returned her embrace, perhaps a bit too tightly. His arms were strong and hard around her. He smelled clean and male, with a faint undertone of cologne she couldn't identify. After a time, she moved back, so she could look at his face.

"Boy, are you a sight for sore eyes," she said.

He smiled, then bent to kiss her gently. "I suppose you were expecting Felicity?"

"Yes, actually."

He sat back down in his chair, pulling her close to him, between his thighs. She sat down on his leg and let him hold her. "She's cut a deal," he said. "You're free to go on two conditions. First, you agree to testify against the EarthFed officers we brought home from Denahault. Second, you can't leave New SanFran until the hearings are over."

She frowned. "Where will I go? I can't afford a hotel, and my mom's in Chicago..."

He squeezed her gently. "You can stay with me."

"I don't want to impose—"

"Oh, please. It's no imposition." He kissed her again, this time letting his tongue trace the space where their lips met. "Besides, I'm sure we can arrange some kind of compensation."

She had reservations—she still didn't like the idea of being in his debt—but, again, she didn't see that she had much choice. "All right. But I want it understood that it's temporary."

Fairfax shrugged. "Sure. Until we can make it legal."

She decided to leave that comment alone. She didn't want to deal with that kind of complication right now. "What else is involved in this deal?"

"After the trial, there'll be a hearing to decide if you should be charged with desertion." He waved off her sudden scowl of concern. "Felicity says it's just a formality. You'll be acquitted."

Trieka swallowed. A few stray thoughts drifted across her mind, swiftly quelled. That was something else she could think about later, when she was calmer, and had some distance from the situation.

"So what do we do now?" she said.

"We go get your stuff," he said, "and we go home."

They checked out her box of possessions. The guards eyed Fairfax with frank curiosity, but were polite enough to say nothing. The MP in charge handed him the sign out sheet and said, "Please sign here, Mr. Fairfax." Other than that, there was no mention of Fairfax's identity.

He signed, then pulled a pair of sunglasses out of a breast pocket. He also drew a hat from under his sweater and donned that, pulling it low over his eyes. It was a soft felt fedora, gray and well made. Trieka found herself wondering if he had anything at home she could wear. If he did, she'd probably be afraid to move for fear of ruining it and adding another thousand dollars to her tab.

It was surprisingly quiet outside the holding facility. Fairfax's car—a late-model Mercedes aircar—was parked at the curb. She'd half expected him to have a chauffeur, but the car was empty.

A handful of TV reporters lingered outside, but they stayed a respectful distance back. No one tried to stick a microphone in her face. Nevertheless, she had a strong urge to cover her face. Instead, she held herself militarily straight and looked right at the cameras, with the expression she used when faced with insubordination.

Fairfax waved at one of the reporters as he opened the car door for her. Suddenly, Trieka noticed what was missing—his left hand was bare. Strangely, she felt tears rise.

He came around the front and settled behind the wheel. Trying not to look at his hands, she rubbed the soft leather upholstery.

"Nice car," she said.

"Thanks."

"The piranhas behaved themselves remarkably well."

He nodded. "I gave them an impromptu press conference beforehand, with the understanding that they'd leave you alone. The ones still there were friends of Kathi's."

"A press conference? What did you say?"

His mouth quirked. "'No comment', mostly. But I did put in a good word for the White Fur People. And for you." He paused, watching the traffic as he eased out onto the highway. "You'll see it tonight on TV."

"You have one?"

"I have four. One's a 3D widescreen, and one—" He broke himself off to adjust the automatic navigator. "One is in the bedroom."

"Why am I not surprised?"

He grinned, leaning back in the driver's seat while the car drove itself. "I'd dim out the windows and suggest we get in the back seat, but we're only about ten minutes from home."

Trieka prickled pleasantly at the thought. "Like you'd last that long."

His soft, warm chuckle increased the prickling exponentially. She reached across to touch his shoulder and he leaned toward her, capturing her mouth with his. He pressed closer, deepening the kiss until she drowned in it. After only two days without him, she felt like a piece of her body had been removed, then returned.

The windows weren't dimmed, and she was sure they garnered a few stares as he slipped his hand under her shirt, but she didn't care. His big hand cupped her bare breast, her nipple hardening against his palm. He shifted a little, his tongue soft but urgent in her mouth, his thumb and forefinger pressing her nipple. She tasted him, fully and insistently, then leaned away from him.

"Harrison—"

A sharp "bing" cut Trieka off, followed by a female voice. "Navigational control will be returned to driver in sixty seconds. Attention—navigational control will be returned to driver in sixty seconds."

Fairfax slid back into his seat, rolling his eyes. "Pushy broad."

He steered off the highway. Two turns later, they had entered what Trieka could only describe as the right side of the tracks.

Wrought iron fences separated immaculately landscaped lawns from the street. The houses themselves were set far back into the yards, some so far back she couldn't see them. Those that were visible were palatial.

About two miles down the road, Fairfax pulled into a driveway. An automatic controller on the dashboard opened the gate that stretched across the drive about a hundred yards from the street. The house itself was set back a good half-acre. Trieka couldn't even begin to guess how much the place was worth, but it had to be in the multi-millions. It was built of gold-colored brick, with white trim. A stained-glass rosette above the wide main doors had been broken in several places and patched with cardboard. She gave a low whistle.

"You like?" Fairfax said. He looked at her, waiting for her reaction, one side of his mouth betraying a smile.

"How many people do you have living in this place?" She pictured a bevy of servants and accountants, groundskeepers and cooks. She wondered if there was a stable behind the house.

Fairfax shrugged. He pushed a button on the dashboard

and the far right-hand door of the four-car garage began to slide open. "Just you, me, a caretaker and my harem."

"Your harem," she repeated, then snorted. "That, I believe."

He laughed, then pointed the car at the open garage door and drove in. There were two other cars in the garage—a two- or three-year-old BMW Aircar 650 and a classic Porsche 944 with actual wheels. "Jealous, are we?"

She peered out the window at the bright red Porsche. "Only of that car. Can we go for a ride?"

"Not today. The engine needs some work." He put the Mercedes in park and killed the engine. "I don't know about you, but I'm hungry. Let's get something to eat."

"I'm not hungry. The prison food pretty much killed my appetite." She followed him to the door leading into the house. He deactivated the security system, and she trailed inside.

The door led into a small anteroom—it would have been a mudroom in a lesser dwelling—which opened into the kitchen. She couldn't help staring. The room was huge, with enough cabinet and cupboard space for three kitchens. Everything gleamed. The pale wooden floors looked like they'd been recently refinished. The countertops were white, the cabinets heavy oak. Fairfax walked straight to the refrigerator.

"Bologna?" he asked.

She shook her head, having expected pâté or filet mignon, not middle-class lunchmeat. "I'm really not hungry."

He fished out a trio of plastic containers and set them on the counter. "Something to drink, then?"

"I'd kill for a cola."

"No need." He took an unopened glass bottle out of the fridge and handed it to her. "Glass? Or do you prefer to drink it the civilized way?"

"Give me a bottle opener and I'm happy."

She sat down to drink her cola, watching him assemble a sandwich out of leftover cold cuts. "You never answered my question."

"Which one?"

"About who's living here."

"Just you, me and Madison."

"Who's Madison?"

"Madison Jeffries. His real name—" Fairfax paused to scrape the last of the mayonnaise from the jar—a task which apparently required no little concentration. "His real name is Robert Berger, aka Brainsucker Bob."

Trieka choked on her drink. Hacking into her hand, she managed, "*The* Brainsucker Bob?" She swallowed, settling her throat. "The guy who hacked four billion dollars from the US government before he was caught?"

Fairfax, having assembled his sandwich, sat down to eat. "That would be him. He also propagated a very interesting computer virus that caused pictures of naked women to appear randomly on the screen. For a virus, it was pretty popular."

"Didn't he get into trouble with the State Department once, too?"

Fairfax nodded. "He hacked into some sensitive documents. He's also been in trouble with the phone company and several major credit card companies for revising his own bills." He took a bite, chewed, then said, quite seriously, "He's gone straight now, though."

Trieka eyed him, trying to read the deliberately blank expression. "Except for maybe a few projects for the guy who got him out of jail?"

"Maybe a few."

"I wondered where you'd learned to hack."

"From the master."

The object of their discussion breezed in just then, coming to a quick halt when he saw he wasn't alone.

"Hey, Fairfax," he said. "I didn't know you were here."

"Captain Trieka Cavendish, meet Madison."

"Hello, Madison." He didn't look much more than twenty-five with his Soul Crushers T-shirt and ripped jeans. The long blond hair and earring didn't help either. Used to military demeanor, Trieka found him a bit offensive.

"Nice to meet you, Captain Cavendish. Fairfax told me you were coming. I went out this afternoon and got some things for you. They're up in the master bath. If you need anything else, or anything different, just let me know."

Well, maybe not so offensive. "Thank you, Madison. That was very considerate of you."

Madison shrugged, grinning. "It's my job." He opened the refrigerator and took out a beer. "I'll be in the study if you need me."

Trieka watched him go, intrigued. "What is he now, your butler?"

"Caretaker." Fairfax finished his sandwich. "Let's go see what he picked up for you. I sent a list with him, but God only knows if he looked at it."

Feeling like she was in a museum, Trieka trailed after Fairfax, across the huge living room and up the wide staircase. It wasn't until she was halfway up the stairs that she realized she recognized the place. She froze, suddenly woozy, grabbing the stair rail for support. Fairfax caught her other arm, looking at her with some concern.

"Are you all right?"

She blinked away the dizzying sense of déjà vu. The dream—or had it been a vision?—swam in broken images behind her eyes. What did it mean? She'd come to him, here, in this room, and then she'd left him, in tears.

"I... I had a dream..." She trailed off. She couldn't tell him. It was too bizarre, too ridiculous. "Never mind. I had a weird déjà vu, that's all."

He drew her closer to him, his hand reassuring on her arm. "Just means you were meant to be here." She still clung to the stair rail; he urged her on. "Come on. You probably could use some rest."

He was right about that. Still uneasy, she let him lead her the rest of the way up the stairs.

Even the hallway was overwhelming, wider than it needed to be and hung with remarkably realistic re-creations of the Bayeux Tapestry. The master bedroom was bigger than most of the apartments she'd lived in. The king-sized bed faced a fireplace. Bay windows next to it looked out over a huge, naturally landscaped yard filled with wildflowers. The bed itself was a massive cherry four-poster.

"This is beautiful," she breathed. "I could get lost in that bed."

"Don't worry. I'll find you."

He opened the door to the bathroom—another oversized room full of marble and gleaming porcelain. Trieka nodded approval at the huge Jacuzzi tub and separate shower stall. The counter was pale lavender with two sinks. Next to one sink sat a collection of masculine toiletries—a razor, shaving gel, cologne. By the cologne was a small pewter dish shaped like a shell, within it Fairfax's wedding ring. She smiled a little, glad he hadn't gotten rid of it.

Madison's handiwork sat in a row next to the other sink: three different shampoos, four conditioners, deodorant, shower gel, hair spray, two moisturizers, a loofah, bath salts, bubble bath and a half dozen beauty bars.

"I guess he wasn't taking any chances," she said.

"Is any of that stuff okay?"

"I'm really not picky." She ran a hand along the slick surface of the sink. "This is very pretty. How long have you had this house?"

"Kathi and I bought it right after we got married. She did most of the decorating."

Trieka withdrew her hand, feeling suddenly awkward. "I'm sorry."

Fairfax shrugged. "It's all right." He embraced her with one arm, gently squeezing her shoulder. "Let's go watch some TV."

Trieka hadn't seen the TV when they'd come in. With good reason—it was inside the cherry armoire. Fairfax picked up the remote and flopped down on the bed. Hesitant, she sat next to him, feeling strange and out of place. This was his territory, the place where he'd lived and loved with his wife. She felt as if he were slipping away from her.

He turned the TV on to the news, which was just starting. "There," he said, pointing. "There I am, making a fool of myself." The station was showing a clip from the impromptu news conference as a teaser for the broadcast. After the preview, the report segued into Fairfax as the lead story. He turned up the volume.

"There's been a great injustice done on Denahault." Trieka sat up straighter, surprised at the strength of his voice and stance. She'd forgotten how he could emote when he needed to.

"Not only have we been lied to, not only have innocent people died, but EarthFed has sanctified a program of genocide. Intelligent life on Denahault is being destroyed wantonly with the approval of the local government. If nothing else comes from this incident, this must be stopped."

The newscast cut away then, to discuss how reliable Fairfax was in his reports of intelligent life on Denahault. They concluded with a brief summary of proceedings in the indictment of Admiral Derocher and his cohorts, and mentioned Trieka's release. A short clip showed her getting into Fairfax's Mercedes, spearing the camera with a direct glare.

"I really don't like being on TV," Trieka said.

"You were lovely. Frightening, but lovely."

He switched channels to a comedy she'd never seen before, then scooted back on the bed, gesturing for her to join him. She slid close, letting him tuck her under his arm. Thinking it would be nice to make love in this wide bed, on the satin sheets, she fell asleep.

Fairfax woke her a few hours later when he got out of bed to go to the bathroom. The lights were off, the TV closed back up in the armoire. Moonlight flooded in through the bay windows, filling the bed with silver light. She got up and slid out of her pants, then climbed back into bed, under the blankets. He returned while she was settling.

"I didn't mean to wake you," he said in a near-whisper.

"It's all right." She pounded her pillow a few times, then tucked it back behind her head. He lifted the blankets to join her. He was wearing dark briefs. Trieka reached across the bed to touch them.

"Silk?" she said. "You wear silk underwear?"

"Only when there's a pretty woman in my bed."

"I like it." She slid her hands down his buttocks, the silk soft-slick under her hands. Her fingers moved forward, molding the thin cloth to his growing hardness. "I'd like it better off."

"Be my guest." His hands slid under her light shirt as she divested him of his underwear, then shed her own. He helped her out of the shirt and folded her to him. She held still a moment, letting her skin soak him up. In spite of her earlier feelings of displacement, she felt right here, like she belonged in his arms. She found his lips in the darkness and kissed him softly.

"I love you," she said, and then neither of them said anything for a very long time.

❋ ❋ ❋

Trieka woke perched on the edge of the wide bed, her back to Fairfax, cocooned in the heavy quilt and satin sheets. She was still naked, and the room had gone chilly overnight. She lay blinking for a few minutes, looking out the wide windows into the lawn full of wildflowers. The sun was up, but the light carried the thinness of early morning. Behind her, she heard Fairfax's breathing, slow and deep. She turned to face him. He showed no signs of waking any time soon. She slid closer to him, until she could feel his heat against her skin.

"Don't touch me," he said, and she jumped a little. "You're freezing."

She scooted closer to him, pressing her cold, bare chest full against his warm one. He shuddered, laughing. "I forgot to turn the heat up in this room last night. I'll be sure to take care of it today."

"In the meantime, I hope you have some good coffee."

"But of course."

The coffee was already brewing when they came downstairs, filling the huge kitchen with its rich odor.

"Madison?" Trieka asked.

He nodded, handing her a mug. She filled it from the pot. "He's been worth every penny."

"And exactly how many pennies is that?"

He grinned a little, filling his own cup. "You don't want to know, and I don't want to admit to it."

She sipped contentedly at her coffee while Fairfax whipped up pancakes. He'd already proven he could cook back on Denahault, and the pancakes were no disappointment. They were huge, though, and he gave her four of them. She barely made it halfway through the stack when she had to stop and stretch. As she resettled in her chair, ready to renew her assault, the phone rang.

Fairfax scooted back his chair and went to answer it. It was a regular kitchen wall phone with no video attachments, though Trieka was certain there was a vidphone in the house somewhere.

To her surprise, he looked up from the call and said, "It's for you."

"For me?"

He nodded. "It's Commander Anderson. He says he has Lieutenant Wu with him. There's a vidphone in the living room. Take it there if you like."

Pleasantly surprised but still a little flustered, she pushed back her chair. "Yes, that'd be good. Where exactly is the living room?"

His mouth twitched with amusement. "Give us just a minute, Commander. I'll have to escort the captain to the other room."

As expected, the vidphone in the living room was a new model, with a nineteen-inch high-resolution screen. Fairfax flipped a switch and the screen flickered on, settling momentarily into the image of Jeff's face. Behind him, Trieka saw Robin hovering.

"Just give me a minute to hang up the kitchen phone," Fairfax said, "and I'll leave you alone." He touched her shoulder lightly as he departed. Trieka turned to watch him, then turned back to Jeff and Robin.

"How did you know I was here?"

"Fairfax called yesterday. He's unlisted, so he gave me the number." Jeff paused. There was a sharp click across the audio transmission—Fairfax had hung up the kitchen extension. "Are you all right?"

"I'm fine," she said. "I'm sorry I deserted you. I take it the *Starchild* made it back without me?"

Robin nudged past Jeff to answer the question. "There was an ex-captain stationed at Prime. He brought us back. We didn't like him much, though." She hesitated, looking at Jeff. "Trieka—I... If you don't want to stay there, you're welcome to stay at my place."

She smiled. "Thanks for the offer, Robin, but I'm fine here. Believe me, there's plenty of room."

Jeff cleared his throat. "Is your lawyer all right with it? Because I'd heard that, even if they clear you, EarthFed might request your resignation due to unbecoming conduct."

Trieka felt herself stiffen, automatically moving into command posture. "My lawyer never mentioned there'd be any problems with the arrangement." She softened a little at the concern in Jeff's eyes. "The food is good, and I couldn't ask for better company."

Jeff moistened his lips. Trieka could tell he was dying to know exactly what was going on between his ex-commanding officer and the billionaire financier. Finally, hesitant, he said, "What, exactly...happened...out there? While you were missing."

"Well, Jeff, in the eyes of the natives of Denahault, I married him."

Jeff and Robin exchanged startled glances. It was Robin who finally summoned words.

"So what will you do now?"

"I don't know. But it looks like I'll have a good deal of time to think about it."

Chapter Twenty-one

She did have time. Much of it was spent lounging around Fairfax's estate while he took care of complicated money matters. As he'd feared, a good bit of his funds had been frozen, and it took perseverance on his part to thaw them. She was fairly certain, too, that Madison had something to do with the recovery of some of the more stubbornly held funds. In any case, it was a slow process.

He was home one afternoon when she returned, sweaty and tired, from a run around the estate. Home and on the phone, swearing quite colorfully in a mixture of English and Swedish. Finally, he slammed the phone down, cutting off the connection. The blond Swede in the vidphone looked annoyed as he disappeared.

"How bad is it?" Trieka asked him when he seemed to have calmed a little.

"Two million in that account." He rubbed the back of his neck. "I've got five million still frozen in another, and the government seized some of my real estate, as well... Felicity says I'll get it all back, but it might take time."

"So what's the hurry?"

"I have plans for that money."

He refused to tell her anything else, even later that night when she caught him, quite literally, with his pants down.

"It's a surprise," was all he would say. When she tried to pose more questions, he distracted her thoroughly, until she forgot why she'd even wondered.

In the meantime, the hearings went on. Trieka and Fairfax were both summoned to testify against Admiral Derocher and the other EarthFed officials brought back from Denahault. She was worried at first. They wanted to hear details of her abduction, and she wasn't sure she could handle it.

Then she sat in the courtroom and watched Fairfax relate the lurid details of Kathi's murder. He went on and on in a quiet, steady voice that never faltered. Throughout most of it, his eyes were on Trieka. When it came her turn to take the stand, she searched out his storm-gray eyes among the observers and told her story to him. It came steady.

That wasn't the only thing about the hearings, though, that she found difficult. Not only the officials of EarthFed were on trial here. EarthFed itself was taken apart and examined piece by piece. It seemed they peeled back layer after layer of veneer, exposing corruption beneath.

With each revelation, she felt more betrayed. She'd made a vow to uphold the principles of EarthFed, and now she was finding that every one of those principles was a lie. She didn't know who she was anymore, or where she belonged.

Because each of the accused officers underwent a separate hearing, Trieka's testimony had been videotaped her first time on the stand. Subsequent prosecutors used the tapes, deciding it was easier and more efficient than calling her to the stand a dozen times. And there was so much other evidence, so much additional testimony, that the horrors on Denahault had become almost a minor issue.

But Admiral Derocher's lawyer, a military lawyer of some notoriety, insisted on live testimony. Fairfax wasn't happy when he heard the news.

"The guy's a bastard," he told Trieka. "He's not going to make it easy on anybody."

Fairfax was right. Trieka took her oath and her seat in the witness stand, and told her story again. Then Ander Garwood started his cross-examination.

"*Captain* Cavendish." He stressed her rank in an almost scornful manner. She ground her teeth and looked straight at him. "*Captain* Cavendish, on the morning in question, how exactly did you know where to look for Mr. Fairfax?"

This had come up before. She'd seen no reason not to be honest about it. "I had met him for dinner in his room at the embassy the night before."

"And may I ask exactly why you met in his room?"

"The restaurant was closed for remodeling."

"And what happened while you were there?"

"Objection." This was Felicity, cool as usual, seeming without fear of Garwood or anyone else. "I don't see how this is relevant."

"If I may be allowed to continue," Garwood said, "that will become clear."

The judge considered a moment, then nodded. "Continue," she said, "but if your point doesn't become clear soon, I'll disallow this line of questioning."

"What did you do that evening?"

"We had dinner," Trieka said. "Then I went back to my room."

"And why did you try to contact him the next day?"

"I discovered he'd committed a security breach while he was on my ship. He had accessed my private logs."

"And, after discovering he'd committed a felony offense aboard your ship, instead of turning him in to the proper authorities, you rushed off to *rescue* him from EarthFed officials, who, as far as you know, were holding him under rightful custody. Why was that, *Captain* Cavendish?"

Trieka felt a rivulet of sweat slide between her breasts, down nearly to her waist. The room wasn't hot.

"Mr. Fairfax had left evidence with me which indicated he'd uncovered misconduct in the upper echelons of EarthFed. Based on this information, I correctly assumed he'd been abducted, and that his life was in danger."

"So instead of reporting his disappearance to the proper authorities, you took it upon yourself to rescue him."

"Under the circumstances, it was impossible to know whether the proper authorities could be trusted."

"So you abandoned your ship, your crew, your *duty*...to follow a hunch. To rescue a civilian from your untrustworthy government."

"I was certain they'd kill him." She was shaking inside now, her stomach and bowels trembling. For a moment she felt sick, then the wave passed.

"When you found Mr. Fairfax, was there any evidence he'd been physically abused?"

"He'd been beaten, yes. His lip was split and he had bruises on his face."

"But none of these wounds were severe?"

"No, not really."

"And it's perfectly possible that the wounds could have been sustained during a struggle, in which Mr. Fairfax protested his rightful arrest?"

"I suppose it's possible, but it's not what Mr. Fairfax told me."

"And what did he tell you?"

"That he was beaten during interrogation, and that he was shown a recording of the torture and murder of Katharine Maier and her father."

Garwood looked at the judge. "I'd like to mention here that no evidence of this alleged recording has come to light."

It went on and on. Trieka had been cross-examined at the earlier trial, but not with such brutality. Garwood twisted her words, discredited her whenever and however possible. And, finally, came his most ridiculous tack of all.

"Is it true, *Captain* Cavendish, that shortly after his rescue, you entered into a sexual relationship with Mr. Fairfax?"

She blinked, waiting for an objection from Felicity. None came. Fairfax was there in the courtroom, waiting to take his turn on the stand. It took an extreme effort of will to keep from looking at him.

The pause went on too long. In a gentle voice, the judge said, "Captain Cavendish, please answer the question."

Trieka swallowed, staring at Garwood. "Yes, it's true. But I didn't—"

Felicity made a quick gesture for her to stop, but it wasn't necessary. Garwood interrupted her.

"So, isn't it possible your assumption that Mr. Fairfax was in danger, your insistence on rescuing him from what you believed to be certain death, all sprang from your own

244

imagination, because you had developed feelings for Mr. Fairfax?"

There was a snort from the courtroom—Fairfax. Again, she had to force herself not to look at him. Anger burned away any hesitation she might have had.

"I am a highly trained officer of EarthFed," she said, her voice level and clear, almost brittle. "For the last ten years I've served faithfully and well. I've dedicated and sacrificed a good deal of my life to my career. I would not—would *not*—put that career in jeopardy because of my feelings for a man."

"Then why did you do what you did? Why did you assume your government—whom you were sworn to uphold—would endanger a civilian?"

The anger was firm and solid, a bright, hard pressure in the middle of her chest. Trieka was glad Garwood had made her angry. Before the anger had come, she'd begun to doubt herself. "I was presented with irrefutable evidence that EarthFed had systematically destroyed ecosystems and perhaps even intelligent life on at least two colony planets. A government that would do that would certainly have no qualms about murdering a man who could expose such corruption."

There was more, but Trieka's anger kept her level. When she finally left the stand, Felicity smiled at her, and Fairfax winked. She sat down next to him, but he didn't touch her. She thought perhaps it was best under the circumstances. And he was called next.

He went through everything he had before, relating his kidnapping, interrogation, beating and finally describing the recording. It wasn't fair that he should have to go through this again just to placate a sleazy attorney. But he was calm, pausing only once to collect himself and drink from the glass of water at his elbow. Trieka winced, too, when he described her condition on finding her in the locker on Denahault. It corroborated her story, but she still didn't like to hear it.

Then Garwood stepped up. Trieka thought she saw Fairfax tense a little, but she wasn't sure. His face was as calm and expressionless as ever.

"Mr. Fairfax, how can you account for the fact that absolutely no evidence can be found to support the existence of this recording you describe?"

Fairfax shifted a little. It was turning into a battle of charisma. Garwood's was formidable, but so was Fairfax's. And Fairfax was better looking. "I'd think that, if they had any sense at all, they would have destroyed it as soon as things started to heat up."

"And you've also failed to present any kind of solid evidence that there really is a race of intelligent man-apes living on Denahault."

There was an interesting approach. The question hadn't come up in the other trials, as far as Trieka knew. There, the prosecutors had focused extensively on the evidence concerning terraforming on Farhallen and similar disgraces performed on Cutter's Star. The evidence had been so strong and indisputable that the defense hadn't bothered attacking either it or the accounts of Denahault. Admiral Derocher, however, hadn't been in charge during the settlement of Farhallen and Cutter's Star, making the Denahault evidence more important to this trial.

"There is intelligent life on Denahault," Fairfax said. Then he lifted his hands to add, in the language of the White Fur People: "You two-faced, flea-bitten son of a half-breed flat-nosed brindle-faced Eater of Carrion."

Trieka clapped her hand over her mouth to quell a very strange sound, halfway between a laugh and a choke of surprise.

"What was that?" Garwood said, appearing genuinely taken aback.

"The natives of Denahault call themselves the White Fur People. They're incapable of complex vocalization, so they communicate through sign language."

"So what was that you said?"

A corner of Fairfax's mouth quirked up. "I don't think you want to know."

The judge leaned toward the witness stand. "Mr. Fairfax, please refrain from insulting the counsel, even if it is in a language none of us understand."

There was a titter in the courtroom, quickly restrained. Fairfax nodded politely to the judge. "I apologize, Your Honor, Mr. Garwood."

"Apology accepted, Mr. Fairfax." Garwood hesitated, looking

at Fairfax, who looked back placidly. Trieka was surprised—and pleased—to see that Garwood actually looked rattled. "Maybe you could demonstrate something that you *could* translate."

Fairfax nodded, then thought for a moment. When he began to speak again, he accompanied his words with the eloquent gestures of the White Fur People. Or perhaps he accompanied the gestures with his spoken words. As the tale unfolded, it sounded more like the latter.

"I was badly wounded and a group of the White Fur People, of the People who Live at the Edge of the Mountain, rescued me and healed my wound. I was then taken into the clan. Fire Hair, who became my mate while we were with the White Fur People, also became of the tribe. I owe my life to the White Fur People, and have pledged to do what I can to ensure that my people and theirs can live in peace."

Garwood nodded slowly. "It's pretty, but it's not proof. Can you show me anything else?"

For the first time since he'd taken the stand, Fairfax looked at Trieka. His mouth twitched, his eyes laughing. Slowly, he stood up and began to unbutton his shirt. The judge leaned toward him again.

"Mr. Fairfax, may I ask what you're doing?"

"With all due respect, Your Honor, I'm disrobing."

The judge didn't object. Neither did Garwood. Trieka glanced at Felicity and found her looking back, a question vying with a smile on her face. Trieka gestured toward Fairfax.

Fairfax shrugged out of his shirt and turned to display the tattoo under his left arm. "This is the mark the White Fur People put on me to show my acceptance into the clan. Now, I know you'll say I could have had it done at any tattoo parlor, but quite frankly, why the hell would I want to? Believe me, I could have afforded a better job."

Trieka smiled. The tattoo was rough and primitive, but still beautiful. She'd lain awake nights, tracing its lines with her fingers. Garwood stepped forward to look at it more closely. After a moment, the judge asked, "Are there any further questions?"

Garwood looked at her, then back over his shoulder at the prosecutor. His face had gone strange and hard. "No, Your

Honor."

The judge called an end to the day shortly thereafter. Trieka caught up with Fairfax outside the courtroom. "How do you think it went?"

Fairfax shook his head. "I don't know. I sure would have liked to've had Six Toes there, though. There's some evidence that jackass couldn't refute."

The jackass in question was only a few yards down the hallway, conferring with one of the other members of the defense team. He looked up as Trieka and Fairfax approached. The hardness Trieka had seen in his face had become flinty and brittle.

"Captain Cavendish," he said in a low voice.

Trieka stopped next to him, holding herself very still and poised. "Mr. Garwood. Congratulations on prompting some of the most interesting evidence of the entire trial." She couldn't keep the edge of scorn from her voice.

"Trieka," Fairfax muttered behind her.

Garwood took a small step forward. His voice came very low, meant for Trieka alone. "You may have won this round, little girl, but, by the time I'm through, you'll never fly another colony ship again."

Trieka swung at him. She couldn't stop herself—it just happened. Luckily, Fairfax was close enough, and fast enough, to wrap an arm around her from behind, to pull her back before the swing connected.

"Just back off," he said quietly into her ear. "Take a deep breath, back off and come with me."

She let him steer her out of the courthouse and into his Mercedes. She said nothing to him, or he to her, until they reached the house. Fairfax pulled the car into the garage and shut off the engine. Only then did he reach across the small space between them to lay his hand on hers.

"Are you all right?"

She shook her head. There were no tears, not even any anger, really, just an emptiness that seemed to have sucked out her soul.

"He was right. He had nothing to do with it, but I'll never

see the inside of the *Starchild* again." She stopped, letting her head fall back against the seat. "I don't know who I am anymore."

"You're the woman I love," he said.

She squeezed his hand hard, until her fingers ached. "Maybe that's not enough."

Chapter Twenty-two

With the ending of the hearings, Fairfax knew the hardest part was over. For him, at least. Trieka seemed to be fighting her own demons, and he didn't know what to do for her.

He had to be absent more often than he wanted, consulting with brokers and accountants, not only recovering his unfrozen funds, but channeling them toward his ultimate goal. He was with an accountant one day when the receptionist buzzed the office.

"Turn on the TV," she said.

The accountant obliged. His business with Fairfax lay waiting on the table while they watched the special news report.

Admiral Derocher had been found guilty, as had all the other EarthFed officials who had been on trial. Control of the colony planets had been removed from EarthFed's jurisdiction. The planets would be transferred to private management until such time as they became self-sufficient. Fairfax nodded. He'd expected as much.

What he hadn't expected was what he found when he got home.

Trieka sat in the living room, in front of the projection TV, flipping channels randomly. Her eyes were distant, red and bloodshot. She'd obviously been crying, hard and long. Fairfax came into the room and sat next to her.

"What's wrong?"

"I resigned my commission."

Fairfax was shocked to silence. She'd been on a mostly involuntary leave of absence since her own hearing, in which she'd been cleared of desertion charges, but he'd never expected this.

"Why?" he finally asked.

She shook her head a little, her mouth trembling. "The dream's gone. Everything I wanted is gone. There's just...there's nothing there for me anymore."

She sounded like someone had wrung her soul dry. Fairfax put an arm around her. He could think of many things to say, but nothing she'd want to hear. So he just held her.

"They didn't even question me," she said after a time. Her channel flipping had stopped on a music channel, and a mournful folk song wound its way between her words. "I think they wanted me to leave."

"You put yourself in a very difficult position. No one knew how it would turn out, least of all us." He paused, studying her face, wishing a mere kiss could take away the ravages of tears. "Do you regret anything you did?"

"No. But I don't even know, now, if it was worth it. Denahault's going to be turned over to private management— who knows how the White Fur People will be treated under those conditions?"

"I've had words in the ear of a couple of senators about that exact issue. There'll be regulations—"

"And that's another thing." Fairfax swallowed the rest of his words, surprised at Trieka's vehemence. "I'm completely useless here. You have more money than God and you can talk to senators. What the hell good am I?"

She pushed away from him, drawing into herself. Fairfax wanted to touch her, but knew she wouldn't want it.

"You could be my wife," he said.

She shook her head. "No. I can't. Not right now."

He let her sit in her silence for a moment, but he had to ask the question. "What are you going to do?"

Her eyes met his, bleak and empty. "I don't know."

Trieka lay alone that night in the big bed, staring out at the moonlight-covered field. She thought of Denahault, of the great wildness and the promise she'd made to the White Fur People. Her life felt like a great, empty stretch of blackness, like a night sky with clouds covering the stars and no moon to light the way.

After a time, she sat up and turned on the light. Her robe lay draped over the cherry footboard; she picked it up and drew it on. It was getting late, and she wondered why Fairfax hadn't come to bed yet.

Quiet, she padded down the hallway, the long, spiral staircase. Halfway there, she heard the soft noises of conversation. Felicity was still here. She'd arrived just after dinner. Trieka had sat in the library with her and Fairfax for an hour or so while Felicity updated Fairfax on the status of a few accounts she was still handling for him. Finally, drifting toward the edge of a headache, Trieka had gone to bed.

The rhythms of the voices no longer sounded like they discussed business. Trieka padded toward the library, her house shoes silent against the muted gleam of the oak floors. The library door stood partly open. Inside, too-bright lamplight glared against maroon velvet, polished mahogany. She saw Fairfax on the couch, back against the high, winged armrest, legs stretched out across the cushions. One hand toyed with a cup of wine. The wine was the same color as the velvet, and Fairfax's eyes seemed to be lost in it.

"I panicked when I found out she was missing," he was saying. His voice was soft, a little muzzy. Trieka stopped by the partially open door and wrapped her arms around herself, listening to his soft voice, his words of little consequence. "I didn't know what to do. I couldn't lose her. And then—" He broke off and sipped at the wine, glancing briefly to where Felicity must have sat. "I'm ashamed to say I thought about it, but I wondered for a while if she'd decided to throw her lot back in with EarthFed." He shook his head a little. "I've been running paranoid for so long, it's hard to put it behind me—"

Trieka must have made a small noise, or perhaps taken a breath, because suddenly his gaze swung toward the door and he saw her.

"Trieka," he said, sounding a little surprised. "Is everything okay?"

No. Nothing's okay. It was for a minute, but never again. "I just wondered when you were coming to bed." Her voice sounded like someone else's, small and without substance.

He looked at his watch, then back at Trieka with a soft smile. "I'm sorry. I didn't realize it was so late. I'll be up in a few minutes."

She nodded and turned away. She took two steps, then ran the rest of the way to the bedroom.

Upstairs, she turned the light back off and buried herself in the quilts. The darkness protected her a little, but not from the sounds of her own breathing. She couldn't keep it steady, couldn't keep the sobs out of it. She swallowed, breathed, swallowed again.

Everything was over. All of it.

She heard the bedroom door open and suddenly there was light, bright enough to pierce even her heavy cocoon.

"Trieka? Are you all right?"

And the anger came. She'd known it would—hoped it would. It was clear and bright and stronger than the helplessness she'd let fill her. She threw back the covers. "How could you?"

He looked at her, perplexed. "How could I what?"

She waited a moment, thinking he might see. But he only looked at her, his hair tousled and his eyes muzzy with wine.

Carefully, her body moving as if she wore a uniform instead of a light flannel nightshirt, she slipped out of the bed.

"I gave up everything for you," she said. "I gave you everything I was, and you still doubted me. I don't understand how you could have done that."

He took a step toward her. She lifted her chin a little and he stopped.

"It was a gut reaction," he said. "I can't defend it. I can't explain it."

She nodded. There was nothing left inside her—all of it had been torn out by the roots. "I'm leaving tomorrow. I'm sure my mom could use some company for the holidays."

"Trieka—"

"No."

She got back into bed. A few minutes later he joined her, but didn't touch her.

❊ ❊ ❊

She left for Chicago the next day, three days before Thanksgiving. The house seemed huge and empty without her, much as it had for so long after Kathi's disappearance. Fairfax threw himself into his fundraising project and tried not to think about her. She'd been so cold when she'd left, cold and angry and empty. He'd tried to understand but he couldn't, so he'd decided to leave her alone. She'd come back if she were meant to.

Finally, in mid-December, he couldn't stand it anymore. She'd left the number for him—he called it and stood in front of the vidphone, waiting.

An older woman answered the phone. Trieka's mother, Fairfax assumed; the resemblance wasn't great, but enough.

"Mrs. Cavendish?" Fairfax said.

"It's Sullivan now, actually. You're looking for Trieka?" She seemed pleasant enough, but there was something hard in her. Flinty-hard, not like Trieka's cold steel.

"Yes," he said. "Tell her it's Fairfax."

Mrs. Sullivan smiled a little. "I know who you are. Thanks for taking care of my daughter."

"Actually, she took care of me."

Mrs. Sullivan softened a bit. "Let me find her."

He waited. A teenage girl appeared in the screen, then ran, talking excitedly to someone offscreen. Then Trieka appeared, carrying an orange cat that clashed with her hair. Around her neck hung the string of amber given her by the White Fur People. She looked happier, but she was different. Softer, more feminine. Fairfax swallowed a surprisingly painful twinge.

"Hi," Trieka said. "I'm sorry I didn't call. Mom's been keeping me busy, and my stepdad—well, I hadn't met him before, so we've been getting acquainted."

Fairfax nodded, beginning to realize just how much she had sacrificed to EarthFed. "It's all right. How are you?"

"Better, I think." The cat wriggled in her arms and she obligingly put it down. "How are you?"

"I'm good." The conversation was strangely awkward, as if he didn't know her. "I was wondering... I know we left things...badly. Do you think it's possible... Do you think you might see your way clear to come back for Christmas?"

She nodded. She seemed very much at peace, and Fairfax found it unsettling. "I've had time to think things through, Harrison. I'll be out to see you next week. We have a lot to talk about."

"Good or bad?"

"A little of both."

"Anything you can tell me now?"

"No. I have to do this in person."

He nodded, a heavy sense of finality settling in his chest. She was coming back to say good-bye. "All right. Take care of yourself, Trieka."

"Yeah, you too."

※ ※ ※

Trieka didn't call when she reached the airport. Instead, she caught a cab. She didn't know if Fairfax would be home, but it didn't matter. She'd rather sit on his front porch all night waiting for him than have to face the interminable ride in his car, making small talk while everything she had to say loomed unsaid.

The time spent in Illinois had been largely a period of reflection. She'd talked more to her mother in those few weeks than she had over the previous ten years. EarthFed had taken so much of her time, her life. She'd missed her mother's courtship, her wedding, the chance to become acquainted with stepsisters, a stepbrother, several nieces and nephews.

She didn't regret it, though. She'd lived her dream, commanding a starship, paving the way to build lives on a new world. And the most ironic part was that, now that the dream had soured, she'd made a decision which would once again separate her from everyone she loved.

"You're nuts," her new stepsister Kylie had told her. "The guy's loaded."

But her mother had said, late one night when they were alone in the quiet living room, "You have to be true to yourself. If you're not, you'll never be happy, no matter how much you love him."

At Fairfax's estate, she pushed the doorbell and waited. There was no answer. She sat on the front step and brooded. Her hand went to the amber necklace, toying with the smooth, warm beads. She'd taken to wearing it again because it made her feel connected to something. When questions weighed on her mind, she always found herself stroking the stones.

She'd gone over the words a million times, but she knew that, when the time came, they'd come out wrong, or they wouldn't come out at all. This was Jake all over again. It would fall apart around her. She'd forgiven him—there'd been no question, once she'd given it rational thought—but he'd never forgive her.

She was about to get up and jog around the block when a car pulled into the driveway—the BMW. Trieka stood. The car stopped outside the open garage door and Madison got out.

"Captain Cavendish," he said.

Trieka shook her head. "It's just Trieka now."

Madison seemed surprised. "Oh. I'm sorry to hear that. Fairfax is at the club. He should be back any time. Do you want to come in?"

Trieka shrugged. "Sure."

He let her in, asked her how the trip was, then left to see to his own business. Trieka wandered the house, admiring the Christmas decorations. They ranged from quaint to obviously expensive, from homey cross-stitched Santas to exquisitely delicate ornaments of blown glass. On the mantle over the fireplace in the living room was a plain silver menorah, the candles unlit. Wondering, Trieka touched the cold metal.

"It was Kathi's." The familiar voice from behind her made her swallow tears. She turned to face Fairfax. She hadn't heard him come in. He carried a gym bag in one hand, and his hair was wet. "I put it out every year but I never figured out when to light the candles."

Trieka stood, looking at him for a moment. No words would come.

Finally, he said, "You look good."

"So do you."

He lifted the gym bag a little. "Let me put this stuff away, and then we can talk."

"I'll come with you."

She followed him up the stairs to the bedroom. He wasn't limping. "How's the leg?"

"I had it worked on. It's better. The scar's still bad, though. I'm trying to decide whether to have it repaired."

"As long as it works, why worry about the scar?"

"More or less what I was thinking."

In the bedroom, he threw the gym bag toward the closet and closed the door behind them.

"I—" Trieka started, but he had her then, his hands on her arms, his mouth hard on hers. She didn't fight him. She couldn't. After a long time, he pulled back. Lifting the string of amber with one finger, he studied her face.

"I think I know what you're going to say," he said, "and I don't want to hear it until I've seen you naked on this bed again."

"Fairfax, please—"

"Please what? Please this? Or please that?"

After the "that", she quit fighting. She'd missed him, and she ached for him. His hands found the ache and turned it to rapture. Her body opened to him without thought, until he owned her, and she him, until they were one soul and one body, enflamed. And finally, inevitably, separated.

She lay next to him on the dampened satin sheets, tracing the lines of his tattoo with her finger. He had his eyes closed, one hand behind his head, the other loose on his chest.

"I missed you," he said.

"I missed you, too."

He opened his eyes, looked up at the ceiling. Trieka slipped her hand away from him, sensing tension as it moved through him. He puffed his cheeks a little, then said, "What are you going to do?"

She looked at his profile, the long nose and beautiful mouth, the lower lip that was almost too much for his face. "I'm going back to Denahault."

He closed his eyes as if in pain, opened them again. "You have plans?"

"I want to help open communication between the settlers and the natives. They need me there. It's what I need to do."

"I can't go with you."

"I know."

"I have things underway here, but I have to stay on top of everything until it pans out—if it pans out."

"I know."

He bit his lower lip. "Is there anything I could do to convince you to stay?"

"No."

"For six months?"

"No."

"Why?"

She swallowed. She hadn't expected his complete acceptance, but she didn't want to fight with him either. "I have to do this." She rolled toward him and he turned his head in response, looking at her. "I defined myself by my military identity. That's gone now. I have to find something to fill that space."

"And I blew it."

She nodded, smiling a little. "Yes, you did, but I've gotten over that. It hurts that you didn't trust me then, but I suppose I can understand."

His mouth compressed a little. "Stay with me. Marry me."

"I can't."

"It's not enough?"

"No, it isn't. I almost wish it were, but it's not."

"I could get you a job—"

"No!" She sat up, fists clenching against the coverlet. "No. Don't you understand? I don't want to be what you make me. I have to be what *I* make me. If you just turn me into your little secretary, or your little wife—" She was shaking now. She rolled out of the bed, grabbed his bathrobe from the headboard and shrugged it on as she headed for the bathroom.

"That's not what I meant—"

"Stop." She paused by the bathroom door, turning toward him. "Just give me a minute, okay?"

In the bathroom, she splashed her face with cold water, then looked at herself in the mirror. She looked solid enough, but she felt ethereal, as if she had no existence in this world anymore. In too many ways, she didn't. As hard as this was, as much as it was hurting him—and herself—she knew it was the right thing to do. She pulled his robe tighter and went back into the bedroom.

Fairfax had pulled on a pair of black sweatpants and was sitting on the edge of the bed, rubbing his eyes. Trieka came to him and laid her hand against his side, her palm covering the tattoo.

"They may not have marked me, but I belong to the White Fur People as much as you do. Maybe more. The Elder charged me to help them. I have to do whatever I can. This is going to be a difficult time for them with the transitions on Denahault, and the changes that'll come about. Only two people in the world can help them. You, and me. Now, I don't know what you're up to, but I trust that it's to the greater good, and that it's what you need to do. You have to trust me, too."

"I do trust you," he said. "And I understand you. But I'm a stinking, selfish bastard, and I don't want to lose you."

She slipped a hand into his hair, her fingers combing into the thick, red-brown strands. "Maybe you won't. Maybe it'll all come together in the end."

He bent his head until his forehead lay between her breasts. "I hope to God you're right."

On New Year's Day he drove her to the spaceport. They said nothing to each other until they stopped, and Trieka got out to unload her two pieces of luggage. Fairfax took the bags from the trunk and passed them into her hands. Then he leaned forward and kissed her, gently. His mouth tasted like tears.

"I love you," he said.

She pressed her face against his chest and let him hold her. Finally, she moved back. Her sinuses burned with unshed tears.

"I love you, Harrison," she said, and then, "Good-bye."

She walked up the sidewalk to the terminal, and didn't look back.

Chapter Twenty-three

Winter held Denahault Prime hostage when Trieka arrived. She went out to Forest Walk in a dogsled, slogging through snow that rose at times to six-foot drifts. The temperature at night dipped to minus fifty and sometimes lower. Grace and Jim Taylor, in immense parkas, greeted her enthusiastically. She moved into the bedroom where their daughter had grown up. The younger Taylor lived down the street now with her husband and a baby girl.

When spring made it possible, Trieka took Jim and his son Randy out in search of the White Fur People. Trieka had little hope of finding them, but on the third day, they found her.

Surprisingly enough, the hunting party who came upon them was led by Six Toes. Even more surprisingly, he grabbed Trieka with a loud hoot and embraced her.

"You came back," he said. "The Elder said it would happen. I doubted him."

"You shouldn't have."

"Where is Long Nose?"

"He's not here. I don't know if he ever will be."

Six Toes touched her face gently. "The Elder said you were lifemates. Keep your eyes open. He will never be far."

Over the next few months, Trieka was too busy to think about Fairfax at all. Or at least not very much. She negotiated the first trade agreements between the inhabitants of Forest Walk and the White Fur People. Other settlements would follow, once more settlers were trained to handle it. She taught language lessons twice a month, once at Forest Walk and once at the embassy in Denahault Prime. After a time, she even convinced the White Fur People to send her an assistant. Violet Eyes was a young, enthusiastic female who'd taught children in the tribe, and she was very good at what she did.

Another pleasant surprise was the lack of animosity toward the White Fur People. But these were colonists, she reminded herself. In spite of the hypocrites in EarthFed, they'd been trained to accept the possibility that they might encounter intelligent alien life. She'd conducted some of that training herself. And now she conducted more, watching as Violet Eyes related the myths and stories of the White Fur People as the settlers sat riveted, and learned.

The days she was in Prime, she heard rumors. The separation of the colony from EarthFed had gone fairly smoothly so far. Who oversaw the planet meant very little to the settlers. Only the embassy personnel were affected in any meaningful way. But stories filtered in from Farhallen, of supplies cut off because of bad management. A company interested in Cutter's Star supposedly wanted every settler registered as an employee. Protests by the settlers led to the breakoff of negotiations. And in Denahault Prime, rumors ran rampant as three separate investment firms bid for control of the planet. Trieka didn't recognize the names of any of them.

Then, one day, when Trieka arrived for her class, there was a new sign over the front door to the embassy. "Denahault, Inc.", it read. She raised an eyebrow. It sounded a little stupid, but at least it left the planet with its own identity. In the hallway leading to the classroom, someone had installed a new electronic message station, with a half-dozen red lights blinking to indicate waiting messages.

Class went as usual. Violet Eyes asked her to stay afterward. She'd seemed distracted through the class. "What does it mean, these signs and names?" she asked. Violet Eyes had begun to learn the significance of the printed word, but it was difficult to teach her to read when she couldn't speak. Phonics was definitely out.

"It only means that someone else will be regulating supplies and overseeing issues with the settlers."

"Will it affect our trade agreements?"

"It shouldn't." Trieka hesitated. "I hope not."

On her way out, the question nagged her. Maybe she

should look into these things herself, just to be sure. There was no point, after all, in getting the government out of the picture just so some other bunch of idiots could come in and screw it up again. She stopped by the reception desk.

"Excuse me. I know this is all pretty new, but is there a department or something dedicated to interaction with the natives?"

"Yes, there is." The woman seemed distracted, poking buttons on her computer terminal. "You're Trieka Cavendish, aren't you?"

"That's right."

"I have a message here from the CEO. He wants to see you about exactly that issue."

"Really?" Maybe this wasn't going to be such a bad deal, after all.

"Yes. In fact, he specifically requested that I try to catch you after class today to see if you could meet with him." She looked up from the terminal. "Are you available?"

"Right now?"

"Yes, right now."

"I guess I am."

"Then you can go ahead to his office." She picked up her phone, cradling it between chin and shoulder. "I'll let him know you're on your way."

"Thank you. Where's the office?"

"Down the right-hand hallway, all the way to the end. There's an alcove there, where his secretary sits. Just tell her who you are." She poked four numbers into the phone. "Hi, Lucy? Trieka Cavendish is on her way. Yes. Tell him she'll be there in just a couple of minutes."

Trieka looked down the right-hand hallway. Suddenly nervous, she gave the receptionist another smile and went on her way.

Lucy, the secretary, was young, blonde and pretty. She was typing at blinding speed on a computer when Trieka approached her desk. Lucy acknowledged her presence with a slight tilt of her chin, finished the sentence or paragraph she was typing and swiveled her chair.

"Sorry about that. I hate to stop in the middle of a sentence."

"It's all right. I'm Trieka Cavendish."

"Yes, of course. You can go right in. He's waiting for you."

For the first time in a long time, Trieka missed the security of her uniform. In her utilitarian jeans and denim shirt, she felt competent enough, but not commanding. Squaring her shoulders, she opened the door to the CEO's office and went in.

She saw the desk first—a big, solid sweep of mahogany. On the desk, next to the computer terminal, sat a piece of driftwood. Draped over the wood was a string of amber beads.

The CEO stood at the back of the room, looking out the window. She couldn't see his face. He was tall and lanky, long-legged, with big, graceful hands clasped behind his back. He wore an immaculately tailored dark blue suit. His hair was brown, verging on auburn. Trieka closed the door behind her and held very still, her heart pattering in her throat like a trapped bird.

He turned around slowly and looked at her, a slight smile on his finely cut mouth. His storm gray eyes twinkled a bit.

"Ms. Cavendish," he said. "Thank you for taking the time to see me."

Trieka swallowed, uncertain whether she was about to laugh or cry. "What the hell are you doing here, Fairfax?"

He grinned. "I bought the planet."

Trieka shook her head slowly. It made sense—he had, after all, come to Denahault in the first place because he was considering investment. "That's what your 'little project' was?"

"That's right. I couldn't say anything because there were so many variables I had to line up to make it viable. But things panned out quite nicely." He shrugged. "Maybe it was meant to be."

"At least I know the place is in good hands."

Fairfax sat down behind the desk and Trieka sat, as well.

"Why did you want to see me?" she asked.

Fairfax steepled his hands, tapping his lower lip with his index fingers. "I have a bit of a proposition for you."

"Please elaborate."

"I've set up an entire department to regulate human-native relations. Unfortunately, there's only one person I could think of, besides myself, who has the knowledge and experience necessary to manage that department. And that person is you."

She chewed her bottom lip. "You want me to work for you?"

"I want you to work for the White Fur People. I want you to continue doing what you're doing, but with the backing of the corporation and with a salary attached." He paused, studying her face. "Nobody can do this but you, Trieka. You already invented the job. I just want to formalize it."

She felt herself smiling, though she wasn't certain where it had come from. It was the perfect solution. She wouldn't be dependent on him—they would work together. She could follow her heart exactly where it led her—both in her duty to the White Fur People and to Harrison Fairfax.

"So how much would this salary be?"

Fairfax opened a desk drawer. "Actually, I have an advance here." He laid a small, velvet box down in front of her.

"What's this?"

"Open it."

She picked it up, searched his face for clues. Finding none, she opened the box. Inside was a ring. A plain gold band carried a half-carat Marquis-cut diamond flanked by small rubies.

"Not very practical for field work," she said. She took it out of the box and slid it onto her finger. It was a little loose.

"Marry me," he said.

She turned the ring on her finger, then looked up at him. "I think I just might be ready for that."

"And the job?"

"Yes."

He sat back in his chair. The look of relief on his face surprised her.

"I can't believe you bought the whole damn planet," she said.

"I had to. I couldn't trust the White Fur People to anyone else. Or you."

The space between them seemed not to exist. Trieka felt as

if she could reach out and not only touch him, but encompass him, take him into her and hold him there forever, just against her heart. The air was full of him, and so was she.

He leaned toward her again, the look in his eyes heavy, like clouds bellied with rain.

"I gave myself a nice penthouse apartment in the embassy hotel," he said. "Would you like to see it?"

Her body prickled at the promise in his eyes. "Yes. Yes, I think I'd like that very much."

About the Author

To learn more about Katriena Knights, please visit http://katrienaknights.kabeka.com. Send an email to Katriena at krknights@kabeka.com or join her Yahoo! group to join in the fun with other readers as well as Katriena! http://groups.yahoo.com/group/KnightsMissive

An assassin can't afford a conscience. It's bad for business.

The Assassin Journals: Hunter
© *2007 S.L. Partington*

Ex-soldier turned assassin Gage Brassan is having a very bad year. First, an unwelcome attack of conscience has him switching targets at the last moment, which doesn't sit too well with the criminal organization that hired him. Then an old girlfriend's betrayal and a trip to prison stir up memories of his military past and a promise left unfulfilled.

Tortured by his haunted past and hunted by the organization he betrayed, Gage seeks the truth behind the execution of the elite military patrol he once commanded. With the help of Jak, a Rigian street kid, and Joanna, the sister of an old army buddy, Gage follows the blood trail from the war-torn Androsian system to the highest echelons of the Galactic Security Force to the corrupt halls of the Rigian People's Palace.

On the run, unsure whom he can trust, he struggles with a growing attraction to Joanna while trying to protect his estranged father from the personal fallout of a life gone wrong.

He knows the answers are out there. The trick will be living long enough to find them.

Available now in ebook and print from Samhain Publishing.

Enjoy the following excerpt from The Assassin Journals: Hunter

I woke to darkness and the certain knowledge that I was in very deep shit.

Light crept in under the door of the windowless room, and I heard muffled voices outside. I sat up slowly, closing my eyes against the pain in my head and shoulders.

Someone had sold me out.

Probably the waitress in the bar.

I really was going to have to stop trusting women like that. The odds were pretty good that Jak the Rigian Rat Boy rotted in the alley along with the garbage while the barmaid spent his cash.

I listened through the pain in my head, trying to figure out where they'd taken me, but the voices outside the door weren't dropping many hints. I could only assume the Guilds had elected themselves a new Grand Poobah, and I was at the top of his shit list.

Shouldn't I be dead?

The heat and stale air in my windowless cell weren't doing much to help alleviate my headache. I heard the sound of a lock rattling and looked up as the door opened. Skinny Sorrellian stood over me with a canteen that he tossed on the floor in front of me. I thought about asking him where I was, but he didn't look like he was in the mood for conversation. He shut and locked the door without speaking. I opened the canteen and sniffed, then took a tentative sip. Water.

Another hour or so passed and I dozed, jerking awake when the lock rattled again. Skinny Sorrellian was back.

"Get up," he said. "The master will see you now."

I got to my feet, and he led me from the room. I wouldn't want to keep the master waiting.

I was led into a large, spacious room, furnished with expensive Terran antiques and hand-blown Lyrian crystal. A log fire burned in a black marble fireplace; above it hung a watercolor painted by a renowned Rigian master, five hundred years dead. A massive rosewood desk sat in the center of the room and a man stood before the French doors leading to a stone flagged terrace. Rigian, older, gray streaked his yellow hair. He didn't turn as I was brought in, just continued staring across the darkening lawn.

"You disappoint me, Hunter," he said at last. "Is there no honor at all among murderers and thieves?"

I didn't reply and he turned to face me. "Tell me why I shouldn't kill you."

"Do I know you?"

"My name is Artur Melardis. I am the Guild Master. I believe you were acquainted with my predecessor. You seemed to have no trouble at all taking the money he paid you to eliminate our esteemed president."

I shrugged. "My shot went astray. Sometimes it happens."

"An interesting argument. It is not often that an assassin pleads incompetence. You took the Guild's money and reneged on your contract. A rather substantial sum provided in good faith with the expectation of results. There are those within our organization who scream for your head, but I believe that would be...unproductive. You owe us a death."

"Who did you have in mind this time? Delaren? Again?"

"Master Delaren is learning, to his frustration, that attempting to transform a system like ours is rather like trying to bail a sinking ship with a thimble—a valiant attempt, but in the end, an exercise in futility. He has made some modest gains, I will admit. Members of the civilian security patrol are less inclined to accept Guild direction, and financial benefit. The general population does not fear us as they once did. These things are inconvenient, but will be overcome with time. His constitutional amendments, however, are making potential business associates nervous. Several have already canceled rather lucrative contracts. This I cannot allow. Since you are directly responsible for inflicting him upon us, it is only right that you correct your mistake. Kill him, and your debt to the Guilds will be cleared."

There had to be more to it than that. They'd never make it that easy.

"I don't suppose refusing is an option."

"Unfortunately, no." Melardis moved to the desk and

switched on the com-link. "Bring in the boy."

He looked back to me. "Equally unfortunate is the fact that we find ourselves unable to trust your word. Once burned, you understand."

The door behind me opened, and Skinny Sorrellian came in carrying Jak the Rat. The boy's hands were bound, and an angry, purple bruise decorated his left cheek. Skinny Sorrellian dumped him on the carpet at my feet.

"A friend of yours, I believe."

I kept my face carefully neutral as I looked from the boy back to the man behind the desk.

"Let him go; he's no threat to you."

"I am afraid that is not possible. He is our guarantee of your good conduct. Once Master Delaren is dead, we will release him to you, and you both may be on your way."

They'd release us all right. Into death.

"You will spend tonight as my guest. In the morning Oren will drive you back to the city. I expect to hear of our esteemed president's death within the month. Otherwise, I fear your young friend will meet an unfortunate end."

Skinny Sorrellian picked Jak up and tossed him over his shoulder like a sack of flour. He drew his weapon and motioned for me to leave the room ahead of him, passing Jak off to a man standing guard outside the door. A nudge in the back with his blaster told me he expected me to precede him down the hallway. I glanced back in time to see the other guard carry Jak through a doorway at the end of the corridor.

Fuck.

I knew I shouldn't have come back here.